Theirs was a need so palpable, it took on an identity of its own

Branson leaned close, his lips inches from hers, his breath warm on her flesh. Her heart raced for a second and then seemed to stop altogether as Branson's mouth touched hers.

The kiss was intense, almost fierce, as if Branson hated himself for letting it happen. When he finally broke away, he lowered his head, their foreheads touching, their hands clasped, holding on for dear life.

"Damn." His voice was a rough whisper. "My job is to protect you, not seduce you."

"Does it matter that I wanted you to kiss me?"

"It matters. It just doesn't make it right."

"And do you always do what's right, Sheriff Branson Randolph?"

"I try."

"Because of the badge you wear?"

He let go of her hands and took a step back, breaking the physical connection that had held them, but not the emotional one.

"The badge is important to me, Lacy, but this isn't about the badge or duty or honor. It's about you. And it's about a madman who obviously plans to be your assassin. If I get wrapped up in wanting you, then I give the killer the edge. I don't plan to let that happen."

A LETTER FROM THE EDITORS
AT HARLEQUIN INTRIGUE

We love to receive mail from our readers. It keeps us honest and lets us know how best to meet your needs. Authors find your encouragement a source of unparalleled inspiration.

Therefore, when Joanna Wayne brought to our attention a letter from a regular Harlequin Intrigue reader—among others—regarding her book *Family Ties*, it was with great appreciation that we had our own editorial instincts confirmed!

Joanna created the Randolph family in that book. Four brothers, all sexy Texas cowboys...but it was oldest brother Dillon who got his girl in that story. Branson, Langley and Ryder hadn't had that dream fulfilled. And boy did they deserve it.

We asked Joanna to give all of the Randolph brothers their very own happily-ever-after, and to make sure their stories had as much suspense, mystery *and* romance.

So thank you for your continued support, and remember we are always looking for new ways to excite you and to maintain your loyal readership. We look forward to more letters of encouragement from you.

Harlequin Intrigue is proud to bring you RANDOLPH FAMILY TIES by Joanna Wayne—enjoy!

The Second Son
Joanna Wayne

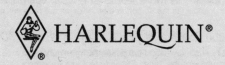

HARLEQUIN®

TORONTO • NEW YORK • LONDON
AMSTERDAM • PARIS • SYDNEY • HAMBURG
STOCKHOLM • ATHENS • TOKYO • MILAN • MADRID
PRAGUE • WARSAW • BUDAPEST • AUCKLAND

ISBN 0-373-22569-5

THE SECOND SON

Visit us at www.eHarlequin.com

Printed in U.S.A.

ABOUT THE AUTHOR

Joanna Wayne lives with her husband just a few miles from steamy, exciting New Orleans, but her home is the perfect writer's hideaway. A lazy bayou, complete with graceful herons, colorful wood ducks and an occasional alligator, winds just below her back garden. When not creating tales of spine-tingling suspense and heartwarming romance, she enjoys reading, golfing or playing with her grandchildren, and, of course, researching and plotting out her next novel. Taking the heroine and hero from danger to enduring love and happy-ever-after is all in a day's work for her, and who could complain about a day like that?

Books by Joanna Wayne

HARLEQUIN INTRIGUE

*Randolph Family Ties

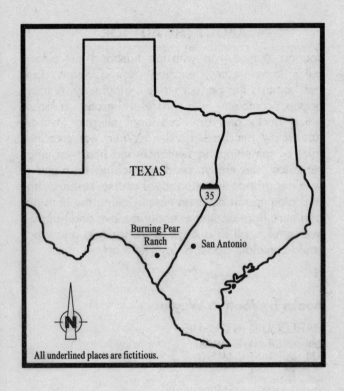

TEXAS

35

Burning Pear
Ranch

● San Antonio

N

All underlined places are fictitious.

CAST OF CHARACTERS

Branson Randolph—Rugged Texas sheriff and part owner of the Burning Pear Ranch. He'll do whatever he has to in order to keep Lacy Gilbraith safe. He's not afraid to face a killer, and he's determined to find out who's Betsy's father.

Lacy Gilbraith—She made a bargain she couldn't keep. Now she's running from a man who's determined to get her back.

Betsy—An adorable baby girl who was dropped off at the Randolph family ranch.

Dillon, Langley and Ryder Randolph—Branson's brothers. They all live by the cowboy code, but can one of them unknowingly be Betsy's father?

Kate Gilbraith—Lacy's sister. She's mixed up in something that may get both her and Lacy killed.

Ricky Carpenter—Kate's boyfriend. Someone wants him dead.

Charles Castile—A San Antonio attorney. He made a bargain with Lacy and he plans to make sure she keeps her part of it.

Joshua Kincaid—He owns a ranch in Kelman, Texas, but his real money comes from the Kincaid Entertainment Corporation. He appears to know a lot more than he's willing to tell.

Adam Pascal—He works for Joshua Kincaid and has dated Lacy, but he's reluctant to cooperate with Branson's investigation.

Milton Maccabbe—He's a cantankerous rancher. It's best not to cross him.

To all the people who enjoyed reading about the Randolph brothers in *Family Ties* as much as I enjoyed writing about them. Thanks for your letters and requests that we not let them go until we had a story for each of the brothers.

And, to Wayne, always.

Chapter One

"You have to make a birthday wish, Gramma, before you can blow out the candles." Four-year-old Petey scooted onto Mary Randolph's lap as the family's off-key rendition of "Happy Birthday" drew to a close.

"I don't know what I'd wish for." She hugged her grandson close. "I have all of you here with me at the Burning Pear for my sixtieth birthday. What more could a mother want?"

She looked around the room. Her four sons, each so different, but all Randolphs through and through. And Ashley, her one daughter-in-law, but she loved her as much as she could have loved the daughter she'd always wanted but had never had.

She blinked as a misty veil fell over her eyes. The moisture blurred the faces that surrounded her and softened the hard lines of rustic wood, Mexican tile and worn leather that characterized the ranch house where she'd lived all of her adult life.

One lone tear escaped the corner of her eye, and she brushed it away with the back of her hand.

"Do something nice for a woman, and here come the tears. I'll never understand the gender," Branson, her second son, said, only half teasing.

"Yeah, and if you sit here teary-eyed too long, the melted wax from the birthday candles is going to be thicker than the icing," Langley added, relighting one of the candles that had already gone out.

Mary paid them no mind. She was used to her sons' good-natured ribbing. "Sixty years of living gives a mother the right to a few seconds of melancholy," she scolded them. "And a little candle wax never hurt anybody." Her tears went on hold as laughter and echos of "You tell them, Mom," rippled across the spacious kitchen.

Her youngest son, Ryder, pushed the cake closer to her. "All the same, you better pucker up and blow—before the smoke alarm goes off."

"You want me to help you, Gramma? I can blow really hard." Petey wiggled around to face her, the excitement dancing in his dark eyes.

"Of course you can help," she told him, lifting him so that his knees rested in her lap and he could lean in closer to the beckoning cake.

Ashley Randolph grabbed her ever-ready camcorder and aimed it at Mary, Petey and the cake. Mary smiled, but kept her gaze low. A woman her age didn't need to have her wrinkles and graying hair preserved for posterity. Besides, she hated to see herself on the TV screen. The woman who smiled back always seemed years older than the one who lived inside her.

"Ready, set, go," Petey announced. He took a deep breath and blew until the last flicker of a flame died. "We did it, Gramma! Your wish will come true." He hopped down from her lap. "And now we can eat the cake. Right?"

"Ashley's chocolate cake, one of the best reasons I know of to grow older," Dillon Randolph said, giving his wife a hug and tousling the hair of his son as Petey scampered past him to get closer to the cake-cutting operation.

"Thanks to Mother Randolph," Ashley said, her tinkling laughter brightening the room. "Don't tell me you've forgotten the way I cooked when I first moved to the Burning Pear."

"No way!" Langley set a stack of dessert plates on the table at Ashley's elbow. "That's the kind of thing follows a man clear to the grave."

"I can't believe you said that," she countered, playfully pointing the tip of the cake knife in his direction. "Even then, *you* were always sneaking into my cookie jar."

"Sure. Those sugar cookies were perfect for target practice. Unless you hit them dead center, the bullet wouldn't even crack them."

The room burst into laughter again as Ashley sliced a large hunk of cake and placed it onto one of Mary's flower-patterned dessert plates.

Ashley could take the teasing of her three brothers-in-law with the best of them. She could dish it out, too. The perfect family. It was just too bad Dillon, Ashley and Petey had to live in Austin so much of the time—part of the price of being a state senator.

Still, if Mary really were to be granted a wish tonight, it would be that Jack Randolph was somewhere in heaven looking down on them, that he would see what fine men their four boys had grown into. That he would know how twenty years after his death she still treasured the time they'd had together.

"Who wants ice cream with their cake?" Ashley asked, handing the cake knife and cutting chores over to Dillon.

"What kind of question is that?" Ryder said. "You can't have birthday cake without ice cream. It's not American."

"Worse," Langley echoed. "It's not *Texan.*"

"I'll get the bowls and spoons," Mary said, stretching to a standing position.

"You most definitely will not." Branson left his post by the door to rest his strong hands on her shoulders. "The birthday girl does not wait tables."

"It's been many a day since I was a girl, Branson Randolph," she teased. "But I'm still a lot better at serving than I am at sittin'."

"You're still my best girl. And the prettiest girl south of—"

"South of the table and north of the door to the living room." She broke in and finished the sentence for him, keeping him honest. "And it's high time you found yourself a real 'best girl.'"

"Whoa." He picked up a fork and handed it to her. "We need to feed this woman fast. She's growing vicious."

"A piece of cake won't convince me you don't need a woman," she said, though her words were practically lost amid the laughter and clatter of dishes.

"Oh my Lord," Langley said, chewing appreciatively on his first bite of cake. "Find me a woman who can bake a cake this good, and I'll marry her tomorrow." He smacked his lips and swallowed. "Nope. Make that tonight."

"Don't say that in front of Mom," Ryder cautioned. "She'll be out combing the county, searching for women who are willing to come out to the Burning Pear and take cooking lessons."

"Now, that's not a half-bad idea," Ashley said. "It would sure give you a break in the kitchen, Mother Randolph. And any woman who'd put up with these guys would get my vote."

"I have a couple of requirements besides cooking," Ryder said, forking another bite of cake.

"Yeah, Ryder would have to make sure she could shine the silver on that World Championship belt buckle and feed his horse," Langley added.

"Now you're talking *my* language of love," Ryder said.

The gang around the table exploded in laughter again. Mary joined in. Being sixty, she decided, was not too awful. Not as long as she had her family with her. All safe. All happy.

She was chewing her first bite of cake when a soft knock at the front door brought an abrupt lull to the conversation and gaiety. "Now, who in the world can that be?" she said, wiping a smear of chocolate from her hands to the flowered cotton napkin.

"Probably another well-wisher," Ashley said. "Half the town's already called or sent cards or flowers. "Of course, none of the bouquets were nearly as extravagant as the one from Joshua Kincaid."

"Good," Dillon countered. "Let him spend his money on lavish flower arrangements. It will give him less money to spend lobbying against every bill I sponsor." He started walking to the door.

"I'll get it," Branson said, laying an arm on his brother's shoulder. "Might be business anyway. Friends never bother walking around to the front door."

Mary saw the muscles in his face tighten, as if instinctively, and felt a twinge of anxiety. She'd never grown comfortable with Branson taking on the job of county sheriff. "You're not expecting trouble, are you?"

He stopped in the doorway that led from the kitchen into the hallway. He forced a smile to reassure her. "I'm always expecting trouble. And always hoping I'm wrong. But there's no reason to think trouble's going to come calling at my front door.''

Mary slid her fork into her cake, breaking off a bite-size chunk of the velvety chocolate, but she only moved it around on the dessert plate. The easy chatter had started up again, filling the space around her. She tried to shut it out, and strained to hear whose voice would greet Branson when he swung open the door.

''Can you help me?'' The voice was low, labored, feminine. Unfamiliar. ''I'm looking for the Randolph home.''

''You found it.''

''Then this belongs to one of you.''

''What the hell?''

Branson's voice rose above the din of kitchen chatter, but not above the cry of a baby. Mary jumped to her feet and rushed to the living room, the rest of the family a step or two behind. Branson was standing in the open doorway.

A tall, thin woman stood in front of him, her face pasty and drawn. She pushed a blanket-wrapped bundle toward him.

''Take the baby.'' The woman's voice was more of a cry than a command.

She swayed and Branson reached to steady her. She pulled away from him and turned to Mary.

''If you're Mrs. Randolph, this is your grandchild. Her name is Betsy.'' The woman's faint voice faded into nothingness.

Mary grabbed the baby from her just as the woman's eyes closed and she collapsed at their feet. It was then that Mary noticed the crimson circles of blood that dampened the back of the woman's blouse.

''Call an ambulance,'' Branson ordered, leaning over the woman. The room erupted in a flurry of activity, but all Mary could understand was that the baby in her arms was crying and that her grandchild needed her.

Chapter Two

San Antonio, Texas
Two days later

Lacy Gilbraith tugged at the scrunch of white tulle. The headpiece tilted where it should have stood at strict attention, bunched up where it should have flared out. And the auburn curls piled on top of her head had already begun their escape, pulling from beneath the myriad pins the determined hairdresser had used to nail them into place.

So much for her attempts to look the part of the perfect bride. In an ideal world her groom wouldn't notice. Unfortunately, Charles Castile *always* expected perfection, at least as far as appearance went.

Lacy turned away from the mirror and dropped to the edge of an upholstered chair. She glanced at her watch. In just a few minutes she'd be marching down the aisle on her way to becoming Mrs. Charles Castile. She'd thought long and hard about her decision to accept Charles's proposal. It was the best solution for everyone. Maybe the only solution.

So why was her stomach churning, her eyes stinging?

Maybe it was because in an ideal world, she wouldn't be sitting alone in the stuffy dressing room just off the church parlor. Her sister, Kate, would be here with her, teasing away her nervousness, joking about the wedding headdress from hell. *Where was she?*

Lacy dabbed impatiently at a tear that had no business making an appearance and glanced at her watch again. Ten minutes before seven. Something had to be seriously wrong. She and Kate had argued, but surely that wouldn't keep her older sister from something as important as Lacy's wedding ceremony.

They'd had occasional differences before, but they'd always managed to work things out. Occasional differences. Who was she kidding? Their whole lives were a series of differences. Monumental differences that had begun to develop that day so long ago when Kate had—

Lacy took a deep, steadying breath. That part of their past was far behind them. Today was a new beginning, for her and for Kate. And this time money and power would be on their side instead of stacked in opposition.

So why wasn't Kate here?

She grabbed the phone and punched in Kate's number again. She'd already tried it a dozen times and all she'd gotten was the answering machine and Ricky Carpenter's recorded message that neither he nor Kate were in. She checked her beeper, but there were no calls.

A knock at the door broke into her thoughts, and Lacy's heart rate quickened. She dropped the receiver into the plastic cradle. Kate had come after all. Pulling up her skirt and petticoats, she raced across the carpeted floor and yanked open the door. Unexpected aggravation nipped at her control.

"You're not supposed to see the bride before the ceremony," she said, shoving the door until all she could see through the narrow opening was Charles's unsmiling face.

"I don't believe in superstitions." He wedged a foot inside the door and then pushed it open enough that he could step inside. "Besides, I wanted to be the first to see my beautiful bride in her wedding dress." He took her hands in his, concern, or maybe chagrin, darkening his deep-set gray eyes. "Have you been crying?"

"No."

He dropped one of her hands and tucked a thumb under her chin, nudging it up so that she couldn't avoid making eye contact. Another rebellious tear escaped to make a liar out of her, and he grabbed a tissue and wiped the moisture from her cheek. "The church is packed with our friends and family. This is no time for second thoughts, Lacy."

"Your family, Charles. Not mine."

"So that's what this is about. Kate, again."

She pulled from his grasp and walked back to the mirror, anxiously pinning wayward curls into the topknot.

Charles stepped behind her and placed his hands on her shoulders. "It's time you accept Kate for what she is."

"She's my sister. She's all the family I have."

"Not anymore. You have me. You'll have *my* family, *my* friends. Kate won't fit in. I'd rather not see her around here."

She twirled to face him. "What are you suggesting, Charles? That I just drop my only sister from my life?"

He leveled her with a determined stare. "It's a decision most sane people would have made a long time ago."

"Then color me crazy." Lacy knotted her fingers into painful fists. "Look, Charles, I don't know what's held Kate up, but she'll be here. She wouldn't miss my wedding. We have to wait for her."

"Let it go, Lacy."

"I can't. A few minutes. That's all I'm asking. I want Kate here when we exchange our vows. It's the only way I can go through with this."

He shook his head, as if he was sorry he had to refuse the request of a spoiled child. "We made a bargain."

"And I'm trying to keep it. All I'm asking for is a little time."

He grabbed her right arm just below the elbow, his fingers digging into her flesh. "Listen carefully, Lacy. That's the church organ playing. The guests are seated and waiting. You *will* walk down the aisle."

The phone rang. She broke from his grasp and dived for it. It had to be Kate.

"Hello."

"Hello, Lacy."

The voice was male, but not one she recognized. It sounded strained, muffled.

"Who is this?"

"A friend. I called to wish you the best on your wedding day. And to tell you that you are going to die very soon."

The connection was broken before Lacy had a chance to reply, but she was shaking when she hung up the phone.

"Who was that?" Charles barked.

"No one. A crank call."

"To a church? Some people are really sick." He took her hand and pulled her toward him. "Let's just forget about Kate for now. Don't let her spoil your wedding day."

"I won't go through with this wedding, Charles, not unless Kate is here."

"Kate's attendance at the ceremony was not a part of our bargain. And I know you are not foolish enough to back out of our agreement." He smiled into the mirror and ran his hand down the front of his tuxedo shirt, smoothing the pleats. "Now, touch up your makeup where your tears mussed your mascara. And for heaven's sake, wipe that look of gloom from your face."

He stepped toward the door. "The next time I see you, I'll expect smiles. After all, this is *your* day."

She stared at the door for long seconds after the back of Charles's head had disappeared from view. Stopping by the mirror one last time, she poked a dab of cold cream on the smeared streaks of black under her eyes. The tears were gone now. She repaired the makeup and smiled at her reflection.

She'd do what she had to do. It was called survival, and both she and Kate had learned the ropes of it a long time ago. They'd just chosen different arenas in which to perfect their skills.

SHERIFF BRANSON RANDOLPH swerved his pickup truck into one of the designated parking spaces for a brick town house in an upper-middle-class area of San Antonio. The house was at the end of a row of similar structures. They backed up to a parklike space with twin gazebos, picnic areas and a pond about half the size of the Alamodome.

Even from the back entry, the building was impressive, two stories with a covered slate patio that looked more like an outdoor living room. Tables, chairs and potted palms as tall as the mesquites that grew in Burning Pear pastures. Not at all what he'd expected.

He pulled a small notebook from his shirt pocket and double-checked the address. There was no mistake. This was the residence of the woman who'd paid a gift-bearing visit to the Burning Pear three nights ago and then collapsed at his feet. Kate Gilbraith, age thirty-three.

At this point, she was still recovering in a hospital across town. The small hospital-clinic in Kelman was okay for minor emergencies and routine health care, but serious bullet wounds required a trip to one of the larger San Antonio hospitals. Kate's injury had been complicated by a serious loss of blood.

The doctors reported she was making a miraculous recovery. In spite of that, she hadn't come to enough to answer Branson's questions. Until she did, he still had no clue as to who had shot her in the right shoulder or why.

To top it off, she'd had no identification on her. Nothing but a key ring with three keys and a few wadded dollar bills, all stuffed into the front pocket of her slacks.

If she hadn't had a record, he might still be trying to figure out who she was. But her fingerprints had told him what she couldn't. Name. Previously arrested on charges of writing hot checks. A few years earlier, she'd done a short stint in the slammer for shoplifting.

Her current address had been a matter of public record. Once you had a name, you could find out a multitude of facts about anyone, if you knew where to look.

What the records didn't tell him was where Kate Gilbraith had come up with the baby she claimed was a Randolph.

It wasn't his. That was for sure. Hell, he couldn't even remember the last time he'd had sex with a woman. No, that wasn't exactly true. He did remember. He only wished he didn't, considering how it had ended up. But it hadn't been with Kate Gilbraith.

And his brothers had all sworn they'd never set eyes on her before the night of the birthday party. And, if a Randolph gave you their word on something, you could take it to the bank. That had been the legacy they'd inherited from their father and his father before him. The Randolph curse, they'd called it growing up on the ranch, but they'd all bought into it.

Nonetheless, his mom had talked Social Services into letting her take care of the newborn baby until Miss Gilbraith was well enough to do the job herself. He'd been against it. He'd been outvoted.

Branson locked his truck, a task he never bothered with in Kelman, and slammed the door behind him. Stepping over a smashed beer can, he headed across the patio and toward the back door. He noticed another beer can on the edge of one of the padded lounge chairs. Looked like the residents' taste, or that of one of their friends, ran to Coors. And no one around here was a neatness freak.

The back door was closed. He knocked. No one answered, but the door squeaked open. Just a few inches, but enough that he could hear someone rummaging around inside. Maybe looters, since he knew the woman of the house was not home. Maybe the person who'd shot Miss Gilbraith. Maybe not. "Police. Come out and identify yourself." No one responded.

Taking the safe approach, he eased his pistol from its holster. Soundlessly, he slipped through the open door and into a shiny kitchen, black chrome appliances, dirty dishes piled in the sink. The noises continued, coming from upstairs. He tiptoed up the stairs and across a carpeted runway that seemed more a loft than a hallway. He peered over the railing and into the lower-level living area.

There was a big-screen TV, a sectional sofa in dirt-brown leather and a bearskin rug thrown down in front of the fireplace. And more empty beer cans scattered about among stacks of magazines and newspapers.

He made his step light, making his way down the hall and past a series of closed doors. A crash of wood on wood, probably the forceful closing of a drawer, alerted him that he was getting warm.

Stopping, he peered through the open crack of a bedroom door. The woman making the noise was facing the other direction, but there was no mistaking the gender. She was in a wedding dress, with rows of minute pearl buttons that went far lower than the tiniest waist he'd ever seen on a full-grown woman. Or maybe it just looked that way above the yards and yards of billowing satin that cascaded over her hips and fell to shapely ankles.

She was bent over, ransacking her way through a dresser drawer. She pulled out a pair of short shorts and held them up for a second before stuffing them back in the drawer. If she was a looter, she had a strange way of dressing for the job, and she was apparently very picky.

The room had French doors that opened onto a balcony and a terrific view of hilly land that sloped to the banks of a sparkling pond. A nice setup. Evidently Kate Gilbraith had changed her ways, or else found that crime *did* pay.

He watched her for a few more seconds before deciding to let the woman in white know she had company. "Police. Keep your hands in plain view, and turn around nice and slow."

She jumped at the sound of his voice and then twirled around lightning fast, the one hand that was in view dangling a lacy scrap of underwear.

"You don't follow orders too well," he said.

"You scared me half to death."

"Not following police orders can get you the other half of the way. Why didn't you respond when I knocked and called?"

"I didn't hear you." She eyed his gun, her eyes flashing suspiciously. "Did Charles send you after me?"

"Afraid not."

"Good." She tossed the underwear she was holding to the bed. "Is this about Kate? Is she in trouble?"

"Right now, it's about you. Do you live here?"

"No way."

"Then why don't we start with you telling me what you're looking for in those drawers?"

"And if I don't, you'll shoot me? You San Antonio police are such a friendly sort. *If* you really are a cop. That doesn't look like a police uniform you're wearing to me. I don't suppose you'd be willing to put that gun away and flash a little ID?"

She twitched her head and an avalanche of auburn curls broke loose to fall around her face. She was prettier than he'd first noticed, a cute nose, full sensuous lips and a long, regal neck. Some guy was missing out on a hell of a honeymoon.

Or maybe they'd already started, judging by a jagged rip in her skirt. So, there had to be a good reason for the bride to be ransacking someone else's home.

He holstered the gun, took out his wallet and shook it open. She stepped closer and peered at the small print on his ID.

"I'd hate to have to shoot a bride," he said when she averted her gaze from the wallet to his face. "Hate to even book one. You'd make too much of a scene at the jail. So why don't you start talking?"

She rubbed the back of her neck, stalling, probably coming up with a story she thought he'd buy.

"I'm looking for my sister," she said, turning back to the drawer and pulling out a pair of jeans.

"I doubt she'd be in one of those drawers."

"A sheriff with a sense of humor. How novel." She threw the jeans across the bed and kicked off a white shoe with a heel high enough to give her a nosebleed. Bending over, she rubbed the ball of her now-bare foot before kicking off the other pump.

"I'm still waiting on an explanation as to what you're doing in Kate Gilbraith's apartment."

"Look!" She accented her call to attention by wildly gesturing with hands that showcased her long, painted nails. "I've already had a day you wouldn't believe. Including a ride across town on the back of the police escort's motorbike."

Lifting the hem of her skirt, she revealed a pair of shapely legs, one with a fresh burn on the calf where an exhaust pipe had apparently caught her.

"What's the matter? Was the traditional bridal ride in a limo too tame for you?"

"Right. But I've had my quota of excitement for the day, so why don't you just be a nice cop and tell me what's going on with my sister?"

Branson studied the woman in white. He didn't notice a family resemblance. His instincts told him she was up to no good and that Kate Gilbraith probably wasn't her sister. But his instincts had been known to be tainted.

"When was the last time you talked to your sister?"

"A week ago. We chatted on the phone. Actually, we argued on the phone. I thought that was why she quit taking my calls. Now I'm not so sure."

If she'd said sometime within the past two days, he'd have known she was lying. Now he had to consider that she might be telling the truth. "What makes you think I'd know what happened to your sister?"

"I take it you're not here doing routine security checks. And the gun you had out a few minutes ago didn't indicate you're here as a friend." She threw her hands up, clearly exasperated. "Look, I know something's up. You can tell me what it is. I just want to know that Kate's all right."

"My turn to see ID," he said. "Do you have any on you?"

Her lips twisted into a defeated scowl. "Afraid not. The only thing I have with me is my beeper." She ran her hands along her hips, smoothing the shiny fabric so that it hugged her curves. "No pockets on these dresses. Of course, you could call Mr. Charles Castile and ask him to identify his missing bride. I'm sure he'd accommodate you."

"I don't believe I know the man, so I don't know why I'd believe him any quicker than I do you." Actually, he had heard of Castile. Nothing good. He was a rich attorney tied to the coattails of Joshua Kincaid. Sleep with a snake, and you probably were a snake. At least that's how Branson saw it. "So, about that ID…"

The woman propped her hands on her hips and glared at him. "Did anyone ever tell you that you're a very unfriendly cop?"

"All the time. But I thank you for the compliment just the same. Now, let's start again. Where would you have to go to get some identification that shows you're Kate Gilbraith's sister?"

"Look, mister. Being Kate's sister is not something you'd want to lie about. At least not unless you were denying it. But it's easy enough to prove I'm who I say I am." She walked to a bookshelf on the far side of the room and stretched to her tiptoes. She was a couple of inches short of reaching the top shelf.

"Let me help you." He stepped behind her and retrieved the photo album she was reaching for. He blew a layer of dust off of it before handing it to her.

She tore into it, turning a few pages and then tapping her finger on a picture of two girls mounted on a painted carousel pony. The younger of the two was skinny with an abundance of reddish-brown hair and a sprinkling of freckles across her nose. The image in the snapshot wasn't nearly as fetching as the woman standing in front of him, but it was obvious they were one and the same.

The older girl in the picture was somewhere in her mid-teens. There was no mistaking her either. It was the same woman who had come calling at the Burning Pear a few nights ago.

She tapped her finger on the picture. "That's us. Me and Kate. See. It says so right under the picture. Kate and Lacy at the county fair."

She turned a couple more pages. "And this was us last year, taken at my apartment." She ran her finger along the edges of the snapshot. "Me and Kate. See. We're sisters. Satisfied?"

But the picture was of a threesome. "Who's the guy?"

"Adam Pascal, my boyfriend at the time. I have extremely poor taste in men." Lacy let the cover slip from her fingers, and the photo album slammed shut.

She looked up at him, concern etched into the fine lines around her eyes and pulled at the corners of her full lips. "I'm Lacy Gilbraith, just like I told you. Now, please, tell me what's happened to Kate."

Branson swallowed hard. He'd bet his best pair of boots the woman wasn't telling the whole truth. But judging from the snapshots in the photo album, she was Kate's sister. Now he wished he had better news to deliver.

"What makes you think anything happened to your sister?"

"She didn't show for my wedding. She would have unless something was terribly wrong."

"Why don't you sit down," he said, motioning to the only chair in the room not draped in articles of clothing.

"No. I'm fine. Just tell me about Kate."

The tremor in her voice and her suddenly drooping shoulders assured him that his words and changed attitude had sucked the fight right out of her, that she sensed something was seriously wrong. In her new state, she looked incredibly fragile. For the first time in a long time, he felt the urge to open his arms to a woman.

Instead, he plunged ahead, explaining how Kate Gilbraith had crashed his mother's birthday party at the Burning Pear with a most unexpected guest. Explaining that she'd been shot, and that she'd dropped to the floor and into a semicoma state that the doctors couldn't penetrate even though her physical condition had improved significantly.

"I'd like to see my sister."

"I can drive you to the hospital."

She nodded, accepting his offer. "But not in this." She held up the skirt of the bridal dress, looping one finger through the unsightly rip. "I can find something of Kate's to wear, but you'll have to help me get out of this dress. It is not a one-person operation." She turned her back to him, her fingers already fiddling with the top button.

Branson's throat grew scratchy dry. Undressing women was not in his job description. Not that he had anything against the task. He was a man, after all. But he doubted seriously his fingers would fit around anything as delicate and small as that row of pearl buttons that stared back at him.

Lacy's fingers made quick work of the top few buttons. "I can't reach much lower, so you're going to have to help or we'll be here all night."

Branson nudged his Stetson back an inch or two to keep it from crashing into Lacy's head. Bending, he forced his fingers to the task, fiddling endlessly with the first reluctant button. He leaned close, and the mind-numbing fragrance of Lacy's perfume worked havoc on his senses, making the task at hand even more difficult.

Long minutes later, he was only three buttons down and dozens more to go. He struggled to steady his breath as his rough knuckles collided with the silky flesh of Lacy's back. Damn. Here he was undressing another man's bride, and his own libido was acting as though it had a honeymoon coming.

Button by button, inch by inch. The opening grew wider, revealing more flesh, finally dipping below her waist to the top lacy band of her panties. His fingers, and other parts of his body, grew stiff and his chest constricted painfully.

She wiggled and stretched her neck as far as she could, trying to see what was taking him so long. "I hope you're better at apprehending criminals than you are at undoing buttons."

"Just hold still. And suck in your breath so I have room to work." His words came out a little gruffer than he'd intended, in an effort not to reveal the effect this undressing act was having on him.

"Yes sir, Sheriff." She held her breath for a few seconds then let it out in a resounding whoosh. "So whose baby was this that Kate delivered to your house?"

"It wasn't mine. I can guarantee you that."

"Oooou. Touché." She wiggled a little more, tugging on the skirt and pulling it lower over her shapely hips. "But I wasn't accusing. Actually, I meant, who was the mother of the baby?"

He stopped struggling with the contrary pearl dots. "Are you saying this baby wasn't your sister's?"

"Absolutely not. I see her at least once a month, whether she wants to see me or not. She's as thin as a rail. I'd have noticed if she were pregnant."

"Then where did she get the baby?"

"I'd think *you'd* know the answer to that if the baby's a Randolph."

"I said your sister *claimed* the baby was a Randolph. There's a big difference."

Lacy twisted from the waist, and the skirt slipped lower still. Branson's breath grew so hot it burned his lungs. He'd seen nearly naked women before, but never one like this. Actually, he hadn't seen all that many, when you got right down to it, and none in many a Texas moon. Still, he would have doubted this type of perfection existed in real life.

"Sorry, cowboy. The show's over." Lacy took him by the shoulders and spun him around to face the door. "You can wait in the hall while I change into something of Kate's."

Branson walked away, thinking Charles Castile had to be one of the luckiest men alive, but wondering why in the world the man wasn't here to undress his own wife on her wedding day. He paced the hall while he waited, forcing his thoughts from Lacy to the newest fact in the case at hand.

If the baby wasn't Kate Gilbraith's, whose child was she? Had Kate kidnapped the infant, left some new mother fearing for her baby's life? Only, if that were the case, why hadn't Kate demanded money? Why had she just placed little Betsy in their hands and fallen at their feet, a bullet firmly embedded in her shoulder?

The best clues as to what happened probably resided with Kate or with the person who'd tried to kill her. And in spite of Lacy's protestations of ignorance, Branson had an idea she knew a lot more about what had happened than she was admitting.

After all, she was here in Kate's apartment when she should be cavorting in some luxurious honeymoon suite.

Branson jerked as the sound of breaking glass ordered him to full attention. He peered over the railing as a tightly wound contraption of glass and metal crashed through the living-room window. It careened across the carpeted floor and slid under the sofa.

Adrenaline rushed through him. "Under the bed," he ordered, racing back into the bedroom. He grabbed Lacy and shoved her resistant body in that direction. A second later, the room rocked with the explosion of a homemade bomb.

Chapter Three

Lacy shifted beside Branson and then dissolved into a spasm of ragged coughing. He turned toward her, the muscles in his arms straining as he pushed against the mattress that had collapsed on top of them. "Are you all right?"

"Probably not." She sucked in a gulp of air and raised her knee, giving herself a little leverage with the mattress. "But I'm alive."

"Good. If you want to stay that way, we should get out of here. Fast." He scooted toward the edge of the bed, holding up the mattress so that she could follow.

He watched while she stood. She was a little unsteady, but he didn't see any blood or signs of bruising. And fortunately, she'd traded the yards of satin for jeans and a sweater, and the nosebleed heels for a pair of loafers.

Grabbing one of her hands, he pulled her through the door and into the open hallway. His eyes stung from the haze of black smoke that hit him in the face. He squinted, making a quick assessment of possible escape routes.

Flames licked and sputtered around the sofa and were racing in a jagged line toward the front door. That left the back door, a path through thick smoke, broken glass and who knew what else. A gas leak from any appliance could send the kitchen portion of the house, including the back door, orbiting into space at any second.

Lacy muttered a word she hadn't learned in Sunday school. "I say we run for it."

She tried to wrestle her hand from his grasp. He held on and turned back to the French doors that led off the bedroom. "How are you at leaping from second-storey balconies?"

"I'll leave that to you and superheroes. I'll take the patio door."

"Too dangerous."

She fell into another bout of coughing. He took that opportunity to drag her back into the bedroom, kicking the door closed behind him. She stumbled after him, tripping once on the dress she'd shed just in the nick of time. He pushed the French doors open and gulped in a lungful of semiclean air. She grabbed the doorknob and held on, resisting his attempts to coax her onto the balcony.

"You're not going to go coward on me now, are you?" Branson pried her hand loose. Manhandling women was not his style, and he got no enjoyment from it. But there was no time to argue when she had no choice.

She shook her head doubtfully. "If we jump from here, we're going to break something, possibly my skull."

"Break or burn. It's your choice." It was a rhetorical option, and he didn't wait for her answer. He let go of her hand and leaned over the railing. It was a fairly long drop, but all they really had to do was crawl over the guardrail, hold on to one of the pickets and dangle until they could wrap their legs around the main support column. From there it was just a fireman's slide to the ground.

He described the procedure to Lacy. She grasped the handrail with both hands.

"Ladies first," he said, not trusting her to follow if he left her up here by herself.

"Always the gentleman." Her voice was hoarse, the effects of the smoke and her recent bout of coughing.

But he could read the resolve in her eyes and the serious jut of her jaw. She'd do what she had to do. He climbed over the railing and then helped her do the same.

"Wrap your hands around my forearm," he said, holding on to the railing with his left hand and extending his right arm.

A shock wave rumbled through the house. The flames had found something they liked. Probably aerosol cans or paint. The result wasn't nearly as strong as the original explosion but enough of a shudder that Lacy dropped her hesitancy.

She grabbed his arm. Her grip was sure, stronger than he'd expected. A second later she was dangling, swinging her long legs until they hugged the post. She let go of him, and by the time she hit the ground he was riding the same stick horse to safety.

She looked around as his feet pounded the earth. "I suppose you have a car around here somewhere."

"My truck is out back." Not stopping for further explanations, he pulled her along, loping over the grass and rounding the back side of the house. The frightening crackle and pungent odor of burning wood dogged their movements.

Branson stood by the truck, checking out the situation. So far, the flames were contained in the one town house, but if the fire wasn't extinguished quickly, the blaze could spread to neighboring residences.

"Who lives next door to your sister? Invalids? Kids? Anyone who would be home during the day?"

"It's vacant. It's been for sale ever since she moved in."

He breathed a little easier. At least no one else was in danger. He ran to the front of his truck, jumped into his seat and reached for his cell phone. But someone had beat him to the 911 call. By the time an operator had answered, the scream of sirens was already closing in on them. He broke his connection just as Lacy slid into the passenger seat.

"Close the door and buckle up. I'd just as soon be gone when the local law officers get here."

She reached for the seat belt. "A cop who doesn't trust cops. I knew there was something I liked about you."

"I thought maybe it was because I just saved your life." He fit the key into the ignition and yanked the gear to reverse. "Besides, I didn't say that I didn't trust cops," he clarified, backing out of the parking space. "I'm just not interested in explaining to them right now why I'm involved in an explosion on their turf."

"That's right. You're not from around here. Not really a cop either. Cowboy Sheriff Branson Randolph. It has a nice ring to it." She put three fingers to her temple and massaged. "Or maybe the ringing is just in my head."

A fire truck came racing toward them. He stopped to let it pass and then took the first left. "So, are you still up for a trip to the hospital, or would you rather call your new husband and get him to take you?" He pointed to the cell phone that rested on the seat between them. "You're welcome to use my phone."

She offered a tentative smile. "You're not backing out on me, are you, cowboy? How was it you put it, turning coward?"

"Why would I?"

"For starters, we almost got killed back there."

"I doubt seriously the explosion was meant for you. Or do you live there, too?"

"No. Kate lives there with her boyfriend. It's actually his place."

Branson kept his eyes on the road, but his concentration was centered on Lacy. He knew that how a person reacted to questions was as important as the answer they gave. "Exactly how much do you know about Kate's life?"

"Kate's thirty-three, six years older than I am. I'm not her keeper."

Avoidance. He wasn't surprised. A bride still in her wedding dress who wasn't interested in even calling her husband probably had a few secrets of her own.

"I didn't mean to offend you with my answer," she said when he didn't question her further.

"You didn't."

"Something did. You've got that hard-as-nails look on your face again, the same one you had when you walked in on me in Kate's bedroom."

"I just don't like playing games when I don't know the rules or the desired outcome. Someone shot your sister and then blew up the house where she resides. You pretend to be all worried about her, but when I try to help, you evade me with 'I'm not her keeper.'"

"See. I knew you were offended. But, you see, Sheriff, I don't know if you're just the good-old-boy lawman you're pretending to be or one of the brutal boys I read about in the paper. I don't know if you're out to help Kate or arrest her."

"And what might I be arresting her for?"

"I'm not sure. You're in the business. You'd think of something."

"I wouldn't say her arrests in the past have been all that creative. Writing bad checks. Shoplifting."

"I never said she was a saint."

"No, you haven't said much of anything. If you really

want to help your sister, it's time you did." He measured his words, wondering what it would take to get through to Lacy. "The stints your sister has done behind bars before would be nothing compared to the sentence she'd get if she were to be convicted on kidnapping charges."

Her forehead wrinkled. "Kate is *not* a kidnapper."

"That's a start. Is your sister involved in something illegal or just something that could get her killed?"

She took a deep breath and exhaled slowly, rubbing a spot under her left ear. "I'm sure you aren't going to believe me, but I really don't know where that baby came from or who shot Kate. All I know for certain is what you've told me, substantiated by the fact that she didn't show up for my wedding."

"So your story is that Kate missed the wedding, you came looking for her, and that's when I hit you with the bad news?"

"Something like that." She clasped her hands in her lap, nervously entangling her fingers. "Believe me, if I'd known Kate was in the hospital, I'd have been right there beside her." Lacy turned to face him. "I just wish I had known sooner that Kate had been shot."

"Even if you'd been at her bedside the whole time, your sister wouldn't have known it," he assured her. "She hasn't been fully conscious since she collapsed at our ranch."

"But she would have known somehow that I was there. And even if she hadn't, *I* would have known." She reached to the ball of hair on top of her head and started pulling out pins. Shiny auburn curls shook loose, falling around her shoulders, wild and tempestuous. She raked through them with her fingers, but her attempts to tame the tangle were futile.

Branson watched the transformation and then forced

himself to look away. No married woman should look that good, especially one sitting in his truck. One he had undressed.

He stuck a finger under the collar of his shirt and tugged it away from his neck. The truck was suddenly way too warm.

Lacy leaned back and closed her eyes. Her muscles were taut, her face strained. She had the look of someone fighting demons in her mind. But were they her demons or Kate's? Either way, Branson had a strong suspicion that they'd become his demons before this was all over.

And the key to Baby Betsy's true identity lay somewhere in the muddle of facts and danger surrounding these two women.

LACY CLOSED HER EYES and tried to deal with the problems at hand. Ricky and Kate's town house going up in smoke. Kate shot and lying in a hospital all alone.

This wasn't supposed to happen. Not after she'd agreed to the bargain just to keep Kate safe. Only now she'd broken her bargain with Charles. But only temporarily. She'd have to go back to him. There was no way out.

"We're about two blocks from the hospital," Branson announced, breaking into her tormenting thoughts.

Lacy sat up straight and pulled down the visor. There was no mirror. Probably just as well since she didn't have a comb or even a lipstick on her. Not that it mattered. Nothing mattered right now except seeing Kate.

"Do you think they'll let me see my sister if visiting hours are over?"

"It shouldn't be a problem. My badge will get us by the front desk, and the floor nurses will be thankful someone in the family is there to visit the patient. You can probably stay the night with her if you like."

"Yes, I'd like that." Anything to put off the inevitable confrontation with Charles. He would be livid. But she pushed worries about Charles to the back of her mind the second Branson pulled into the well-lit parking lot.

SEVERAL MINUTES LATER, Lacy and Branson were trotting along behind a tall nurse who had introduced herself as Carol Roust. The intimidating woman had jumped right in and taken control of the situation, insisting she talk to them before Lacy saw Kate.

Lacy was only a step behind her when Carol stopped at the door to the nurses' lounge. "We can talk in here," she said, standing back while they entered. "There's fresh coffee in the pot on the counter. Help yourself if you'd like some."

Lacy dropped into the nearest chair, nodding yes when Branson poured a cup for himself and offered to pour one for her. Carol declined his offer of the same and took the chair opposite Lacy, crossing her legs.

She waited until Branson joined them at the table before she started talking. "The doctor was here earlier. He said Miss Gilbraith was making a remarkable recovery in every way but one."

"Which way is that?" Lacy asked.

"She is still not responding to questions or to any attempts to get her to talk. She appears not to be aware that we are in the room with her."

Branson took a sip of his brew. "So, she's still in some sort of coma?"

"Not exactly." The nurse pursed her lips. "Ideally, the doctor should be talking to you about this, but he just left the hospital and I don't think he'll be returning tonight. He stressed before he left that any family member visiting Kate be advised of the situation. He wanted you to know about the problem as well, Sheriff.''

''What problem?'' Lacy spoke the question quietly, though she wanted to scream it at the nurse. The woman's passion for melodrama had Lacy's stomach churning and her patience strained to breaking.

''We think your sister's inability to respond to verbal stimuli may not be physically induced.'' She lay her hands on the table. ''To put it bluntly, we think she may be faking.''

Kate, performing? That certainly sounded like the sister Lacy knew and loved. For the first time since she'd heard of Kate's injury, she felt a little relief.

''That would be a good sign, wouldn't it, Miss Roust? I mean, if Kate is only faking a coma, then she is recovering in that area as well.''

''Playing games with a hospital's medical staff is never a good thing, Miss Gilbraith.''

Lacy straightened her shoulders, more than ready to be finished with the conversation. ''I agree that it's probably not the best scenario, but someone did attempt to kill my sister. *If* what you suspect is true, maybe Kate has her reasons for not talking.''

Lacy looked over at Branson and then stood up. ''Now, if there's nothing else you feel you *must* tell me, I'd like to see my sister. And I'd like to talk to her doctor as soon as possible.''

The expression on Nurse Roust's face left no doubt that Lacy had made a new enemy. But what was one more to a list that was growing steadily as the day wore on?

Speaking in clipped tones, the nurse gave them directions to Kate's room and sent them on alone. The room was the third from the end of the hall. Lacy stopped for a second and read her sister's name from the card at the door along with instructions that Kate was to have a soft diet with extra liquids.

Lacy knocked softly on the closed door. She didn't expect an answer and didn't wait for one. Taking a deep breath and trying to prepare herself for seeing Kate in this condition, she pushed through the door and walked to the side of the bed.

"Kate, it's Lacy. I would have been here sooner. You know I would have been with you if I'd known you were injured."

The bulge under the covers didn't move. A motionless lump without even the top of Kate's sun-bleached blond hair poking out.

Suspicion tugged at Lacy's mind. She stepped closer and clasped the edge of the hospital blanket. She knew what she would find when she jerked the blanket down, but she held on to the hope that she was wrong.

She wasn't. Kate Gilbraith was gone.

LACY STOOD at the top of the stairs in front of the hospital. A young couple hurried down the steps in front of her. An elderly gentleman, shoulders bent, stared at her as he shuffled past.

She envied them that they had somewhere to go, a purpose to their movements. She had none. Had no clue as to where to find Kate. All she knew was that her sister was in danger and that she had to find her.

"Do you have any idea where your sister might have gone?"

Lacy jumped at the sound of Branson's voice. She'd been so lost in her misery, she'd forgotten he was still standing beside her.

"No. The only one she's really close to besides me is

her live-in boyfriend, Ricky. That was his town house that just got blown up, so there's no telling where he is."

"She must have friends."

"Not really. She's pretty much a loner, except that she's always involved with a man. The only female I remember her being close to moved out of town about a year ago and never got back in touch with her. Kate took that as a betrayal. And most of her life has been a series of betrayals."

"Maybe she needs to pick a different kind of friend."

Lacy looked up at Branson. The artificial lights cast shadows on his face, highlighting his rugged features. For the first time she noticed how young he was. Probably in his early thirties at the most, but the aura of authority he wore made him seem much older.

He shifted his stance, and she realized he'd grown uncomfortable under her assessment.

He tugged his hat a little lower. "I put out an APB on her. I want her picked up as quickly as possible. Kate could be involved in a kidnapping. Even if she's not, she's likely still in real danger."

She swallowed hard, but for once didn't try to camouflage her true feelings. "I know she's in trouble. I just don't know how to help her."

"I might, if you'd level with me."

He glanced at the parking lot for a second and then stepped closer. "You think because I carry a badge that I'm the enemy, Lacy. You need to think again. I'm not the dirty coward who shot her in the shoulder. Not the one who airmailed a bomb through the window of her town house."

Lacy took a step backward and leaned against a concrete pillar, suddenly so tired she could barely stand. Branson wasn't totally right, but he wasn't totally wrong either. She didn't think he was the enemy. She *knew* who he was.

He was the law, and the law had never protected or

looked out for her or for Kate. Besides, she knew the law from the other side, from the office of attorney Charles Castile. The law favored the people with money and clout.

No matter that she ached to trust someone, she couldn't let it be Branson. She couldn't be taken in by his seeming concern. Couldn't respond to the strength of him or the rugged charms of the cowboy who'd saved her life.

Branson placed a hand on the pillar, a spot just above her left shoulder. "I think you're making a big mistake, Lacy, but I can't force you to talk."

"I never thought you law types admitted that."

"Is that what you want, Lacy? Do you want me to take you to some intimidating interrogation room and harass the truth out of you? Would that make you feel justified in choosing not to help your sister just because helping her means talking to a cop?"

"No."

"Good, because that's not my style. And, I don't know why I'm worried about helping you or your sister when you're so dead set against working with me." His eyes softened. "Maybe I'm just not used to saving brides on their wedding day."

He reached over and took her right hand in his. The unexpected intimacy of the touch surprised her. Even more, she was amazed that she wanted to tell him the truth, at least as much of it as she knew.

But she didn't dare trust the law. Not in this. Ricky had warned her. The only one she could go to now was Charles and pray he would forgive her for running out on their bargain.

She shifted her gaze from Branson to her feet. "I can't tell you anything."

He let go of her hand. "Then I guess we may as well call it a night. Can I drop you somewhere?"

Her insides quaked sickeningly at the thought of returning to her future husband.

Branson's gaze was fastened on the darkened parking lot. He was probably convinced she and Kate were both kooks. Frankly, she wasn't sure at this point that he was far from wrong.

Branson took her by the elbow and led her down the steps and over to the parking space where they'd left his truck. "Don't look now," Branson said as he opened her door, "but we have a fan sitting a few cars to the right of us in a red Jaguar. He's been watching us ever since we walked out of the hospital."

Her heart plunged to her knees. "Early forties, sandy hair and wearing glasses?"

"Bull's-eye."

She twisted in her seat and located the last man she'd expected to see in the hospital parking lot. The reality of the fact twisted in her brain, sending stabbing pains to both temples, destroying her resolve. Did Charles know Kate was in this hospital? And if he did, how did he know it and why hadn't he told her that Kate had been shot?

Branson brought the engine to life. "I take it the man is someone you know?"

"Apparently not well enough. That's Charles Castile."

"Your husband?"

"No. The groom I left at the altar." She lay a hand on Branson's arm. "I've changed my mind, Sheriff. Buy me a steak, and I'll tell you everything I know."

Well almost, anyway.

Chapter Four

Branson sat across from Lacy, sipping his iced tea and watching her chew appreciatively on a bite of her filet. She'd ordered it rare, with a baked potato and salad. A real meal and she was eating like a real person, not nibbling at it as if a normal-size bite would choke her delicate system.

He liked that about her.

He shifted in his chair and scanned the room. He didn't need things to like about Lacy Gilbraith. He needed to do his job. In the few hours he'd known her, he'd already found out that she was not the kind of citizen who went out of her way to help a lawman.

But something had changed her mind in a hurry tonight. One minute she didn't have a thing to tell him, the next she was promising "will talk for food." The dramatic change had come as a result of finding her jilted groom in the parking lot of the hospital. The second he'd mentioned a red Jag, her eyes had grown wide, and the muscles in her face had clenched.

Fear, anger, irritation? Maybe a little of all three. Which made him think that whatever had precipitated her running from the wedding had to do with more than just the absence of her sister at the planned ceremony. Especially since she'd run before she had exchanged the vows.

Branson had expected Charles to follow them when they left the hospital, but apparently he'd seen enough. He hadn't caught sight of the Jaguar again. Branson would make it a point to find out a lot more about Charles Castile tomorrow. As for tonight, he had yet to learn any more from the beautiful woman in front of him than what she'd told him initially.

"You do know how to feed a woman, Branson Randolph."

He turned back to his dining companion as she put down her fork and took a sip from the tall glass of iced tea at her fingertips. "You're not giving up now, are you? There's still food on your plate."

"If I eat another bite, I'll never be able to button Kate's jeans around my waist. They're already seriously interfering with my breathing capabilities."

"Then you better stop eating. It wouldn't do to pass out from lack of oxygen. As you already found out, buttons are not my strong suit."

Lacy smiled as she picked up her napkin and dabbed at the corner of her mouth. The red lipstick she'd been wearing when he'd first encountered her had all worn off, leaving her mouth a dusty pink. Delicate. Paired with the wild mass of auburn curls that framed her face, she was a picture of innocence.

He stretched his legs under the table. Pictures might be worth a thousand words, but that didn't mean they couldn't lie.

"Are you ready to answer a few questions now, or would you like dessert first?"

Her smile disappeared. "You know, for a few minutes there, Sheriff, you had me going. I thought there was a real man sitting across the table from me instead of a cop."

"I'm real enough." Too real, and too much a man, although he'd almost forgotten the fact himself until he'd started disrobing her this afternoon. He fingered the end of his fork. "But I don't think you accepted this dinner invitation because of me at all, Miss Gilbraith. I think it was the steak you were courting."

She nodded. "I admit it. I was famished. I hadn't eaten all day and I'm not sure about last night."

"Wedding-day jitters?"

"Or as it turned out, my unwedding-day jitters." She wadded the napkin in her hand, squeezing the fabric between fisted fingers.

"I guess it's rough on a woman when her dream day turns disastrous."

"My dream day?" She took a deep breath and let it out slowly. "My dream day would involve walking on a secluded beach somewhere. I'd have cool waves splashing around my ankles and a blue sky overhead."

She released the napkin, letting it slide from her fingers and drop to the white tablecloth. "Actually." Her tone grew agitated. "You could throw in a couple of sharks, and it would still beat the ceremony I almost had."

So his assumption had been accurate. "It sounds like this match was not made in heaven."

"To say the least." She pushed her plate back a few inches. "Castile came into this world with a silver spoon in his mouth. Me, I was gagging on trouble from the day I was born."

"Does this story go back that far?" He patted the small notebook in his shirt pocket. "If it does, I'll need a bigger pad of paper."

"No." The spark of life and humor he'd glimpsed earlier gave way to shadowy sadness. "Some pasts are better forgotten, or at least buried."

He moved the flickering candle from the center of the

table to one side so that he could study her reactions that much more closely. "Why don't I order coffee and you tell me what you know. Your sister is obviously in danger, but it might not be quite as bad as it seems."

"You're sugarcoating, Sheriff. You're not very good at it."

"You're right." He finished the last of his iced tea. "And you didn't let me buy you dinner just because you wanted to cooperate with the law. You're scared for your sister."

"Well, at least we understand each other."

"The motivation, not the facts. What's Kate involved in?"

"It's not the what, but the who." She lifted a tangle of hair from the back of her neck. "It's stuffy in here. I feel like I can't breathe."

"We could stroll along the Riverwalk if you like, talk out there. It's a good night for it."

"A stroll in the moonlight—while I squeal on my sister and her boyfriend." She pushed back from the table and stood up. "Why not? I'll go to the ladies' room while you pay the bill. Next time, I'll treat."

"Don't try to slip out on me."

"I won't. You already called it. Kate needs help, and right now you're the only game in town."

Branson watched her walk away, her back straight and her head high, though he knew fear and regrets were choking the life out of her.

And for the first time since he'd pinned the badge on his chest, he wished it wasn't there. What Lacy Gilbraith needed was a friend, a man to stand by her the way that snake she'd almost married apparently hadn't.

Damn, he was doing it again. His family was obviously wrong when they claimed he didn't have a romantic bone in his body. It was just that his romantic inclinations were few and far between. And not to be trusted.

Here he was, letting a woman mess with his mind. Again. Convincing him she was who and what he wanted to believe when the facts said differently. Only this time he would not be taken in.

Lacy Gilbraith was part of the job. She might need a man to stand by her. But he was not that man.

LACY STEPPED through the open door and into the night air. She and Branson had exited the restaurant on the lower level, putting them directly onto San Antonio's famed Riverwalk.

It was a beautiful May night, and the paved walkway that bordered the narrow, shallow river bustled with the Friday-night crowd of work-worn revelers. A couple passed them, their arms entangled, their laughter adding to the chorus of chatter and music that spilled into the night. Lacy wondered if her heart had ever felt that light, if her laughter had ever bubbled that freely.

She shivered and hugged her arms around her chest.

"We can go back inside if you're cold."

"No, it's not the temperature," she said. "I like it out here, but I'm not sure it's conducive to serious talking."

"Not here in the midst of hotels and restaurants, but there's a quieter area if we follow the river for a few blocks. Are you up to the walk?"

"I could use it after that meal," she said.

Branson was right. A few blocks north, the crowd thinned considerably. He led her to an unoccupied bench a few feet from the water's edge. "Is this quiet enough for you?" he asked.

"It will do."

Branson sat down beside her. "I know you're finding

this extremely difficult, Lacy, but you don't have much choice. Bullets and bombs can be deadly. Your sister is keeping vicious company.''

He was right, of course. Kate had a history of bad choices in friends and lifestyle, but a lot of those had been a matter of survival. The truth was, Kate had a heart of gold. But that kind of thing never showed up on a police rap sheet. That's why people like Branson couldn't begin to understand a woman like Kate.

But Lacy didn't need him to understand her. She needed him to find her and protect her.

''I'm not sure where this story begins, Sheriff, so I'll give you a little of the background.'' She searched her mind for the right words, the right facts to share with the eager lawman. The right ones to keep secret.

''Kate moved back to Texas a year ago. She was broke. I asked Charles Castile if he could help her find a job.''

''Your fiancé?''

''Only he wasn't my fiancé then, just my boss. He pulled strings, got her a job in spite of her lack of skills and her police record.''

''What kind of job?''

''She went to work as a waitress out at Joshua Kincaid's San Antonio nightclub. Charles does a lot of work for Kincaid, and he hired Kate on as a favor. I know a lot of people don't like Mr. Kincaid, but he's been nothing but nice to my sister and to me when I've been around him.''

''I don't think anyone complains about Joshua Kincaid's social skills. It's his lack of scruples that brings the criticism.''

''Anyway, Kate went to work for Kincaid and through that job she met and got involved with Ricky Carpenter. Apparently he's a friend of Joshua Kincaid's. He played pro football until he suffered that career-ending injury a couple of years ago.''

''So how does Ricky enter into all of this?''

''He and Kate have been a thing ever since they met. She's crazy about him. He acts like he's just as crazy about her. She moved into his town house a few months ago.''

''The one that just got bombed?''

She nodded.

Branson crossed an ankle over his knee, man style. ''So, tell me how Ricky enters into Kate's taking a bullet in the shoulder.''

Jittery spasms attacked Lacy's nerves. Charles and Ricky had both warned her that this should go no further, that if she talked to the police, she might well be signing Ricky's and Kate's death certificates. But now she couldn't trust Charles, and even before she'd run out on her bargain with him, someone had tried to kill Kate.

''I can't help you, Lacy, unless you talk to me.''

''I'm not sure you can anyway.''

''Someone is trying to kill your sister. How much worse do you think it can get?''

Branson was right. She'd tried to play by the bad guys' rules. She couldn't afford to do that any longer. She sucked in a shaky breath and forced herself to talk. ''Ricky came to see me one night about four weeks ago.''

''What about?''

''Trouble. He showed up at my apartment about midnight, ringing the doorbell and banging on the door. I probably wouldn't have let him in at that time of the night had he not looked as if he might die on my doorstep if I didn't.''

''Was he ill?''

''No. His face and arms were bruised and blood was caked on his forehead and matted in his hair.''

"Did you call for help? An ambulance? Police?"

"No, he begged me not to. And instead of being cocky and arrogant the way he usually is, he seemed fearful, desperate."

"What explanation did he give you for the bruises?"

"He said he'd been jumped and attacked by two men who had beaten him within an inch of his life and promised more would return if he didn't come up with the fifty thousand dollars they said he owed them. A gambling debt. Only next time they promised it wouldn't stop with a beating. It would end in a death—Kate's."

She was shivering again, inside and out. Branson touched a hand to her shoulder, and it was all she could do not to lean into him, not to bury her head against his broad chest. She trembled but didn't give in to the tears that pushed at the back of her eyelids.

"Take it easy," he said. "Just get the story out. Then we'll decide what to do."

"I'm not usually like this." Her voice broke.

"You don't usually have to worry about the safety of your sister."

"More often than you know. It's just that this is the first time I haven't been able to at least talk to her."

"Still, it's no crime to show emotion."

She bit her bottom lip. It might not be a crime, but she'd learned long ago what showing weakness got you. And she doubted if the good sheriff sitting beside her ever indulged. He was too much in control, too unruffled by explosions to believe him capable of ever losing his cool or exposing his vulnerabilities.

"Did you give Ricky the money?" Branson asked, his gaze fastened on her face.

She lowered her own gaze to the concrete walk beneath her feet. "I would have in a second if I'd had it. I didn't.

But I didn't have to think about it long. Ricky begged me
to go to Charles and ask for the money.''

"Four weeks ago. By that time you and Charles must
have been engaged?''

She nodded, knowing it was the same as lying. She drew
into herself, alone with the rest of the secrets, the ones she
didn't dare reveal. Branson would find out soon enough,
and when he did, he'd do what any good officer of the law
would. He'd throw her into jail.

"And did Charles lend him the money?''

"Yes.''

"What did Ricky use for collateral?''

"I don't know. I didn't get into the details with them.
They worked it out between themselves.''

Branson fingered the brim of his hat. "So, let's see if I
have this straight. You asked your wealthy fiancé for a loan
of fifty thousand dollars because you thought it would save
your sister's life. He agreed and the two of you went back
to the business of planning a wedding.''

"That pretty much sums it up.''

"So, if the men got their money, why would they still
be trying to kill Kate?''

"That's the same question I've been asking myself ever
since you told me she'd been shot.''

"Where's Ricky now?''

"I have no idea.''

"When was the last time you talked to him?''

She shook her head and then raked flyaway wisps of hair
from her cheeks. "Ricky called me on the phone a few
days after the beating and thanked me for getting Charles
to lend him the money. That's the last I've heard from
him.''

Branson stared straight ahead. "This makes absolutely
no sense.''

"I agree, but I've told you everything I know. So, if you'd lend me a few dollars, I'll catch a cab and go see if Charles will at least let me back into the house to get my things. I'll pay you back. Of course, you'll have to take my word on that."

"I'm not a trusting sort. Besides, I have a better idea. You can go home with me."

"I don't think so, Sheriff."

"It's not what you're thinking," he added quickly. "It's the family ranch down in Kelman. You'll have a room of your own and the most diligent chaperon in the state of Texas—my mom. So you won't have to worry about your virtue not being as intact when you leave as when you arrive."

Suspicion edged along her nerve endings. "Why would you invite me to your home? You don't know me or anything about me."

"I can't resist coming to the aid of a beautiful woman in danger."

She didn't buy that for a second. "I'm not in danger. I'm an innocent bystander."

"Then come with me for the sake of the investigation. I'm looking for your sister. I'll need to know everything you know about her life and her habits if I'm to find her before her would-be killer does." He stood up, taking her hand and tugging her to her feet as well. "Besides, Charles isn't your husband. There's no honeymoon to hurry back to."

"How long are we talking about?"

"How long can you spare?"

"Let's see, at this point I'm sure I no longer have a position at Castile's law firm, I gave up my apartment already, and I doubt Charles is going to welcome me back into his home in the hills with open arms."

"Then I guess you can stay as long as I need you."

As long as he needed her. That was as long as she'd ever stayed with any man before. Her visit to Kelman would surely be short.

"Of course, I can't promise you a good night's sleep," he said, walking along beside her in the direction of where they'd left his truck. "There's a baby in the house."

"The mystery baby that Kate delivered to your door?"

"That's the one."

Lacy's nerves tightened again. She hated to even think how her sister had come up with a baby. Especially one whose father was a Randolph. Maybe Branson's, though he'd vehemently denied the possibility.

There were probably many a woman enamored of the handsome cowboy lawman. Especially if you went for the intelligent, pensive type. Or if you liked the feel of his strong hand when it closed over yours. Or the sensation that crept into your senses when his hip accidentally brushed against yours as you walked side by side.

Some women might like that. Probably only the ones who were breathing.

Kelman, Texas

BRANSON TURNED OFF the main highway and onto the road to Burning Pear. He probably should have called his mother and alerted her he was bringing a guest with him. She'd welcome Lacy with open arms, but she'd expect an explanation. She'd demand to know why he was providing bed and board to the sister of the woman who'd delivered Betsy to their door.

And that was probably the reason he hadn't called. The only explanation he could offer was the one he'd given Lacy, and that one held about as much water as the feed pail he'd shot full of holes last weekend when he'd found a rattler inside it. He could easily question Lacy about her sister without having her sleep under the same roof as he did.

But he didn't want her disappearing on him the way Kate had. Besides, he wasn't convinced that she'd told him the whole truth. And he was even less certain that she wasn't in danger herself.

"What will your mother say when you come waltzing in on a Friday night with a woman in tow?" Lacy asked, breaking the silence that had ridden between them for most of the ninety-minute trip.

"First of all, I don't waltz. I have two left feet. Second, with any luck, she'll be asleep. Langley will likely be asleep as well, and Ryder will probably be out at the Road-house courting one of the local ladies."

"Langley and Ryder?"

"My brothers. Langley runs the ranch with some help from Ryder and me and a few hands. Ryder was on the rodeo circuit, but he's been sidelined with an injury for almost a year. He's healing nicely, but he still has a slight limp and the doctor hasn't given him the okay to return to the suicide circuit. My older brother, Dillon, is in Austin."

Lacy sank back against the seat. "A big, close-knit Texas family, and I'm just going to barge in on them. I don't think this is such a good idea, Branson."

"Too late to worry about that now."

"It's never too late to worry."

He lowered his window a notch. "Just breathe that air."

She did. "Smells like any other air to me, minus the city pollution, of course."

"Dust, cattle, cactus, mesquite. Smells like home to me."

"Not something *I'd* want to bottle." Still, she lowered

her window a couple of inches as well. "Haven't you ever wanted to escape from your rural roots, move to the big city, be blinded by the bright lights?"

"Once. When I was about twelve years old, I had my heart set on becoming an astronaut."

"What changed your mind?"

"The colt my dad gave me that year for my very own. I wrote to NASA. They said they didn't have any plans for sending horses on space missions. How about you? What did you dream of when you were young?"

Branson was sorry he'd asked the question before it had cleared his tongue. It was as if he could see Lacy sink into a sheltering hole.

"I had no dreams." Lacy turned to stare out the window and into the moonlit shadows that marched by them. "My mother died when I was ten."

"That's tough when you're a kid. I was fourteen when my dad died. I thought my world had come to an end."

"That's the difference between you and me, Sheriff. Mine had."

Her tone left no doubt that the conversation was finished. It was just as well. Sharing dreams and disillusionments was something close friends did, people who had more vested in their relationship than finding a missing sister and her would-be killer.

Lacy Gilbraith was part of his job and nothing more. Strange, but he'd never had trouble separating the two before. He turned off the road and stopped at the gate to the Burning Pear.

"Let me get the gate," Lacy said, opening the truck door and jumping out before he had a chance to protest.

She moved lightly over the ground in front of him, her agile frame caught in the beam of his headlights. Unexpectedly, his mind leaped back to the sight of her as the voluminous wedding gown had parted, revealing delicate curves and satiny skin.

He shuddered as his body responded in ways it shouldn't, the feelings inside him so foreign to the way he normally reacted that they almost frightened him. He worked on regaining control of mind and body as he drove through the open gate.

A spray of lights from an oncoming car illuminated Lacy as she swung the gate closed and latched it. The vehicle slowed, and Branson's muscles tensed instinctively. For a second, he thought the driver was going to stop, but he accelerated again and darted off before Branson had a chance to identify the car or the driver.

"I thought for a minute Charles had come to haul me back to his place," Lacy said, climbing into the truck and buckling her seat belt.

"I couldn't tell the make of the car, but it wasn't his Jag."

"So you had the same thought?"

"The possibility sprang to mind. It was probably a couple of young people looking for a spot to pull off and neck. I've found them in the driveway before on a Friday or Saturday night."

"And like the good sheriff you are, I'm sure you sent them home."

"I've even been known to take them myself if I catch a whiff of alcohol. The exciting life of a Texas county sheriff."

"Then you should thank Kate and me for dropping into your world. We seem to be real short of dull moments lately."

"So I've noticed." Branson guided the truck around a rut in the road. He slowed as a young deer stepped out of a cluster of mesquite and into the peripheral glow of the headlights. The deer froze for a second, just long enough for Lacy to sit up and take notice, before the startled animal darted back into the brush.

She watched in the direction the fawn had disappeared and then turned to look at him. "What's that?"

"The fawn?"

"No, those lights."

She pointed past his head, out his side window.

Branson shifted his gaze and caught a glimpse of the sprawling two-storey ranch house where he'd lived all his life. "That's home. I told you it was too late to turn back."

"You mean you actually live there!"

"A man's got to sleep somewhere."

"But it's so big!"

"Yeah. My dad leaned to the grandiose. We pretty much fill it up when we're all home, though." Branson rounded a curve in the road, and clusters of heavy brush and scrubby trees blocked the house from view for the next hundred yards or so. When it appeared again, Branson realized why the size looked so impressive from a distance.

The place was lit up as if there were a party going on. Only there wasn't. The birthday party had been two days ago.

Past midnight and all the lights burning could only mean trouble. He speeded up as much as he dared with the prospect of a deer or a cow stepping into his path. Still, it seemed to take forever to cover the last of the distance down the dusty road.

Forgetting Lacy Gilbraith, Branson skidded to a stop and jumped out, hitting the ground at a run and not slowing until he was inside the house.

One look at Ryder's face, and he knew his fears had been well founded.

Chapter Five

"It's Mom!" The explanation spilled out of Ryder's mouth before Branson had a chance to question him. "She was having chest pains. Langley called Dr. Ramirez and he sent an ambulance for her. He's meeting her at the clinic in Kelman for now. If it's serious, they'll stabilize her and move her to San Antonio."

Branson handled the bad news like he handled everything. Outwardly, he was calm. Inside, the dread burned like acid. "How long ago was that?"

"They probably haven't been gone a good half hour yet."

"Where's Langley? I saw his car out back."

"He rode with Mom in the ambulance. She was still insisting she'd be fine, but she looked scared. She was pale as a sheet. And shaky." Worry pooled in Ryder's eyes. "I've never seen her like that before."

Branson rolled the news around in his head. Other than the winter she'd had pneumonia, he didn't remember his mom ever going to bed with an ailment. If she'd willingly left Burning Pear in an ambulance, she had to be in serious pain.

He buried his hands in his pockets, hating the feeling

that there was nothing he could do. "Why didn't you go with them?"

The answer came from the newly created nursery in the form of a high-pitched wail. Betsy. In the panic of the moment, he'd forgotten all about the baby. And Lacy. He glanced toward the back door. Apparently she hadn't followed him in.

Betsy's cries increased in volume.

Ryder backed toward the hall door. "Mom's in good hands, Branson. Good spirits, too. She was still giving orders as they strapped her to the stretcher."

But in spite of his attempts to reassure Branson, Ryder's lips were drawn into tight lines, his muscles bunched, as he turned to walk toward the crying infant. He stopped at the door and turned back to face Branson. "Mom will pull through this. She *has* to."

And more than ever before, Branson wished he were half the optimist his brothers had always been.

LACY STEPPED to the back door where Branson had disappeared a few minutes earlier. She had no idea what had gotten into him, but something had struck him like a lightning bolt, changing his whole demeanor in a matter of seconds.

The wooden door was open. She wasn't used to just walking into people's houses, but she had been invited, even if the sheriff had apparently forgotten that she was with him. Besides, Branson hadn't exactly waited on an engraved invitation before he'd busted in on her in Kate's home earlier today.

She pushed through the screen door and into a large kitchen that smelled of spices and onions and... She sniffed again. And baby lotion?

Naturally, Kate's gift to the Randolphs.

Branson turned as the screen door closed behind her. "Lacy."

"Well, at least you remember my name." But Branson was showing signs of stress that hadn't been evident a few minutes earlier. She was sorry she'd responded so flippantly. "Is something wrong?"

"It's my mother. They think she may have had a heart attack."

Lacy listened as Branson gave her the report he'd just gotten from his brother Ryder. His voice was steady and strong, but she could read the concern in the depths of his dark brown eyes.

He was worried about his mother. It was a different side of the sheriff, a softer side, one that made him seem more human.

"I'm sorry," she said, feeling the inadequacy of the words. "Does she have a heart condition?"

"Not that we were aware of." He pulled the hat from his head and slid it into place on a shelf by the back door. "Actually, we're not sure of anything yet except that she was having severe chest pains."

"That's reason enough to worry." She stood awkwardly by the door. Branson had saved her life and bought her dinner, but they were still virtually strangers. She felt like an intruder, standing here in the Randolph kitchen, like a voyeur, peeking into family matters she had no right to share.

"It's a bad time for you, Branson, and too late for us to do much more talking tonight. If I could get a ride back into Kelman, I could stay at a local motel and meet with you in the morning."

Branson narrowed his eyes and stared at her as if she'd suggested something totally out of the question. "How

would worrying about you in a motel make dealing with
my mother's sickness easier?''

"You don't have to worry about me, Branson. I can take
care of myself. It's my sister who's in trouble.''

"You weren't taking care of yourself too well when
someone hurled a bomb through the window this afternoon.
Besides, we have plenty of room here." He turned his back
on her and started toward the kitchen counter and an au-
tomatic drip coffeemaker that was half-full of an extremely
dark brew.

"And you're the only decent lead I have in an attempted
murder and a possible baby-abduction case.''

He threw in the last sentence as if it were an afterthought.
She knew it wasn't. Even under family stress, Branson Randolph held tenaciously to his responsibilities as sheriff.
That's why he had no intention of giving her the chance to
disappear on him the way Kate had.

"You didn't tell me you'd brought company with you,
big brother.''

Lacy jerked around to find a tall, handsome cowboy
parked in the open door frame behind her. His hair wasn't
quite as dark as Branson's but it was every bit as thick, and
his eyes were the same piercing shade of cocoa brown. He
cradled a baby in his right arm about as proficiently as she
might have handled Branson's six-shooter.

"I'm not exactly company," she volunteered. "More
like a homeless suspect he found wandering around a crime
scene.''

"Ah, that explains it. You're lucky he didn't zip you
into a plastic bag and mark you as evidence.''

"This is my brother Ryder," Branson said, nodding his
head in Ryder's direction. He stepped over and dropped a
hand to the small of her back. "And this is Lacy Gilbraith,

the sister of the woman who delivered Betsy to our door-step.''

The curious but accepting look on Ryder's face vanished as comprehension sank in, replaced by a ''What-the-hell-are-you-doing-here?'' expression. He stared at her as he switched the fretting baby from one side of his body to the other.

''I hope you come bearing answers,'' he said, his tone a shade less than friendly. ''Your sister seems to be mixed up about who fathered this baby.''

His attitude grated on Lacy's control. He didn't know anything about her or her sister, but he was willing to jump to accusing conclusions. ''My sister's mixed up about a lot of things right now,'' she answered.

''I don't wish your sister any ill will,'' Ryder said. ''It's just that she's a stranger to all of us. We don't know her and we're not Betsy's family.''

''So I've been told.''

Betsy started to cry, and Ryder paced the kitchen, moving his arms in a rocking motion. He limped slightly, favoring the right leg, but he was a muscular, intimidating man by any standards.

''What's wrong with the baby?'' Branson asked. ''What did you do to her?''

''Exactly what Mom told me to do.''

''Well, you must not be doing it right or she wouldn't be crying.''

''If you know so much about babies all of a sudden, why don't you take her? Better yet—'' his gaze moved from Branson to Lacy ''—if you're Kate's sister, then you must be Betsy's aunt. You take her.''

''I'm sorry to bust your bubble, but Kate did not give birth to this or any other baby.''

Ryder's eyebrows rose to a questioning arch. "Then who did?"

Branson stepped toward Ryder. "Hold on a minute. Lacy's here as an invited guest, Ryder. My guest. She's not here to be interrogated by you."

Lacy put up a hand to stop his lecture. "It's all right, Branson. I can handle Ryder's questions." She was usually mild-mannered, especially when she was a guest in someone's home, but she'd taken more than enough garbage for one day. Charles, a mad bomber, a rude nurse and now a cowboy who was taking out his frustration on her.

"I don't know the identity of the mother or the father of the baby you're holding," she said, forcing a civility she didn't feel to her tone. "But if Kate said the baby was a Randolph and risked her life to bring her to you then I'd be inclined to believe she's a Randolph. So, unless you and your brothers have been celibate for the past ten or so months, I wouldn't be so quick to unequivocally deny anything."

She turned and caught a glimpse of Branson. He was leaning against the counter, watching the show. He'd backed off and let her have her say. She liked him more by the minute.

Ryder adjusted his hold on Betsy, moving her from the cradle of his arms to rest on his shoulder. He supported her tiny neck with a broad hand that swallowed the infant. "I guess I deserved that. I did kind of jump to conclusions."

"If that's an apology, I accept." Lacy stepped closer so that she could sneak a peek at the baby who seemed to be the center of all the secrets and danger. Raising on tiptoe, she pushed aside the edge of the pink fuzzy blanket.

Betsy quieted the second Lacy ran a finger along her pudgy, red cheek. "She's beautiful. And so tiny."

Branson stepped close behind her, peering over her

shoulder for a peek himself. "Her lungs don't seem all that tiny," he said. "Especially when she hits top form about two in the morning."

"The duty I'll probably draw tonight," Ryder said. "But I think it's your turn to play uncle now."

Ryder handed Betsy off to Branson, a tenderly awkward exchange that brought a smile to Lacy's face and a strange tightening in her chest. Two rugged cowboys who were probably expert at everything else they did, yet so inept at baby handling that they were laughable.

Branson managed to untangle his hands from Ryder's, but he was still holding Betsy as if she were an egg that might crack if he moved the wrong way. She wiggled and let out a plaintive cry.

Branson shrugged, bewilderment hanging like weights on his hunched shoulders. "You're going to have to do better than that, baby Betsy, if you expect me to understand you. Are you hungry?"

"I've fed her and changed her," Ryder said. "Just exactly like Mom said to do. She quiets down for a minute or two and then starts crying again. You don't think she could miss Mom already, do you?"

"It could be. I do." Branson picked up a rattle from the table and shook it. Betsy screamed as if he'd insulted her. "Maybe she just doesn't like cowboys much."

"Give her time," Lacy said. "Right now she'd probably prefer a sure hand to virility."

"There's not a surer hand in the county than mine," Branson protested, shifting the crying infant to his other shoulder. "Go get that certificate I won in last year's shooting competition, Ryder. That should convince Betsy she's in good hands."

"Branson Randolph," Lacy taunted. "There is a big difference in holding a baby and a weapon. Babies like to be coddled, cooed to.''

"Well, thank God, newborn calves don't need that kind of pampering," he said. "We'd have to sell the ranch."

Betsy took a few shallow, baby breaths and then started bawling all over again.

"You don't suppose you could show us how that pampering and cooing stuff works, do you?" Branson asked, staring at Lacy over the top of Betsy's bobbing head.

"Give her to me," she said, more than willing to have a turn at holding the unhappy infant. "I can give it a try."

Branson shifted the bundle of kicking and squalling humanity into Lacy's arms before she had a chance to change her mind. Lacy shifted her hold on the infant so that Betsy rested in the cradle of her arms, her tiny head snuggled against her breast.

Betsy stretched, suddenly showing signs of contentment, and Lacy cooed baby love words to her. "You little sweetheart. You just need some loving, don't you, precious? These big, old, tough cowboys don't know how to treat a tiny, little angel like you."

Betsy snuggled against her, and Lacy's heart did a flip-flop of its own. A baby without a mother. Without a father. Did Betsy know she'd been deserted by the person who'd carried her inside her for nine months, the woman who's very heartbeat had sustained Betsy's life?

Or had she been deserted at all? Had she been abducted instead, stolen away from the arms of her mother? Was some woman somewhere tonight slowly dying of a broken heart, aching to hold Betsy to her chest the way Lacy was doing right now?

Oh, Kate. How could you have become part of this? After all we went through when we were young. All the pain. All the hurt.

But Kate wasn't here to answer her questions.

Lacy swallowed hard, forcing her mind to deal with the here and now, with the only world she had any control over. She held Betsy so that she could study her delicate features. Her eyes were beautiful, chocolate brown and bright as moonbeams. Her lashes were thin and silky, the same dark shade as the soft fluff that covered her perfect head.

Lacy touched her lips to the soft baby flesh of Betsy's cheek. "She's so precious."

"She is now." Branson peeked over her shoulder, pushing the blanket lower for a better look. "What did you do to her? If it's some kind of trick, you'll have to teach it to me."

"It's no trick. Babies sense when the person holding them is nervous."

"Kind of like a horse knows when a rider's afraid of him."

"Yes, only Betsy's not trying to get the upper hand. She only needs to feel safe."

"How did you get so baby smart?"

"I'm not. I've just shared with you my one scrap of newborn knowledge."

"And Betsy thanks you for that." Branson reached over and touched one of the baby's hands. Betsy circled one of his large, tanned fingers with her petite pink ones. "So, you like me now that you've dumped me. Just like a woman."

His voice was light, not quite cooing, but close. Betsy lost her grip and he moved his hand away.

"Now that you've got her quiet, I can take her back if you like, let you get some rest."

She held Betsy closer. "I'd like to hold her until she falls asleep. We both need it. So if you'll point me toward a rocking chair and the nursery, we'll wait for the sandman together.''

''You're sure?''

''Absolutely.''

Branson led the way to a nursery that housed an antique baby bed, a new changing table, a black iron daybed and a collection of toys, some new, some evidently holdovers from the time the Randolph men were babies.

Lacy eyed the daybed with a covetous stare. ''I see a spot that has my name on it.''

''There's a real guest room upstairs. You'd be a lot more comfortable there.''

''I'd rather stay here so that I can hear Betsy if she needs me.''

''You don't have to do this, Lacy. I didn't bring you here to baby-sit.''

''Why not? Ryder was right, you know. My sister *is* the one who brought Betsy here. The way I see it, until we know who the real parents of this baby are, she's as much my responsibility as she is yours.''

Lacy settled into the rocker, Betsy in her arms. ''Besides, she's the first person in a long time who needs something from me I can actually deliver. Now, go try again to explain to your brother what in the devil I'm doing sleeping at the Burning Pear. And I hope you do a better job of convincing him than you have me.''

She closed her eyes, dismissing Branson. He was eager to help her now. That would all change soon enough. As soon as he got wind of the details she'd omitted. As soon as he realized he was harboring a thief.

BRANSON AND RYDER both jumped at the first ring of the telephone. Branson beat him to it, grabbing the receiver and punching on the speaker button as he said his hello.

"How's Mom?" he asked as soon as he heard Langley's voice amplified into the den.

"It looks good. Dr. Ramirez says the indications are she didn't have a heart attack."

Two sighs of relief filtered through the tension. "That's great. Does he know what caused the pain?"

"No. That's why he wants to send her to the hospital in San Antonio for a few days. He wants to run a full battery of tests, pinpoint the problem so he can treat it effectively."

"Can he get her to agree to that?" Ryder asked. "I can't remember her ever having spent the night in a hospital."

"That's where we come in. Dr. Ramirez says we have to convince her. She's resting now, thanks to some drugs he gave her to ease the pain."

Branson listened more than talked throughout the rest of the conversation. The gist of the message was that the doctor didn't know what had caused his mother's problem, but he thought stress might have been a major contributing factor.

Mary Randolph had worked hard all her life, putting in as many hours as her husband did when he was alive and as her sons did now. In the beginning, with four young sons to care for and a struggling ranch, she probably hadn't had a lot of choice.

She did now. They had all begged her to hire help with the housework and cooking, to let one of the hands help her in her vegetable garden, to give up some of the responsibilities at church.

She'd refused even to listen to their pleas. She was a rancher's woman and "not afraid of raisin' a few blisters." One of her favorite sayings that meant she would do as she pleased. And staying busy pleased her.

His mother was a hardheaded woman. She'd proved it once again when she'd insisted on taking care of Betsy.

She'd claimed Betsy needed her, but Branson wasn't fooled for a second. His mother adored Dillon's son, Petey, and she missed him terribly at times like this when the Senate was in session and Dillon and his family had to live in Austin. She wanted more grandchildren.

Lots more, and her three youngest sons had shown no signs of heading down the aisle. That's why she'd grabbed on to the possibility that Betsy was a Randolph like a motherless calf to a teat of milk.

He and his brothers had been certain the baby did not belong to them. None of them had ever seen Kate Gilbraith before. But now that they'd found out Kate wasn't the mother, their denials held a lot less substance.

Unless you've been celibate for the past ten months or so...

Ten months or so. A hot July night. And a woman he'd thought he knew.

"How about some milk and cookies to celebrate the good news?"

Ryder's question jolted him back into the present. "I'll join you, but I think I'll make my snack liquid. Bourbon, to be exact." He needed it.

"Okay by me," Ryder said, "and then I'll toss you for who pulls the two o'clock feeding."

"Only if we use my nickel. I don't trust yours."

"You, my dear brother, never trust anyone."

"In today's world, it's a sign of intelligence." Branson poured two fingers of the amber liquid and downed it, appreciating the burn as it anointed his throat. But one drink was enough. He needed to wake up with a clear head.

A woman needed to be located. A would-be killer needed to be apprehended. Questions needed answers.

And baby Betsy needed an identity.

BRANSON ROLLED OVER, groggy, but forcing his mind to focus. Something had wakened him from a sound sleep.

"Branson."

He looked up to find a woman standing in his bedroom doorway, the light from the hall shining in her hair and filtering through the pajama top that stopped midthigh. *His* pajama top.

"Branson, are you awake?"

"I am now. Is something wrong, Lacy?"

"I'm worried about Betsy."

The strain in her voice finished the job of waking him. He kicked free of the tangling sheet and sat up in bed. "What's wrong with her?"

"She's just sleeping."

He rubbed his eyes. "It's the middle of the night. Sleeping sounds good to me."

"But it's not the middle of the night. It's almost four and she hasn't made a peep all night. I heard you talking about her two o'clock feeding, and she hasn't had it."

"I don't think it's required." He rubbed his eyes. "Do you?"

"Well, I'm up and can't go back to sleep, so I thought I'd wake her and feed her."

"Be my guest." He fell back to his pillow.

"I can't. I looked in the refrigerator, but there's no baby bottle."

He sat up again and swung his legs over the side of the bed, tugging the sheet so that it covered his boxer shorts. "It's dry formula. Comes in a can. You mix it with boiled water right before she takes it." He stretched a kink out of his shoulder muscles. "Mom wrote out all the instructions. They're on the counter in the kitchen, right next to the formula."

"I'm sorry I woke you, but no one told me." She backed

toward the door. "I'm glad your mom is not seriously ill. You must be relieved."

"Extremely."

"She's lucky to have sons who worry about her so."

"We learned our worrying from her. But how did you know my mom was better?" he asked. "You had already gone to bed when Langley called."

"Voices carry well in this house."

"I'll have to remember that."

Lacy touched a hand to the footboard of his bed. Streaks of moonlight through the blinds painted her in silvery stripes. A mystical figure, dreamlike. One that smelled of lilacs.

Branson rearranged the sheet as his awareness level spiraled upward. He raked his fingers through his hair, imagining what a wild mess it was and wondering why his never looked as good uncombed as Lacy's did right now.

"I vote we wait until Betsy wakes up on her own to feed her," he said. "You go back and try to get some sleep. I lost the coin toss with Ryder, so this feeding's mine anyway."

Lacy stepped closer. "A coin toss to decide who feeds you. A nursery full of antiques and bright-colored toys. Three cowboys and a grandma. A baby could do a lot worse."

"Four cowboys, actually. I have another brother."

"Senator Dillon Randolph."

"Do you know him?"

"I know about him. He's not very popular in the Kincaid camp."

"Or vice versa. They ride opposite sides of the fence when it comes to saying what's best for Texas."

"I've really only heard Charles's take on the situation, so I'm sure I've only gotten one side."

Lacy leaned against the bed rail. Branson decided the innocent movement was far more sensual, more seductive than she could possibly know.

"I imagine Charles would think you've taken complete leave of your senses," he said, "if he could see you now. Hanging out at the Burning Pear when you could have been the mistress of the manor."

She stared at her bare toes. "You don't hear me complaining."

"Not now," he said. "Give yourself time. Most city women find ranch life a little dull for their liking."

She sat down on the bed beside him, so close her thigh brushed his through the thin sheet. Pleasure erupted inside him—hot, like water that had set too long in the south Texas sun.

The situation clawed at his gut. He was sitting on his bed with a half-naked woman, his body reacting to her every movement, to the very essence of her. But he was still a lawman, and she was still a woman with too many secrets.

This was a first for him. The only time he'd compromised his position as sheriff. And the first time in a long time he'd let himself feel anything for a woman, even something as fleeting as desire. The first time in almost ten months.

He should learn from his mistakes.

"Lacy, I'll be calling Charles Castile first thing in the morning. If there's more that I should know about him, something related to Kate's shooting, it would go better if I hear it from you."

She looked away from him, her expression suddenly grim. It supported what he believed, that she hadn't told him the whole truth. The fact stuck in his craw.

"All I know is what I've already told you."

"I'm only asking, Lacy. It's my job."

The phone rang. He grabbed it and barked a hello.

"I hate to wake you, Branson…"

"You didn't. What's up, Gordon?"

"A bunch of kids from the high school went out partying tonight. You know how they get when school's almost out."

"I know."

"Well, they were down at the creek that runs just west of your front gate, the one on Maccabbe's side of the fence. They had two cars full of them down there from what I could judge and a couple of them on motorbikes."

"Any trouble?"

"Yeah. You're gonna love this."

Branson bit his tongue to keep from yelling at his inexperienced but well-meaning deputy. The man loved a good story. "How about some facts, Gordon?"

"Old Hank's boy called about an hour ago. Said they saw a vehicle down there, run off into the creek. Just the nose of it's underwater."

"Have you checked out his story?"

"I'm at the spot right now, not that I can see that much before the sun comes up, but I wanted to make sure no one was in the vehicle."

"I take it the vehicle's empty."

"It's empty, but the car's registered to Kate Gilbraith. There's what looks like a couple of bullet holes in the back window. And Kate Gilbraith's purse is still in the car."

"Stay there, Gordon. I'll be right out."

Branson stood up and grabbed for his jeans, doing a balancing jig while he stuffed in one leg and then the other.

"What happened, Branson? Is it Kate?"

"They found her car, but she's not in it. Partly submerged in a creek."

Lacy rushed toward the door, stopping only to throw a parting comment over her shoulder. "Wait for me, I'm going with you."

"I'd rather you stay here."

It was a waste of breath, he knew. Lacy Gilbraith didn't follow orders. At least not his.

Chapter Six

The early-morning wind cut through Branson's light jacket and nipped at his ears. By midmorning, it would be shirtsleeve weather, but now the sun was no more than a band of gold along the horizon and had not begun to warm away the night's chill.

Lacy was standing apart from Gordon and Branson, hugging her chest and staring at Kate's partially submerged car as if she thought by will alone she might somehow cause her sister to materialize. She looked waiflike, the shoulders of the jacket Branson had lent her drooping halfway to her elbows, the length of it reaching to the tops of her knees.

Branson wished there was something he could say to ease her worries. But any way you looked at what was going on, it spelled deep trouble for Kate. He'd thought that before Gordon had found Kate's car at the creek. And nothing he'd discovered in their daybreak examination of evidence had changed his mind.

"Not a lot more we can do out here this morning," Gordon said, grinding the toe of his boot into the ground. "Do you want me to have the car towed before I go off duty?"

"Yeah, and dusted for prints."

"The car's obviously been sittin' and soakin' for several days. What's your take on how it ended up in the creek?"

"The bullet holes are in the back window and the left rear tire. My guess would be that someone came up behind Kate on the highway and shot at her. She took off through the brush and then got caught in the mud of the creek bank, losing control and sliding in."

"Lucky for her, the creek was practically dry. Probably wouldn't have even been muddy if we hadn't caught those thundershowers Wednesday afternoon."

"Yeah, lucky for her." Lucky for Betsy, too. Kate must have grabbed the baby and tramped through the brush, bleeding from her wound and carrying a baby all the way to the ranch house.

Which would explain why she'd lost so much blood from the shoulder wound and why she'd collapsed at their feet. It was a good mile hike. A spunky woman. And one determined to get Betsy to the Randolphs.

Gordon turned and let his glance linger on Lacy. "Kate Gilbraith's sister seems nice enough, but she sure looks like she's hurtin'. I don't understand why that Kate gal don't hightail it to the police if she's got folks aiming to kill her, or at least let her sister know what she's up to."

Branson kicked at a rock, sending it hurtling into the water to the left of the partially sunken car. He didn't understand Kate's actions either. It would have been easy enough for her to beep Lacy if she'd wanted to let her know where she was. So apparently she didn't.

Of course, Branson would have a better chance at figuring this all out if Lacy would tell him the full truth. He still had the distinct impression she was lying to protect somebody. Probably Kate, but it could be to protect herself or even her recently jilted fiancé.

"I reckon I'm gonna git on outta here, go down to the

café and catch me some breakfast," Gordon said. "You and Miss Gilbraith want to join me?"

"No, I think Miss Gilbraith probably needs a little more sleep. We didn't get back to the Burning Pear until very late last night."

Gordon crammed his right hand into the pocket of his khaki pants and dragged out a fat ring of clattering keys. "I still don't think it's a good idea, your putting that woman up at your house. You don't know anything about her. It's asking for trouble. That's what it is."

"I'm just trying to find a few answers and hoping Lacy Gilbraith can help me."

"Yeah, well, you're the boss, but I don't think I'd be able to concentrate on finding her sister if I had a shapely little stray like that one parking her boots under my roof. I just might forget why she was there."

"I'll work on honing my memory skills." Branson tugged his hat a little lower, his gaze nailing his young deputy. "You just take care that you don't lose any evidence from the interior of that car. We need every scrap of a clue we can find."

"I'll be more careful than a heifer at a bull convention," Gordon drawled, turning to head across the clearing toward his truck. He turned before he reached it. "You know where to find me if you need me?"

"A phone call away."

"Yeah, so don't keep all the fun to yourself. This is the most exciting thing we've had around here since Matilda Moxley found her husband in bed with that traveling saleswoman and took after him with a branding iron."

Gordon waved to Lacy and tipped his hat as he crawled behind the steering wheel. Branson doubted if Lacy noticed. She appeared lost in her own thoughts, fighting her own fears.

He watched the dust settle from Gordon's departing car and then walked over to where Lacy was standing. Even in the soft glow of sunrise, her silhouette reflected the doom that had settled over her.

The urge to put his arm around her drooping shoulders was much too strong. Gordon had probably called it right. He should never have brought her home with him, should never be feeling the emotions that were stripping him of the hard edge this situation demanded.

But he wondered if it would have mattered where they were. In his bedroom. Here in the isolation of the Texas brush country. He doubted if even the sterile environs of the county jail would have altered the level of awareness that hovered between the two of them.

He couldn't explain it, nor could he deny it. He felt tied to her, an accomplice, a friend.

Only he was none of those things. He had met her mere hours ago. He only knew what she told him and what he had surmised from her actions. For some men that might have been enough, but the truth was, he had never been that good a judge of character where women were concerned.

Look at the mistake he had made last summer. Had that mistake been the catalyst for all that was going on right now? A baby in the house, Kate Gilbraith's shooting, Lacy's shivering in the first light of day?

Hopefully, he'd know the answer to that question soon. Right now, he had work to do. "Let's go back to the house, Lacy. We can talk better there."

"We have to do more than talk, Branson. We have to find Kate before the man who riddled her car with bullets finds her."

It was only the word *we* that worried him. He wasn't going after a would-be killer with her at his side. He climbed into the driver's seat, but before he could fire the ignition, his cell phone rang again. This time it was Langley delivering a message from Charles Castile. Branson turned to Lacy when he'd broken the connection.

"Looks like you're going to have company at the Burning Pear."

"Me? No one even knows I'm staying there."

"Apparently, Charles Castile does. He called a few minutes ago. He wants to see you, says it's urgent."

Lacy grew pale. "How did he find me?"

"He went in and talked to the nursing staff after he saw us leaving the hospital last night. They identified me for him. At least that's what he told Langley, and it sounds likely enough."

"And he just assumed that you would bring me to the Burning Pear. That doesn't make sense."

"I suspect it was a lucky guess. He was probably fishing for information about where I'd dropped you last night and caught Langley off guard."

"Why is he so desperate to talk to me?"

"He didn't say. He only said that it was important that he see you at once. I'd like to have him drive down here."

Lacy lay a hand on his arm. "Can we talk for a minute before we go back to the Burning Pear?"

"Can't it wait?"

"No. I need to tell you now. While I'm convinced that you're different from every other man with authority and power that I've ever known. While I still believe you're really interested in helping Kate and me."

Maybe it was her hand on his arm, the tightness in his chest or the feeling that she wanted something from him he couldn't give. He wasn't sure which. He only knew that he felt anxious and more than a little inadequate.

"I'm a sheriff, Lacy. My job is to uphold the law." He

should stop there. He couldn't. He lay a hand over hers. "But I'm also a man. I'm not immune to feelings."

"I know. I realized that last night when I saw you holding little Betsy in your arms."

Lacy sighed audibly and Branson sensed the struggle going on inside her. He'd dealt with lots of hesitant witnesses and frightened suspects, but none that he'd felt was so torn apart about talking to him. Lacy Gilbraith was a very complicated woman.

She stared out into the monotonous landscape of cacti and brush and windblown grasses. "I'm still amazed that your mother—your whole family—have embraced a baby whom you all seem so sure that neither you nor your brothers fathered."

Branson felt a sharp stab of guilt. A day ago he'd been certain that Betsy could not be his daughter. Now doubt had crept in, settling inside him somewhere between his heart and his head. Besides, he couldn't take the credit Lacy was offering. He'd never wanted his mother to keep Betsy in the first place.

"We have a lot of room at the Burning Pear, Lacy. Taking in a baby isn't that much of a sacrifice."

"You have a lot of love at the Burning Pear, Branson. Even when you and Ryder were fussing about who would take care of Betsy, it was evident in the way you both worried about her crying and in the way you held her. Not to mention the concern you had for your mother."

"We're a family."

"A family. You say that word like it has some magical power. It doesn't."

"You're right. I've seen enough of life to know that. But you and your sister obviously share some special bond."

"She's a special person. Mixed-up, but special." Lacy turned from the window and back to face Branson. "That's why I was willing to do *anything* to help her when Ricky Carpenter came to me four weeks ago and asked me for the money.''

Anything. Branson wasn't at all sure he'd like what Lacy was about to tell him, but this time he hoped it would be the whole truth. ''You said you asked Charles to lend Ricky fifty thousand dollars and that he agreed.''

''That's not exactly the way it happened. Charles didn't agree to a loan. Instead, he made an offer I couldn't refuse. He said he'd *give* me the money.''

''I would have never taken him for the generous type.''

''He isn't. The gift had strings attached. In return for the fifty thousand dollars he wanted me to become his wife.'' She turned back toward Branson. ''We made a bargain. The rest is history.''

''So, when you didn't go through with the wedding, you broke the bargain.''

''Yes. That's why you have to help me. Fast. Before Charles has me arrested. I'm sure that's why he's coming out here. He wants to talk to you, not me.''

''Jilting your fiancé is not a crime, no matter how much he's paid for you.''

''Stealing fifty thousand dollars is.''

Branson's suspicious nature shifted into overdrive. Lacy's story was fishier than the trout he'd had for lunch yesterday.

''How is Charles going to make a case against you if he gave you the money? I doubt that he had you sign a legal document saying you were selling your body and allegiance to him for fifty thousand dollars.''

''No, but Charles doesn't hand over good hard cash without safeguards. He had me write the check and forge his signature. If I backed out, he'd claim I wrote the check without his approval. All part of the bargain we made.''

So Charles Castile bought himself a beautiful bride and planned on using blackmail to seal the deal. It was a fascinating story, but was it the truth? Or was Branson being played a fool?

Only time would tell. And time was ticking away fast.

"There's one other thing I didn't mention last night."

Branson turned back to Lacy. "Go on."

"A man called me on the phone in the church parlor the other day, just before I was to walk down the aisle. I didn't recognize the voice. Actually, I thought it was a crank call at the time. Now I'm not so sure."

"What did the caller say?"

"That I was going to die—very soon."

KATE GILBRAITH LEANED against a tree in the park that ran behind what was left of the town house she'd shared with Ricky. She hugged her arms around her chest and fought the shudders that shook her frail body. In the past few minutes she'd experienced a rollicking collage of feelings. Shock. Anger. Frustration. Fear. Now the feelings merged and coiled inside her with the force of a tempest.

The town house had been the closest thing to a real home she'd ever known, worlds nicer than the apartment she had been able to afford on the salary and tips she'd made working for Joshua Kincaid.

Now it was gone. So was everything else she'd owned. Her clothes, her jewelry—if you could call costume earrings jewelry—her pictures.

Along with most of her determination and all of her physical prowess. Her head felt as if someone had hit her upside it with a two-by-four, and the arm that had received the incessant IVs ached like crazy. Thankfully, the rest of her body was numb.

Still, she'd been amazed how easy it had been to steal a

set of scrubs from the laundry area and just walk out of the hospital. It had been easier still to hot-wire a car in the hospital parking lot. Another trick she owed to the expertise of an old boyfriend. She could write her own book. *All I Need To Know, I Learned from Jerks in Knights' Clothing.* It would probably never make a bestseller list.

Kate froze against the tree as low voices broke the early-morning silence. The voices were male and coming from the street in front of the town house. She waited, her heart hammering against her chest.

It could be anybody, but then so could the man, or men, who were after her. So, once again it was time to disappear, to run away from everything she knew. Only this time she would be totally alone. She would not drag Lacy into the path of a killer.

LACY WOKE to the smell of meat frying and the sound of voices drifting under her door. She opened her eyes and squinted from the glare of sunlight that tunneled through the window. For a minute, she struggled to get her bearings. Then the wooden railing of the crib came into focus and served as a focal point to ground her thoughts.

Branson had insisted she lay back down for a while when they'd returned to the ranch. For once she hadn't argued, though she hadn't expected to sleep.

She twisted in the narrow bed, scooting to a sitting position and looking for a clock. She finally located one on the brass and glass tea cart that had been rolled into the makeshift nursery to hold diapers and various other baby paraphernalia.

Nearly noon. She looked at the clock twice to make sure she hadn't misread it. She hadn't slept this late in years. She slid her legs over the side of the bed and sank her toes into the carpet.

Charles was supposed to be here around one. A sense of urgency and dread pushed her to action. She needed a shower, needed to pull herself together and prepare for whatever Charles planned to hurl her way.

Her mind slipping into gear, she stood, stretching her hands over her head until she could feel the strain to her muscles. Still barefoot, she tiptoed across the room, stopping at the edge of the crib. It was empty. Apparently Lacy had slept through Betsy's wake-up cries and the sounds of someone coming to get her.

Had it been Branson? Had he been in here while she slept, tending the precious baby whom her sister had dropped into his and his family's lives? A light tap at the door broke into her thoughts.

"May I come in?"

The voice wasn't the booming bass she'd expected but a softer feminine one. She turned the knob and swung the door open far enough that she could see her guest. The woman was striking, with thick, dark hair that swirled around her shoulders, classic features, full lips. If she had on any makeup at all, it was so scarce as to appear natural.

"Hi. I hated to wake you, but Branson asked if I'd tell you lunch was ready. He insisted you wouldn't mind, that you were expecting a guest."

"Thank you. I didn't mean to sleep this late."

"You must have needed the rest. Branson said you'd had a rough day yesterday."

"One I wouldn't want to relive."

"Still, I heard you were a godsend last night. Both Branson and Ryder have been singing your praises ever since Dillon and I drove up. By the way, I'm Ashley Randolph." She extended a hand.

Lacy took it and was surprised at the firmness of Ashley's grip. Only the smile seemed strained.

"I'm Lacy Gilbraith. You're probably wondering why I'm here."

"Branson explained everything. He also mentioned that you could use some clothes." She stepped inside the door and studied Lacy from top to bottom. "You're a tad shorter than I am and a few pounds slimmer, but I think you could wear my jeans and shirts without a problem. I took the liberty of spreading out some choices on the bed in the upstairs guest room."

"I appreciate that." Lacy raked her fingers through her hair, tangling them in unresponsive knots. "I could use a shower, too, and some shampoo."

"Already taken care of. I put a supply of toiletries on the counter in the guest bathroom. Deodorant, a new toothbrush, some body lotion. Dillon and I have a bungalow here at the ranch, although we live in Austin much of the year, so I probably have pretty much anything you need."

"You're very thoughtful."

"I have to be if I'm stepping in for Mother Randolph. She's a jewel. I hope you get to meet her."

Mother Randolph. Something in the way Ashley said the name made it seem almost like an endearment. The sentiment made Lacy uneasy, made her more aware just how much an intruder she was at the Burning Pear.

She and her sister were bringing the Randolphs nothing but trouble, and yet they were all going out of their way to make her welcome.

"I guess I better get out of here and let you shower and dress," Ashley said, her hand circling the doorknob. "And I better make sure Ryder is not burning the chicken. I gave him the frying chores while I woke you."

"Where's Betsy?"

"Langley walked her over to the corral to introduce her

to the horses. She's so adorable, and I swear she's grown since I saw her Wednesday night.''

Lacy's interest piqued. ''Were you here when Kate dropped her off?''

''Yes. We all were. It was Mother Randolph's birthday.''

''Then you saw my sister?''

''I saw her. I didn't get to talk to her.'' Ashley walked behind the rocking chair and propped her arms across the back railing. ''Branson told me to stay out of this, but I have to ask you, Lacy. Why would your sister do this?''

So Ashley wasn't as trusting as she'd first appeared. She'd been gracious and helpful for Branson's benefit, not for Lacy's. Strange, but now that Ashley's honest feelings were out in the open, Lacy felt more comfortable with the situation. She could understand reasonable doubt a lot easier than she could comprehend blind acceptance.

''All I know is that my sister is in danger, and I plan to do whatever I can to help her. I have no clue as to how Betsy fits into the puzzle.'' Her voice rose, probably too loud.

''I'm not judging you or your sister, Lacy. I can't. But I'm asking. Please don't bring danger to the Randolphs.''

''That's not my intention. Coming here wasn't my idea, but I can't turn down Branson's help in finding my sister.''

''I understand. I really do.''

Lacy was shocked to see the depth of sadness reflected in Ashley's eyes.

''Ask Branson to tell you about my past sometime, Lacy. Then you'll know why I understand exactly how you feel about your sister.''

Lacy watched Ashley walk away and then she raced upstairs to shower and dress. She was suddenly fully awake, famished and anxious to deal with Charles and get it out of the way so she could go searching for Kate. That is if she didn't end up in jail.

But one thing she knew for certain. She had to get out of this house quick. The Randolphs were growing on her. First Branson, then Betsy, and now Branson's sister-in-law.

And it was still less than twenty-four hours since she'd bolted from a wedding to Charles Castile. A man who undoubtedly would make sure she paid for not keeping her bargain, even if it took him another fifty thousand dollars to secure his revenge.

LUNCH HAD BEEN on the table when Lacy finished showering and dressing in Ashley's clothes. Like everything else at the Burning Pear, the meal had been a family affair. The men had laughed and talked and eaten as if they hadn't had food in days. Ashley had joined right in, but Lacy had mostly listened, feeling every bit the intruder she was.

Now lunch was over and everyone was ready to spring back into their busy, focused lives. Dillon and Ashley had left their son with his other grandmother for the day. They were picking up Mary Randolph at the clinic in Kelman to drive her to the hospital in San Antonio to undergo a series of tests. She'd refused to ride in an ambulance again, saying they were for dangerously ill patients and she wasn't one.

Langley and one of the hands called Riff were heading over to Eagle Pass to pick up some cattle he'd bought at an auction last week. Branson was back on the phone. He'd spent half of lunch taking phone calls, getting the scoop on Ricky Carpenter. It was amazing how many sources he had for collecting dirt. He'd put a vacuum cleaner to shame. And Ryder had drawn baby-sitting duties. Lacy considered him the luckiest of all.

Finally Branson hung up the phone. "A nice break," he said, circling the table and stopping behind her chair, "albeit a small one. A San Antonio police officer found the car we believe your sister stole from the hospital parking lot last night.''

Hope quickened Lacy's pulse. ''Was she in the car?''

''No, it was abandoned in the parking lot of an all-night grocery store.''

''But she might be inside getting food. Did they check?''

Branson lay a hand on her shoulder. ''They checked. She's not in the store. But there's an officer staking out the car. If she comes back to it, they'll nab her.''

Lacy went back to the table and started gathering dishes and taking them to the sink.

''Leave those, Lacy. Ashley's hired a woman from town to come out and help with Betsy and the housework until Mom is back on her feet.''

''Or until Mom gets home and fires her,'' Ryder added.

Lacy kept working, not so much for the sake of cleanliness as to do something with her hands to keep from beating them into the wall. She had counted on the highway patrol locating the car while Kate was still in it.

They would have arrested her for stealing the car, but at least she'd have been safe while she was in custody. And she would have gotten the medical care she needed.

''Looks like your guest has arrived,'' Ryder said, peering out through the screen door. ''Driving way too fast. He'll slow down quick enough if he comes face-to-face with one of those Hereford bulls in the middle of the road.''

Ashley walked over and watched the sleek, red Jaguar bouncing down the dirt path, raising a choking cloud of dust as it sped toward the house.

''Looks like the man can't wait to see you again,'' Branson said, stepping behind her.

''Can't wait to see me behind bars.''

''Then he's about to be sorely disappointed.''

Branson's words of support were appreciated, but even they couldn't stop the quaking inside her. Branson might represent the law, but Charles manipulated the law, used it to suit his own purposes. Give the devil his due, he'd said on more than one occasion, and the devil would make you his partner.

Only this time, *she* was the devil's due.

Chapter Seven

Branson decided on the massive office at ranch headquarters for the meeting with Charles Castile. It was the perfect choice, about a quarter of a mile from the house, and a world away from the high-powered business setting Charles was most comfortable in.

The stucco building blended perfectly with the south Texas ranch land. Lacy had ridden over in the truck with Branson and they'd stopped twice to wait for a cow to mosey off the road. Charles had followed in his expensive Jaguar, and she had a visual image of him stringing trails of profanity all along the way. Today was probably the first time the wheels of his car had ever seen a dirt road.

Branson's cell phone rang just as she hopped out of the truck. She walked over to the building without waiting for him, but didn't go in. Charles followed her.

"That was an extremely thoughtless stunt you pulled yesterday, disappointing me and all our guests."

"I'm sure you didn't track me down to complain about my manners, Charles."

"No. You know why I'm here."

"You want your money, but you know I don't have it. The worst part of all of this is that giving the fifty thousand dollars to Ricky didn't help. I'm not even sure he gave it to the men he owed. If he did, they tried to kill Kate anyway.''

''That's what happens when you deal with trash.''

Charles's whispered put-down stopped when Branson joined them and opened the door to the ranch headquarters. She stepped inside, then waited while her eyes adjusted to the lack of bright sunlight.

The room surprised her, or, maybe *seduced* her would be the better word. If rooms had gender, this one was definitely male. The walls were unfinished, the floor a brick-colored Mexican tile. There were huge antique desks at either end, not the glossy, mahogany variety Charles had in his office, but rugged pine desks with a brand she assumed belonged to the Burning Pear burned into the wood.

Antlered heads of bucks lined the walls and unframed snapshots of various prizewinning livestock dangled from randomly inserted pushpins. Only the two computers and array of business machines gave the truth away. The Burning Pear was a modern ranch.

''Come on in, Mr. Castile, and have a seat.'' Branson's voice denied the welcome of his words. It was gruff, authoritative.

''I don't see any reason for this meeting, Sheriff. I've come to pick up my bride. I know she's upset, but I'm sure she'll see things my way if you'll give me a minute to talk to her in private.''

''The lady doesn't seem to want that. And, to tell you the truth, even if Lacy did choose to go with you, I wouldn't allow it.''

''You won't *allow* it?'' Charles fingered the silk tie around his neck and puffed out his chest, stretching the buttons on his designer shirt. ''I'd like to know what gives you the mistaken idea that you have any authority at all over Lacy.''

Branson maneuvered around her and sauntered to a large, wooden, claw-foot table in the center of the room. He rolled out one of the captain's chairs for her and waited until she'd slid into it before responding to Charles's question.

"Have a seat and we'll talk about this sensibly, Charles. Lacy can't leave the ranch unless she leaves with me or one of my deputies. She's in protective custody."

She swallowed, her body stiffening, her buttocks pressing against the hard bottom of the chair. Branson had warned her to let him do the initial talking, to give him a chance to figure out what Charles was up to. But this was the first mention she'd heard of protective custody.

Charles slid into a chair next to hers. "You surely don't think Lacy's in danger from me?" He sounded offended, the consummate gentleman.

Branson propped a booted foot over his knee, a manly gesture, open, unassuming. The total opposite of the arrogant, intimidating posture of the man facing him. "I never considered that possibility, Charles. I mean, you're a well-respected attorney. My neighbor's right-hand man."

"Your neighbor?"

"Joshua Kincaid."

"Joshua lives in Austin."

"Most of the time, but he owns a ranch not ten miles from here as the crow flies. I'm sure you've visited there before, since you work for the man."

"I don't work for the man, as you put it. I'm my own boss."

"True, but your firm is on retainer by the Kincaid Entertainment Corporation, and they are by far your highest-dollar client."

"Not anymore. Joshua Kincaid likes to spread his money around."

"At any rate, to answer your first question, I'm sure Lacy has nothing to fear from a gentleman such as yourself."

He was baiting, and Charles knew it. But Branson had the advantage of the badge behind him and Lacy was sure Charles knew that, too. That was the only reason he wasn't spouting fire the way he did on his home court when someone tried to one-up him.

Any someone except Joshua Kincaid.

Charles turned and faced her, their gaze locking for the first time since he'd entered the room. Her blood ran cold at the anger that smoldered just below the sheen of his steel-gray eyes. She couldn't help but compare the two men at the table.

Charles was cruel where Branson was considerate, cunning where Branson was intelligent, deceitful where Branson was honest.

She should never have let Branson fight this battle for her. He would win this round, but he wouldn't win the war. Charles would find a way to get what he wanted and to punish anyone who tried to stop him. He always did.

She lay her hands out flat on the table in front of her. "I know what you want from me, Charles—fifty thousand dollars. I'll pay you back, every penny of it. It may take me a while."

"Darling, you don't have to pay me back. I'm your husband. What's mine is yours."

His words, his attitude, even the look in his eyes had a frightening madness to them that made her feel sick. She took a deep breath and tried hard to maintain her control. "No games, Charles. We all know there was *no* wedding. Even your guests would have to testify to that fact."

"They know you became ill, an attack of nerves. That's why we held a private ceremony, just you, me, a couple of witnesses and the justice of the peace."

"I don't know what you're trying to do, Charles, but I'm not going with you. I'm *not* your wife, and I'm not afraid of you."

The last statement wasn't entirely true, but she wasn't so frightened of him that she was still willing to go through with a sham wedding. Charles reached for her hand. She jerked away.

"You're embarrassing the sheriff, sweetheart, placing him in an awkward position. I'm sure he's enamored of you. What man isn't? But he doesn't need to become embroiled in our marital difficulties."

Branson leaned forward. "I don't see how you can have marital difficulties if there was no wedding."

Charles shook his head, smiling nervously. "There *was* a wedding. Lacy's just angry with me, that's all. I spoke harshly of her sister. My timing was poor." He pulled a legal-size envelope from the inside pocket of his suit jacket and dropped it to the table. "The license is here, signed, sealed and delivered." He pushed it toward Branson.

Branson examined the document and then inserted it back into the envelope. "Documents can be faked."

"They can be. This one isn't."

Branson shoved the envelope in front of Charles. "If you're not interested in the money that Lacy admits to owing you, then why are you here? What does Lacy have that you want?"

All traces of a smile disappeared from Charles's face. "What do I want from Lacy? Probably the same thing you want, Sheriff. Only with me it will be legal." He pushed his chair back and stood up. "Now, I'd like to take my wife home with me."

His words were cut off by the sharp ring of Branson's cell phone. Branson excused himself, then walked away from the table to take the call.

Charles moved over to stand behind Lacy. He dropped his hands to her shoulders, and his fingers fell into a rhythmic massage. "I'm sorry I upset you yesterday, my darling." Bending over, he touched his lips to her ear. "A bargain, Lacy. Keep it. For your sake and Kate's. And the sheriff's."

The words were whispered, yet they echoed like thunder in her brain. Charles wasn't pleading. He was threatening.

"By the way, Lacy, Kate sends her love."

The statement hit like a blow. "Have you talked to Kate?" Her voice was shaking. She didn't care anymore, couldn't play the game of nerves the way Charles and Branson could.

"Better than that. She's at my house waiting for us to return."

"How did Kate get to your house?"

"I don't know what manner of transportation she used, but she was there when I got in last night a little after midnight." He patted her on the shoulder. "Your sister is eager to see you, Lacy, and she'll be very upset if I come back alone. We both will."

"You're lying about the wedding. How do I know I can believe you about Kate?"

"Call my house, *our* house. See for yourself."

"I will." She walked to the desk at the far side of the room and picked up the phone. In seconds, she had dialed the number to Charles's house. His housekeeper answered.

"I'd like to speak to Kate Gilbraith," she said without identifying herself.

"She's asleep right now. Would you like for me to wake her?"

"No, that's okay. Let her sleep." Lacy hung up the phone. She still wasn't positive Kate was there, but she had to face Charles sooner or later anyway. It might as well be now. And this was her battle, not Branson's.

"Okay, Charles. I'll go with you."

Satisfaction released the tightness in Charles's face, stiffening his stance, stretching his lips into an arrogant smirk. "I thought you'd see it my way."

Branson rejoined them at the table. "You look upset, Lacy. What's going on?"

"I appreciate what you've done to help, Branson, but I have to go with Charles. Kate's at his house, and she needs me."

"Is that right? And when did Kate show up on your doorstep, Charles?"

"Last night. Around midnight."

Lacy watched the change in Branson's expression. He was disappointed in her. The truth of that hurt a lot more than it should have. She swallowed hard and followed Charles to the door. There was nothing left to say. Nothing that Branson would understand.

It wasn't until the knob turned in Charles's hand and he'd jerked the door open that she heard Branson's voice challenging them.

"I don't think you hear too well, Mr. Castile. I said Lacy is in protective custody. She will *not* be leaving the Burning Pear with you."

She turned and put up a hand to silence him. "It's okay, Branson. I'll be all right." Her voice gave her away, shaking so that she barely got the words out.

"It's *not* okay." Branson pushed past them and stood in the open door. "Now, you can leave the Burning Pear real nice like, Mr. Castile. *Alone.* Or I can throw you off my property. Your choice."

The muscles in Charles's face clenched, and his Adam's apple bobbed like a bouncing ball. "You talk awful high and mighty as long as you're wearing that gun at your waist. But even country cops are accountable to the law. You better have damn good cause for holding my wife against her will. Believe me, she will not thank you for this.''

Panic pitched against the walls of Lacy's chest. Branson thought he was helping, but he wasn't. She needed to go with Charles, needed to know for certain that he would not throw her sister back to the man who had tried to kill her. She needed to make sure Kate stayed alive.

Branson touched Lacy's arm. Possessively. Charles exploded.

''Take your hands off my wife, Sheriff.''

Branson stood in front of Lacy, too close, crowding her space. He stared unflinchingly until she met his gaze. ''Does he have a wife, Lacy? Is that marriage license he's touting false, or have you been lying to me all along?''

She wilted under the scorching heat of his gaze. There was no use to lie. She'd never been good at it, and she was sure Branson could see right through to her soul.

''I'm not married to him.''

The wind picked up outside the building, blowing dust in their faces. Lacy blinked and squinted, but still she could see the fury rolling over Charles.

He knotted his hands into tight fists, the muscles in his arms bulging against his suit jacket. ''You will live to regret that statement, Lacy.''

She fell against the open door as he stormed away, his feet pounding against the hard earth. Branson stepped outside and nudged his hat lower, blocking the bright rays of the noonday sun, but not turning away until Charles had revved his engine and roared back down the narrow dirt road.

"You shouldn't have stopped me from going with him, Branson. I have to go back to him anyway."

"Because you think Kate is with him?"

"I can't be sure that she isn't. And I need to know she's safe. Besides, I can't stay here. I can't bring my problems into the Randolph home." Tears burned the corners of her eyes. She tried to hold them back, but they seeped from her eyelids and rolled down her cheeks.

Branson took her hand, but she yanked it away. She didn't need his fake assurances. She'd seen what these men had done to Ricky. They'd beaten him mercilessly. And then they had come after Kate just as they said they would, leaving her with a bullet in the shoulder. Who knew what they would do next?

Branson wrapped his hands around her wrists, pinning them to the wall at the side of her head. "Listen to me, Lacy. Charles is lying. Kate is not at his house."

"How can you be certain of that? Kate could be anywhere around San Antonio. You said so yourself."

"That phone call just now was from the San Antonio Police Department. One of Kate's neighbors reported that he saw Kate sneaking away from her town house around dawn this morning. That would have been hours after Charles claimed she showed up at his place."

Branson released his hold on her but didn't step away. "I don't know what Charles's role is in all of this, Lacy, but you can't trust him. And you don't have to worry about me or my family. I'll take care of that."

Lacy struggled for a deep breath and a lungful of cleansing air. "So what do we do now, Sheriff?"

"You could tell me you're going to listen to what I say from now on. You could say you're going to act like I know what I'm talking about. That I'm not some country-bumpkin sheriff who's never met up with the kind of big-city predators you're dealing with.''

''Have you?''

''No, but I've watched a lot of movies.''

His comment brought an unexpected smile to her lips. He was teasing, but he wasn't taking her or her situation lightly. Already she knew him too well to believe that.

The fingers squeezing at her heart loosened ever so slightly. For once in her life she wasn't struggling alone. Thanks to a tiny baby girl, Sheriff Branson Randolph had adopted her cause. And if anyone could find Kate, it would be Branson.

He lingered, so close she could feel the heat of his breath on her flesh. So close that if she wanted to she could lift her mouth a few inches and touch her lips to his.

And she did want to.

She raised on tiptoe and feathered his mouth with hers. No more than a brush, a tickle, but she felt it all the way to her toes.

Branson didn't pull away, but he didn't kiss her back either. Suspicion clouded his eyes. ''What did I do to deserve that?''

The man was worse than her. He never took anything without questioning the motives behind the action. ''It's not what you *did*,'' she assured him, ''but what you're about to do.''

''Which is?''

''Find my sister.''

''I probably won't be the one who finds her, but she will be found. Like I said, I have an all points bulletin out on her now. Cops all over Texas are on the lookout for a woman who matches her description.''

''But *you'll* be the reason we find her.''

Branson touched a hand to the small of her back as he

guided her to his truck. "Your sister is a very lucky woman to have someone like you as her champion."

"I don't know that luck has ever played a large part in our lives, unless you count bad luck. But I know that if the situation were reversed, if I needed Kate, she'd be there for me."

"Right now, it would just be nice if she'd call. You're sure that beeper of yours is still working?"

She touched her finger to the beeper at her waist and pushed the button so that it vibrated beneath her fingertips. "It's still working," she said.

But there were no messages from Kate. For the past few years, Lacy had prayed that Kate would get her life together, that she'd quit calling on Lacy to bail her out of one predicament after another. That she'd quit laying her troubles at Lacy's feet, expecting her to have all the answers. Now, of all times, she appeared to have done just that. Lacy would have to be very careful what she wished for in the future.

"If we could locate Ricky Carpenter, we might be able to get some answers," Branson said. "But no one seems to know where he is."

"Does he even know that his town house was bombed?"

"I doubt it. He hasn't gotten in touch with the insurance company. Did you know that he was three months behind on his monthly payments, and that the place was about to be repossessed?"

"No. But I'm not surprised. He hasn't worked at any steady job since his injury knocked him out of football two years ago. Kate said he'd gone through a major part of his savings, that medical care after the injury had taken a big hunk of it."

"And I guess his gambling habits took care of the rest."

"Yes, but he told me he'd learned his lesson, that the

fifty thousand dollars would pay off his gambling debts and that he was going to find a job and make a clean break from his past life.''

"Maybe he changed his mind, decided to take the money and split. At any rate, when he finally shows up, the cops will be taking him in for questioning on possible insurance fraud. When a house that's about to be repossessed goes up in smoke, it raises a lot of red flags.''

"Then he probably won't show up. I just wish I knew if my sister was with him.''

"She wasn't as of this morning. She was alone when the neighbor saw her.'' Branson stopped a few feet from his truck. "With any luck, I may find out something new this afternoon. I'm going into San Antonio, to Kincaid's night-club. I have an appointment with your ex-boyfriend.''

"Not Adam Pascal?''

"That's the man.''

"You do take care of your homework. How did you find out that I used to date Adam?''

"*You* told me. He was in the snapshot with you and Kate, the one you showed me when you were trying to prove your identity. But that's not why the appointment's with him. Adam's in charge of employee relations. I'd like to see if he knows anything about Kate or her friends that might help us locate her.''

"I doubt very seriously that Kate tells Adam anything about her personal life.''

"Then maybe he'll tell us about Ricky. I talked to a detective friend of mine in San Antonio. He hangs around Kincaid's place sometimes and he gave me the scoop. Said he thinks Adam and Ricky are friends.''

"A detective. He wouldn't be undercover, would he? Kate said there had been some cute guy in the club lately asking a lot of questions.''

"I never give away my sources. Anyway, Adam may know something about Ricky's gambling habits. That might lead us to identify the man, or men, responsible for shooting Kate."

"Let me warn you up front. Adam is not a cop-friendly sort of guy."

"That's okay. I'm not looking for any new friends."

"I think Charles Castile would vouch for that."

Branson walked over and opened the passenger's door of the truck.

"What time do *we* leave for San Antonio?" she said as she climbed in.

"I was afraid you were going to ask that."

BRANSON AND LACY arrived at Joshua Kincaid's San Antonio nightclub around four, well before the Saturday-evening crowd started pouring in.

Branson had heard a lot about Kincaid's, but he'd never visited it before. Now that he was here, he didn't know what all the fuss was about, unless it was just the enormity of it. It was big enough you could pipe in sunlight and raise a few head of cattle on the dance floor.

Branson took Lacy's elbow as a saucy young waitress ushered them past the bar, past the motorized bucking bronc with the missing ear and across the gigantic dance floor. The place was mostly empty, except for a few early happy-hour groups sipping on beers and margaritas and nibbling on some of Kincaid's famous chips and extra-hot salsa.

They left the bar for a narrow, dimly lit corridor lined with signed pictures of famous personalities who had visited the club. Most of them had been posed with Joshua Kincaid front and center.

"I'll let Mr. Pascal know you're here, Sheriff Randolph,'' the waitress said as she opened the door to a rectangular office. ''He's talking to the waitstaff now, but I'm sure he'll be with you shortly.''

Branson drawled his thanks and the waitress flashed him a smile as she closed the door behind her and, hopefully, went off to fetch Adam Pascal.

''Looks like Adam's moved up in the world since he dated me,'' Lacy said. ''He was more bodyguard than administrator back then.'' She sat down in one of the straight-backed chairs that faced the desk.

Branson walked over and stood behind her. ''He must do something the big man likes.''

''He's great with people, oozes charm, and he's got a degree in accounting. He's probably a valuable employee.''

''Sounds like a nice guy. So why did the two of you break up?''

''He's also compulsive, and more than a little possessive. I liked a little more breathing space than he could handle.''

''He was probably in love with you.''

''So he claimed when he asked me to marry him. But it always seemed to me that it was himself he loved, and I was a possession he needed to make him happy. He was a lot like Charles in that respect.''

''So you broke up with Adam and started dating Charles?''

''What can I say? I'm a slow learner. Besides, both men can be extremely charming on the surface. It's not until you get to know them better that you see their less desirable qualities.''

''I'm not casting stones. I've had a few problems making character judgment calls myself.''

''Anyway, Adam didn't take our breakup well. He made a lot more of the relationship than it had ever been. But I've run into him at the office several times lately when he was picking up or delivering files for Kincaid, and he seems to be well over me.''

Lacy stopped short when the door opened and Adam Pascal stepped into the room. He was a big man, deep-set eyes, an abundance of wavy brown hair.

Adam extended a hand to Branson as they exchanged greetings and introductions. Then he turned to Lacy. ''Hello, Lacy. It's nice to see you again.''

''Thank you, Adam. And thanks for agreeing to talk to us.''

''No problem, but I am pressed for time. Saturday's a big night around here. Why don't you have a seat, Sheriff, and we'll get to business. I'd like to help if I can.''

''We won't keep you long, Mr. Pascal,'' Branson said, taking the chair next to Lacy's. ''I'm just looking for a few answers and hoping you can supply them.''

''You said on the phone, you wanted to see me concerning Kate Gilbraith, but I can't imagine what I could tell you that Lacy can't,'' he said, seating himself behind the desk. ''Basically all I know about Kate is that she works well when she's here. She calls in sick a little too often, but I've talked to her about that and she's promised to do better.''

''I'm more interested in who her friends might be. You know, who does she pal around with after hours?''

''Ricky Carpenter. I've never seen her with any other man. And as far as I know, she's not much for partying with the other waitresses after work. Lacy can probably tell you a lot more about that than I can.''

''Then there's no *one* person she seems to spend more time with than others, maybe a customer?''

''No. We don't allow a lot of fraternizing at Kincaid's. There's too much work to be done, and if you favor one table you're neglecting another. Of course, the customers flirt with the waitresses and they flirt back. It's how they make their tips, but I haven't gotten any reports of Kate's overdoing it.''

''What about Ricky Carpenter? Do you see much of him these days?''

''He still comes in.''

''And are you still friends?''

''We talk. Ricky's a friendly guy. Everyone likes him.''

''But you were close friends at one time, weren't you?''

Adam leaned back in his chair and leveled his gaze at Branson. ''I don't know who you're getting your information from, Sheriff, but it's not too accurate. Ricky and I used to party together on occasion, but we were never what you'd call close. And I don't have a lot of time for partying anymore.''

The last question had put Adam on edge, but still they were getting nowhere. Branson decided to go straight for what he wanted. ''I hear Ricky's gambling on everything that comes down the pike. Do you know who's taking his money?''

Adam scowled. ''Why don't you ask him?''

''He's not around.''

''That's interesting. Neither is Kate. She called in and reported that she's sick and doesn't know when she'll be able to return to work.''

''She is sick, she was—''

Branson silenced Lacy with a look. They were here to get information, not give it. ''When did she call?''

''Friday afternoon, about the time she was supposed to report to work.''

Friday, two days after she'd collapsed in the Randolph's entryway. ''Did she make the call herself or did someone call for her?''

''She made the call. At least that's what I was told.''

Adam toyed with a giant paper clip, stretching it out straight and running his fingers down the length of it. "Look, Sheriff, I'd like to help you, but I don't know anything about Kate's friends or who Ricky hangs with now. So if he's losing his money, I wouldn't have the slightest idea who he's losing it to."

"But you are aware that Ricky has a gambling problem?"

"Ricky has a lot of problems. Gambling is one of them."

"And you have no idea where I might be able to find him?"

"I'm afraid not." Adam dropped the paper clip to his desk. "I'm sorry I can't help you any more, but, like I said, all I do these days is work. And I really need to get back to it."

Branson stood and placed a hand on Lacy's shoulder. "Then I guess there's no use in our wasting any more of your time, Mr. Pascal." Lacy got up and stepped toward the door.

Adam beat her there and opened it for them, shaking Branson's hand and saying again he was sorry he couldn't be more help. But when he took Lacy's hand, he held it. "You do look like a million dollars, Lacy," he said, bending down to give her a peck on the cheek. "One thing about Charles Castile, he knows his cards and how to play them."

"If you're talking about my wedding to Charles, it's been called off."

Adam let go of her hand. "Too bad, for Charles, that is. Looks like our attorney friend just learned like the rest of us that all's fair in love and war."

Lacy ignored his parting comment as they walked down the narrow corridor and back into the spacious bar.

A country ballad was blaring from the jukebox as Branson and Lacy made their way back across the dance floor. A romantic, belly-rubbing song about the kind of love that lasted forever and ever.

Lacy stuck her arm through Branson's. "May I have this dance? It would keep our trip from being a total loss."

"I'm not much of a dancer."

"We'll have the dance floor to ourselves. And I promise not to yell if you step on my feet."

The offer was too tempting to refuse. One dance. A few minutes to hold a woman he had no business holding. And then he'd make a call to another woman. One he *used* to know. Or, more accurately, a woman he'd thought he knew. A woman he hoped like hell hadn't given birth to Betsy.

All's fair in love and war, or so Adam believed. As for Branson, he wondered if he'd ever be able to tell the two apart.

Chapter Eight

True to Branson's word, he wasn't much of a dancer. Lacy didn't mind at all. She didn't want to spin and dip. But it was nice to move around the floor in Branson's arms.

The bar was dimly lit, so much so that she could almost forget that outside the sun was glaring and that people were rushing around finishing their Saturday chores and preparing evening meals. She closed her eyes, not only to the sights around her but to blot out the fears and worries that haunted her mind. In here there were only a country love song, a sawdust-strewn dance floor and Branson.

Branson tightened his hold on her. His shoulders were broad, his manner easy, the sheer virility of him almost overwhelming. She leaned into him, wishing the music and the moment would never stop. They both did.

"Speak of the devil," Branson whispered in her ear as the singer took the last words of the song to a torchy finale. "Your sister's boss just walked in the door."

Lacy jerked her head off Branson's shoulder. Joshua Kincaid was strutting across the floor, every silvery-gray hair in place, his suit immaculate, his expensive boots shined to a high gloss.

He met them at the edge of the dance floor. "Good to see you again, Lacy." Joshua took her right hand, not shaking it but just pressing it between his two as if they were the best of friends. They weren't. She'd met him several times when she'd dated Adam and she'd crossed paths with him on several occasions in Charles's office. Nothing that suggested friendship.

When Joshua finally let go of her hand, he extended his to Branson. "This is a surprise, Branson. I didn't think you ever came into the big city to play."

"On rare occasions."

"Then I'm impressed you chose Kincaid's to visit. How was your mother's birthday?"

"It was just a small family gathering, but she seemed pleased. Your flowers were a big hit, but I'm sure she'll thank you herself if she hasn't already."

"I'm glad she liked them, though I can't believe Mary's sixty. Seems like only yesterday she and your dad were getting married. I always said she was the best thing that ever happened to him. I don't know how I let him beat me to the sweetest and prettiest catch in the county."

Lacy noted that Branson sidestepped the fact that his mother was in the hospital. They talked for a few minutes more, cattle business, and then Kincaid turned his attention back to Lacy.

"Don't tell me the honeymoon's already over." His lips suggested he was teasing. His eyes didn't.

His comment caught her off guard, but, of course, Charles would have told Joshua the same lie he'd told them. After all, Joshua had been one of the invited guests at the spoiled wedding. "Charles is…is—"

"Lacy and I are here on business," Branson broke in, stopping her stammering. "I was here to talk to Adam Pascal about a case I'm working."

"One that involves Lacy?"

"One that involves her sister, Kate. She's an employee of yours."

"I hope nothing serious. But even if you're here on business, why not stop at the bar and have a drink?" Joshua said. "On the house."

Branson declined his offer, but Lacy didn't breathe a genuine sigh of relief until they'd made it out the door and into the parking lot. It wasn't dark yet, but the neon sign that flashed Kincaid's was already glaring brightly.

"I need to go by the San Antonio Police Department while we're in town," Branson said, "and chat with a buddy of mine about Kate's case. After that, I'd like to stop by the hospital and see my mother, if that's okay with you."

"What kind of information are you expecting from the local police?"

"I'm calling in a couple of favors. Got someone checking on the streets to see if we can scrounge up some info about Ricky's so-called friends with the guns and fists."

Conversation died as they got into the truck and Branson edged his way into a line of snarled traffic. Lacy leaned back, the same questions that had plagued her the past two days pummeling her mind. If Ricky had given the men the fifty thousand dollars, why had they shot Kate? And if they weren't the ones who had shot her sister, who had? And how did Betsy fit into this?

Questions without answers. Lacy brushed her fingers across the beeper at her waist, the way she did a hundred times a day. But touching the beeper had no magical powers, couldn't connect her with Kate until her sister chose to dial the number and link the two of them together.

She turned and stared at Branson. Strange that her life had shifted focus so completely in the past two days. Long ago she'd learned to fear anyone in law enforcement. Now a cowboy sheriff was the only man she dare turn to.

LACY STRUGGLED to keep pace with Branson as they walked down the hospital hallway. It wasn't that he was in a particular hurry. It was just that his long stride had her taking two steps to his one.

His cell phone rang again. He answered it without slowing down. Lacy heard enough to know that the caller was Gordon, but this time the call was short.

"I never knew sheriff work required so much time on the phone," she said when he broke the connection.

"Cellular phones and computers. I can't imagine how the West was won without them."

"Sounds safer than six-shooters."

Branson smiled. "Well, ma'am," he drawled in his best John Wayne imitation, "I don't reckon I'd like to go face-to-face with a killer if I was just totin' my cell phone."

"And I don't want to go face-to-face with a killer, period."

Branson touched her shoulder. "I don't plan for you to. That's why you're in protective custody."

"You're not serious about this protective-custody stuff, are you?"

"Absolutely."

"Why? I'm not the one in danger."

"I'm not so sure of that. You received a threatening phone call at the church. Besides, I don't think any of this is as black-and-white as it appears."

"I don't understand."

"We'll talk about it later, after we visit with Mom."

A talk about a killer. A visit with Mom. This was Branson, as comfortable in his own life as a snake in his new skin. He was a sheriff, a rancher, a Randolph.

She envied him that certainty of knowing who and what he was. She'd tried to find her niche all her life but never felt she truly belonged anywhere. She'd grown up wishing desperately she was someone else. Wishing that there was a mother in the next room, one she could run to when the nightmares came.

But wishing hadn't changed a thing, and she'd learned to accept what was and make the best of it. She needed to remember those lessons now. Branson made her feel like someone special, but that was just his way. She was a job to him. No more and no less.

"Why don't I go down to the cafeteria and grab a cup of coffee while you visit with your mother, Branson?"

"Don't you want to meet her?"

"There's really no reason to. More than likely, I'll be gone before she returns to the Burning Pear, and I'm sure you don't involve her in all of your cases."

"I don't involve her in *any* of my cases. I didn't have to involve her in this one, though. Kate and Betsy did that for me."

She wondered if she imagined the resentment that seemed to tinge his voice. "How much does your mother know about my sister?"

"Nothing yet. Not even her last name. All I've told her is that I haven't had any luck as yet in discovering who Betsy really is. I'm not going to mention that you're Kate's sister. If I do, Mom will have to know every detail about how I found you, and I don't want her getting upset unnecessarily."

"So who will you tell her that I am?"

"A friend."

A friend. A friend who had him searching for a would-be killer and dodging bombs. The plea Ashley had uttered earlier today echoed in her mind. *Don't bring danger to the Randolphs.*

"We won't stay long," Branson said, stopping at the door to his mother's room. "She's supposed to be resting. I'd just like to check on her, make sure she's not driving the hospital staff nuts. If they don't watch her, she'll be down in the kitchen showing them how to cook."

He knocked, and waited until his mother invited him in. Then, hat in hand, he stood aside so that Lacy could go first. Mary Randolph offered Lacy a tentative smile, but her whole face lit up when Branson stepped inside, her blue eyes shimmery as a summer morning.

"Branson. I didn't know you were coming."

"Wild horses couldn't have kept me away. Unless, of course, someone had stolen them and I had to go find them." Branson walked over and kissed his mom's forehead. "How are you feeling?"

"Like I need to get up and go home." She looked from Branson to Lacy. "Are you two together?" She sounded as if she had serious doubts that might be the case.

"Of course we're together. You act like you've never seen me with a woman before."

"Not in a month of Sundays."

She untangled her hands from the covers and lay them on top of the drab hospital blanket. They were work-worn and thin in spite of the fact that her arms were almost pudgy. Branson took one of her hands and held it. "This is Lacy Gilbraith. She's a friend of mine, and she's helping with an investigation I'm doing."

"So that's why you're here with a woman." Mary scooted up a little higher in the bed, giving Lacy a thorough once-over.

Branson smiled sheepishly. "You make me sound anti-social."

"Not at all. It's just nice to see you with someone who doesn't carry a gun or chew tobacco." She patted Branson's hand. "And I want to hear all about what you and Lacy are doing in San Antonio. But first, how's Betsy?"

Lacy listened while Branson shared Betsy stories. His mother hung on every word. Another heart the precious newborn had stolen. Lacy's own heart felt as if someone were pressing on it with a steel ball. She couldn't bear to think what Kate's role might be in this.

She'd done a lot of things in her life that Lacy had disapproved of, but nothing so deceptive as this might turn out to be. Lacy could only imagine the heartbreak Mary Randolph would suffer if this baby she believed was her granddaughter were suddenly ripped from her life.

And the longer the hoax was allowed to continue, the worse it would be for everyone. One more reason that they had to find Kate and soon.

They visited for a few more minutes, sharing easy talk, the kind that wouldn't upset the patient. Lacy realized quickly where the Randolph men had learned the art of making people feel welcome.

Mary Randolph was the expert. When they were ready to leave, Lacy leaned in, kissing Branson's mother on the cheek. It felt natural and right.

But this was Branson's life. Hers was still out there waiting for her. At least what was left of it.

"ARE YOU HUNGRY?" Branson asked when they'd left most of the city behind them.

"A little. I'm more interested in finishing the conversation we started before we arrived at your mother's hospital room. What do you think is not black-and-white about this investigation?"

"Too many pieces to the puzzle that don't seem to fit.

Actually, they don't even seem to belong to the same puzzle. They're only related by time, space and personalities.''

"Meaning?"

"Just meaning that I don't necessarily believe that Ricky's gambling debts are at the root of everything. The problem is, I can't put my finger on any other motivation."

"I know. I just keep thinking about Kate. Do you think she really called in sick?"

"I'd say no. She wouldn't have made a long-distance call from the hospital when she was either unconscious or pretending to be."

"So who made the call?"

"Another question we probably won't find an answer to until we locate her."

"I just hope it's soon." She shifted in her seat. "How well do you know Joshua Kincaid? I notice he called you by your first name."

Branson leaned back, one hand on the wheel, the other resting on the back of the seat between them. "He and my dad grew up together in Kelman. They were friends all through high school and college. After they graduated, they both went into ranching, but Kincaid didn't take to it the way Dad did. He branched out and went into the nightclub business. Now that's his bread and butter."

"A *lot* of bread and butter. He's a very rich man."

"That depends on how you count wealth. How about you? Do you know him well?"

"Fairly well. We wouldn't classify as friends though."

"Good for you. He's not friend material. He'd climb a tree to tell a lie when he could tell the truth standing on the ground. Never trust a man like that."

Branson Randolph, a man who told the truth and expected others to do so, no matter what the consequences. She'd never known a man like that, had never even suspected they existed. Even now she had a hard time believing the sheriff was for real. "What did you find out back at the San Antonio Police Department?" she asked.

"That Ricky Carpenter still has friends in the poor neighborhood where he grew up. Word on the street is that he has a lot of bad habits. Some drug use, expensive cars, cheap women. Not that I'm saying anything against your sister, but he is not known as a one-woman man."

"What about his gambling connections?"

"None. Two reliable informants reported that he never gambles, that he prides himself on avoiding the local bookies."

"But some men beat him up over gambling debts. He told me so himself. I saw him after it happened."

"I'm just telling you what I heard. I don't have all the answers yet." Branson stretched and rubbed the back of his neck. "I vote we get a bite to eat. We could get something fancy, or we can grab some semi–home cooking at the café back in Kelman. The atmosphere leaves a lot to be desired, but the food's good and the service is quick."

"Do they have onion rings?"

"Some of the best in Texas. And great pecan pie."

"In that case, I vote for dining in Kelman."

LACY WAS GLAD she'd made that decision the second they walked inside the door of Gus's Corner Café. The grill behind the counter sizzled and the aroma of onions and peppery spices filled the room. A pert young waitress who knew Branson by name greeted them as they walked in, and several other people smiled and waved or called out a greeting.

Branson and Lacy took a booth against the wall, and she ordered a cheeseburger and onion rings. Branson opted for the dinner special. Chicken-fried steak with white gravy, creamed potatoes, black-eyed peas and corn bread. They both wanted coffee, the sooner the better.

The waitress returned a minute or two after she'd taken their order and set water in oversize plastic glasses in front of them. The silverware was wrapped in white cloth napkins that showed signs of wear and an abundance of bleach.

Lacy unwrapped her napkin and laid out her utensils neatly, knife and spoon to the right, fork to the left. For some reason, order seemed important tonight. Predictability, routine, in a world that had changed so drastically in the past few days she barely recognized it.

The waitress came by with the two mugs of hot coffee they'd ordered and an intriguing smile. Lacy noticed that the young woman had applied fresh lipstick since they'd come in. Fluffed her hair as well. She placed the coffee on the table. "It's kind of late on a Saturday night for you to be having dinner, Branson."

"I had some business to take care of in San Antonio."

"And you came back to have dinner with us?" She smiled and leaned closer. "You are a homeboy."

"No city food like Gus cooks it up here."

"The food should be up in a few minutes." She lingered, standing at Branson's elbow.

"Thanks, Mary Jane." He dismissed her without even a look.

The smile faded from the waitress's face. But the truth was, he probably wouldn't have given her any more notice if she'd been green and had antennae growing out of her head. He shut out everyone when he had something on his mind. Another of his idiosyncrasies Lacy had picked up on in record time.

Branson leaned toward Lacy, resting his elbows on the table. "Tell me about Charles Castile."

She stirred her coffee. "Where do I start?"

"Jump in anywhere. How long have you worked for him? What's he like in the office?"

She considered her answers, mentally adding up the months since she'd graduated from the paralegal program. "I went to work for the Castile agency just under two years ago. One year, eleven months to be exact. I was thrilled to get the job, especially since Charles gave me interesting work to do from the very start. He said I was a rare find, intelligent and industrious."

"I'd agree with him on both counts. I'm sure gorgeous didn't hurt either with a man like Castile."

"Thank you, Sheriff."

"I'm just stating the facts, ma'am. Did you know him before you went to work in his office?"

"No. The school-placement office arranged for me to interview with him. My first meeting left me awestruck. He fairly oozed the essence of power, gave a whole new meaning to the word *charisma*."

"I can see why a woman might like that."

"Power and wealth are very seductive, especially to someone like me who'd been relegated to the have-not side of the socioeconomic curve all my life. He offered me a job that day, and my feet scarcely touched the ground until I showed up for work the next Monday."

Branson was a good listener, and she found herself providing information she would have normally considered too private to share. Background distractions—the laughter and conversation, the clatter of dishes—all faded into obscurity while she recalled one experience after another of working with Charles. The good and the bad.

But it was the bad that Branson seemed the most interested in. That and some of the seemingly insignificant details she'd all but forgotten until she started talking. Like the night last week when she'd come back to the office after hours to pick up some work she'd forgotten.

"Charles was on the phone, arguing about something, but I didn't hear what. I could tell he was flustered the minute I walked by his office. He followed me into my office and demanded to know what I'd heard."

"And what had you heard?"

"Nothing really. A comment about someone getting what they deserved. I wouldn't have thought anything about it if Charles hadn't gotten so upset. The next day he apologized for his actions. He blamed fatigue for his lousy attitude."

Branson nodded, his lips pulled tight, as if he was mulling over the information and meshing it with what he already knew or suspected about Charles Castile.

Their talk was interrupted when the food came. Branson's plate was platter size, with a huge steak that covered most of it. The creamed potatoes were piled into a mountainous heap, and the gravy that covered them and the steak was thick and plentiful.

This time he did flash the waitress a heart-stopping smile. Food was definitely the key to making him sit up and take notice. That was not good news for Lacy. Her greatest culinary accomplishment was salad. And cowboys were not known for the greens they ate. The cattlemen's association probably had some requirement that dropped them from the rolls if they went a day without beef.

Not that any of that mattered, she told herself while she lifted the top bun from her burger and applied a dash of salt and a liberal shake of pepper. When this was over, she'd be eating her salads alone and the good sheriff would be eating his steak and potatoes back at the Burning Pear surrounded by his family.

She bit into her burger. The juices squirted into her

mouth, awakening every taste bud she possessed. Talk died between them while they ate except for occasional ums and ahs and exclamations of how good her cheeseburger was.

Branson finished before her, though she had no idea how. He'd had twice as much food, and the only thing left was half a spoon of peas and a little gravy.

He waited until she chewed and swallowed her last bite before he started with the questions again. "Did you date Charles before you became engaged, or were you just the prize he won with his fifty-thousand-dollar entry fee?"

She picked up her coffee cup and twirled it, watching the black liquid swirl around the bottom. "We started dating about a month after I broke up with Adam. At first he only asked me out to parties, mostly big formal affairs like the ones Joshua Kincaid hosts. I didn't have the clothes to wear, so he'd give me one of his charge cards and send me on shopping sprees. When I said I wasn't comfortable spending his money, he insisted, saying it was more for him than me. He needed me to make a good impression."

"Were you in love with him?"

Branson's tone had changed, gone from nonchalant to serious. Lacy pushed the coffee cup aside and raised her gaze to meet his. "I thought so, at first. I was definitely awed. But I wasn't in his league. I started to feel more a trophy for his arm than a significant other."

"Was he serious about you?"

"I suppose so. He asked me to marry him. Repeatedly. He got angry when I refused his proposals, just couldn't seem to accept that I wasn't thrilled at the chance to become his wife. I finally had to quit seeing him socially altogether."

"Doesn't quite understand the word *no*. I got that impression of him this morning."

"What about you, Branson?" She waited until he looked

up from the dregs in his coffee cup. "You're much too good a catch to still be single. Haven't you ever been in love?"

She was sorry she asked. His answer came too slowly, his look too distant.

"Once. I got over it."

"I don't think love is like a cold, a virus that you let run its course and then forget."

"No. It's more like a stampeding herd of cattle that runs you down and then waits around until you climb to your feet so that it can regroup and come back for another go at you." Cynicism added grit to his words.

"You sound like a man who's been burned big time."

"To a blackened crisp."

"I'm sorry."

"Don't be. You weren't the cook. Besides, I'm not the marrying type. I'm happy with my life just the way it is."

He reached in his back pocket and pulled out his wallet, pillaging through it and lifting out a twenty-dollar bill. "Would you mind taking care of the check when the waitress comes? I need to use the pay phone outside, and I'm anxious to get back to the ranch."

"Is the battery dead on your cell phone?"

"No."

So the phone call was personal—one he didn't want her to overhear. She wasn't surprised and she shouldn't be disappointed. She was a job to him, and he was doing his job well.

"I'll pay the bill and meet you in the truck," she said. "And if I ever manage to get hold of all my belongings, I'll even pay you back for all the meals you've bought me."

"You already have. Having dinner with a beautiful woman is payment enough. Besides, you're the only one

who can handle Betsy.'' He smiled and touched his fingers
to his hat as he walked away.

A devastating smile that left her weak. And suddenly she
ached to go home with him, to go back to the Burning Pear.
To hold Betsy in her arms.

It wasn't her life, and it wasn't permanent, but she would
borrow it for a while longer. And pray that Kate was somewhere safe tonight as well.

LACY SAT SILENTLY beside him as Branson turned off the
highway and onto the road that led to the Burning Pear.
The lone star state had outdone itself, studded the sky with
hundreds of sparkling lights, so close he felt he might reach
out and grab a star for keeping. But even the beauty did
little to lift his spirits.

The phone call to Marilyn hadn't produced the results he
was hoping for. He'd reached her answering machine and
a message that she was out. Low and seductive, even her
recorded hellos had once made him ache to take her in his
arms.

Tonight the feeling had been far different. It stung and
then rolled inside him, hitting a hollow spot where all he
knew was dread. He'd gotten over her for good ten months
ago, but it was more than that. He didn't respect her, would
never trust her, couldn't bear to think she might have given
birth to his child.

If she had, he couldn't even imagine what kind of sick
game she must be playing. Drop Betsy into his life. Let her
capture his heart and all the rest of the Randolphs'. But
then what? Ask for money? For marriage?

He shook his head and pounded a fist on the steering
wheel. There was no use to speculate. He couldn't begin
to figure it out. But if he didn't hear from Marilyn soon,
he'd go to a lab and have a blood test. DNA—truth in

labeling. The last way he'd ever dreamed of finding out whether or not he was a dad.

"You seem extremely agitated for a man with a full stomach."

"It's been a long day, for both of us. You must be bone-tired."

"I could use some rest. I only wish we'd uncovered some real answers."

"Well, at least there's been no more bad news. No word of shootings or bombs exploding."

"No clue as to where Kate is."

He pulled up to the gate and stopped. Lacy started to jump out. He grabbed her arm to stop her. "I'll get it."

She turned to face him, and the glow of starlight danced in her hair. Suddenly his body ignited with awareness. His hand tightened around the soft flesh of her arm.

He loosened his grip, but made no move to get out of the truck. Lacy inched closer to him, her gaze seeking his. He could see the same desire that burned inside him reflected in her look. He knew it was all wrong as he leaned over, knew kissing her was a big mistake, but he couldn't stop himself.

He touched his mouth to hers. She parted her lips, and his insides crumbled with a hunger so intense he felt he might never let her go.

His hands splayed across her back and he pressed her closer. It was the wrong time and the wrong place, but now that he'd succumbed to the desire he'd been trying to deny, he couldn't stop. Finally, it was Lacy who pulled away, her body trembling.

"I'm not sure I'm ready to feel this way." Her voice was shaky, but her hands were still locked around his neck, and her breath was warm on his skin.

"And I know I'm not." But he kissed her again, this

time slower, sweeter. And by the time he forced himself to stop, his body was on fire.

Pulse racing, he climbed out of the truck and walked to the gate. His nose wrinkled as a sickening odor hit him head-on. Something dead. He let his gaze follow the odor. He saw the face first, discolored, bloody. And then he saw the rest of the body, stretched out on the grass. He heard the truck door slam behind him as he walked toward the body.

In a second, Lacy was beside him. He grabbed her as she fell toward him, her choked cry drowning in her sobs.

One less person to look for. Death had come calling at the Burning Pear.

Chapter Nine

"It's Ricky." Lacy closed her eyes and held on to Branson, afraid she was going to be sick.

"You don't need to see this, Lacy. I'm going to walk you back to the truck. I'll call Langley to come and get you."

"What will you do?"

"This is a crime scene. It has to be photographed, investigated fully. I'll call Gordon in to help, but it will still take quite a while. Then the body will have to be picked up and delivered to the morgue for an autopsy."

Lacy wanted to scream, or to cry, or to beat her fists against something hard and unforgiving. Instead, she walked with Branson, her legs so shaky that she almost collapsed more than once. Branson all but lifted her into the passenger seat.

"I'll find out who did this, Lacy. It just takes time."

"But Ricky had the money to pay them. Why did they have to kill him? Why are these monsters doing this?" The words burned her throat and she struggled to breathe.

"I don't know. I don't know what drives anyone to take another person's life."

He held her close and buried his head in her hair. She could feel his anguish. He was so strong, and yet death wasn't easy for him either. It was only easy for the bad guys, the ones who killed and killed and killed. She was shaking again, and she didn't think she could stop. "I should have gone to the police earlier."

Branson held her for a long moment. When he let go, he tucked a thumb under her chin and forced her to look him in the eye. "This isn't your fault, Lacy."

"But—"

He put his fingers over her mouth. "No. Just no. You didn't get Ricky in trouble and you couldn't get him out."

The rest of the night passed in a blur. Langley came to get her and took her back to the house. He was upset, too, but still he had taken care of her. He'd persuaded her to drink a glass of sherry to help her sleep and had tried to get her to go upstairs to the real guest room so that Betsy wouldn't wake her. She was tired, almost numb, but she insisted she sleep in the nursery.

She needed the comfort of Betsy's soft breathing. Needed the solace of her innocence.

But still sleep was a long time in coming.

"DON'T COME IN HERE, Lacy." Kate stood in the doorway to their mother's bedroom, barring the entrance with her tall, slender body.

"I want my momma."

"Well, you can't have her. Go back to your room. Now!"

Lacy shivered in her thin cotton nightshirt. "You're not my momma, Kate. You're not my boss."

"Don't be such a baby, Lacy. Please don't. Not now."

But it was Kate who was the baby. She was crying. Something was horribly wrong. Lacy butted her head into her sister's side, shoving her out of the way. She wanted her momma.

But her momma was on the floor, her arms and legs spread out as if she were making snow angels.

"Momma, what's wrong?"

Now Lacy was crying, too, and Kate was pushing her away. But she couldn't stop crying. She tried to scream. She opened her mouth, but nothing would come out.

Lacy jerked awake and sat up in bed, her body drenched in a cold sweat. The nightmare had returned.

She took deep breaths and stared straight ahead until the shadows around her coalesced into reality. Swinging her feet to the floor, she padded to the crib. Betsy was sleeping soundly, her tiny chest rising and falling with the gentle movements of breathing.

Lacy stood in the dark and watched her for a long time. Watched the precious baby girl until her own heart rate slowed to near normal. The nightmare could still terrify her and leave her shaking, but she wasn't a little girl now. And she wasn't going to run. Not from the past and not from a killer.

Especially not when she had Branson on her side.

LACY ROLLED the wheeled chair across the floor of Branson's small office. It was a two-room affair that fronted on Main Street. Wooden bookshelves filled with law-enforcement handbooks lined the walls, and the one window was uncurtained. An oblong of bright sunlight poured through and painted a small section of the dingy floor.

She had been here with Branson since just after breakfast, and it was almost two now. He had put her through an exhausting interrogation session, trying to see if she could remember anything Ricky had said the night he'd made his midnight call that might lead them to his killer or killers. But she had already told him everything she knew.

The fax machine started clicking and humming, and Branson stopped in front of it, waiting for the first page of the transmission. He grabbed the page the second the machine spit it out.

"Just as I thought. Ricky had been dead for several days when we found him. But he didn't die at the Burning Pear. He was killed somewhere else and then dumped there."

Lacy stood up and read the preliminary forensics report over his shoulder. Branson had already told her this wouldn't be a complete report, but it would give some basic facts. It did, in ugly detail. The words twisted in her stomach, and she was thankful this was not the type of reading material that went with her job.

Correction. Her ex-job.

"Why would they dump his body at the Burning Pear?" she asked, picking up the first sheet when Branson dropped it to the desk.

"A bloody little warning for me to stay out of this."

"I think you should. These people are dangerous."

"I'm a sheriff, Lacy. This is my job. And even if it weren't, shooting a woman under my nose and delivering a body to my front gate would make sure I didn't stay out of it. If the killer had done his homework he would have known that."

"So what do we do next?"

"I've got a couple of stops to make this afternoon, local problems I have to see to. I thought I'd drop you back at the ranch. You can stay with Langley and Ryder and play with Betsy for a while. I know you'll like that."

"But you'll call me if the police find Kate?"

"The second I hear anything. And it has to be soon. No one just drops off the face of the earth."

"Kate can. She's done it before." And Lacy held on to

that fact with every bit of hope that she could muster. She had to believe that Kate had gone into hiding and wasn't—

No, she couldn't even think that word. Kate was alive.

RYDER STARTED begging for help with his young charge as Branson and Lacy walked through the door. He was parading back and forth across the kitchen, holding Betsy on his shoulder. "I put her on my shoulder and patted her on the back, just like Mom said to do, but she won't burp. Do you think we should call the doctor?"

"I vote yes," Langley said, one step behind Ryder in the parade. "She might have something wrong with her. Maybe she *can't* burp. After all, she can't tell us if something's wrong with her."

Lacy watched as Betsy's head bobbed off Ryder's shoulder, cradled by his strong, supportive hand. The baby's eyes were bright and shiny, her cheeks pink and pudgy. She showed absolutely no sign that anything was wrong with her. Ryder and Langley, however, were having a serious panic attack.

"She looks awful healthy to me, guys," Lacy said. "How much of her bottle did she take?"

"Two ounces, but Mom said be sure and burp her after she took a couple of ounces," Langley explained. "When I fed her, she burped big. Either Ryder did something wrong or something's the matter with Betsy."

Lacy sighed in pure amazement. It had happened again. She had walked through the door at the Burning Pear and her anxiety level had taken a heart-healthy plunge.

Nothing had changed. The danger was still waiting. The fear was still real. But the house had an aura all its own, an all-pervasive one that touched everyone inside its walls.

"Why don't you let me finish feeding Betsy?" she offered, shedding her sweater and draping it over the back of a kitchen chair. "I think your mom was just giving you a guideline. Babies have their own schedule for burping. It's kind of on an as-needed basis."

"Now why didn't Mom say that?" Ryder said, transferring Betsy to her arms. "We could have saved ourselves a lot of worry, and Betsy wouldn't have had to listen to our pleading with her for the past twenty minutes."

Lacy didn't point out that Mary Randolph probably thought it went without saying, that she hadn't expected her rootin', tootin' cowboys to be transformed into such klutzes the second they were left alone with a baby.

Langley handed Lacy the baby bottle and she settled in the man-size recliner/rocker to the left of the hearth. The second the nipple touched Betsy's lips, she latched on to it, sucking as if she was afraid Lacy would try to take it away at any second.

Branson propped a booted foot on the hearth. "How is Mom?"

"Ashley called a half hour ago," Ryder answered. "They don't have all the results back from the tests, but they haven't found anything major. One of the doctors thinks it might be a stomach condition."

"Ulcers?"

"Ashley didn't mention ulcers, but I guess we'll get a full report later."

"I'm sure Mom won't be staying in the hospital long," Langley said. "She'll be chomping at the bit to get out. She already had Ashley call twice to check on Betsy. She's more attached to that baby than she is to us."

"Which is the last thing we need," Branson reminded them. "With any luck, Betsy will be reunited with her real parents soon."

"Unless we find out she really is a Randolph." Langley picked up a stack of newspapers from the couch and dropped them on the coffee table. He settled into the clean spot.

"Are you trying to say something, Langley?" Branson's voice had adopted a biting edge.

"Not me. Lacy said it all. Her sister's not Betsy's mother and we don't know who the mother is. So unless you've been celibate for ten months, blah, blah, blah. I don't have a reason to be concerned, but I can't speak for the rest of you."

"Well, I don't have time to chitchat all day," Branson said. "And it looks like you guys have everything under control here anyway."

"We do now that Lacy's back. I hope you're not planning on dragging her off again. We need her more than you do," Langley insisted.

"Hey, don't fight over me, guys. I'm enough woman to go around for everybody," she joked, although her mood was far from jocular. Her mind had switched to Branson and the fact that he had gotten visibly edgy with just the mention of Betsy's parentage. For a man who seldom showed emotion, his reaction didn't quite compute.

But it wasn't her problem, and she surely didn't need any new ones to take on. She leaned back in the chair and rearranged the angle of the bottle.

"I thought Ashley found someone to stay here and help out with Betsy," Branson said, leaving his post at the hearth and walking to the table and a stack of unopened mail.

"She did," Langley answered. "She hired Mrs. Brown, but she can only work until two. That's when we change from ranchers to nannies."

"Yeah. We're going to have to do a better job of training Betsy," Ryder complained. "Mrs. Brown walked out the door at two. At five minutes after two, I'm holding Betsy and I smell something a little funny." Ryder held his nose to make his point.

"Score one for Betsy!" Branson said. He stopped scavenging the mail long enough to make an imaginary mark in the air. "Ryder's on dirty-diaper duty. Now that we know he can do it—"

"Wrong. This is an equal-opportunity family. From now on we toss for the privilege."

"No way, man. If you're herding the cattle, you take care of the coyote," Langley said. "And Lacy's doing the herding right now."

Lacy slipped the nipple from between Betsy's lips and set the bottle on the table beside her. She threw a cloth diaper over her shoulder and hoisted Betsy up for another attempt at eliciting a burp. The baby whimpered instead.

Branson walked to the back of the rocker and hunched down to Betsy's eye level. "Don't let these guys hurt your feelings, Betsy. As much time as they've spent in cow manure, a little baby poop will not hurt them."

"Won't hurt *us?* How about you, big brother? You don't think you're getting off the hook. You can't chase criminals all the time."

He stretched back to a standing position. "I can if I don't do a better job of catching them than I did today."

Betsy broke up his complaining with a resonant burp that got everyone's attention.

All three men broke into wide grins and Betsy smiled as if she knew she'd impressed the heck out of them. Actually, Lacy felt a little cocky herself. Not that she'd done anything special, but the Randolph men didn't think that. She could tell by the way they were looking at her.

Ryder wrapped an arm around Branson's shoulder. "I'll tell you what, Branson. You've brought home stray dogs, orphaned calves and once even that wounded buzzard. But you haven't ever brought home something as nice as Lacy before. She's worth keeping. Make a note of that."

Lacy felt the burn in her cheeks, knew they were probably flushed a bright shade of red. She turned to Betsy and hoped Ryder and Langley didn't notice. If she was going to stay here, she couldn't let anyone think there was something between her and Branson. It wouldn't be fair to him.

Even more important, she couldn't start believing there was something between them. Last night's kiss had been the result of proximity and the emotional aspects of the situation they were in. Nothing more.

Branson dismissed Ryder's comment without so much as a response. "Try to put up with these guys while I'm gone, Lacy. I've got work to do."

"I'll walk out to the truck with you," Langley said.

"Good idea. Why don't you come too, Ryder? Give Lacy and Betsy a minute's peace."

The three men clattered out of the house, their easy chatter and laughter following them. But she knew it would stop soon enough when they were out of her hearing. Branson would tell them the details of the forensics report, let them know that Ricky hadn't been coming to see either Branson or Lacy when he'd gotten shot. The killer had hauled the body out to the Burning Pear to make a dangerous point.

She wondered if she'd be able to tell the difference in Ryder and Langley's attitude when they walked back inside. She wouldn't blame them a bit. Sheriffing was Branson's job, not theirs. And *she* wasn't even sure where she fit into his job requirements.

All she knew was that she was glad she didn't have to face this without his help. As it was, she had to make herself believe that Kate was okay. After all, Kate was a survivor. They both were. But then, Ricky had probably thought of himself as a survivor, too. Right up until the time someone put a bullet through his heart.

Betsy grew still on Lacy's shoulder. She moved her to the cradle of her arms. Betsy's eyes were closed, her expression cherubic. A soothing warmth tucked itself around Lacy's heart.

She was caught between two worlds. Hers and Branson's. Hers was filled with unspeakable terror, with a nightmare that didn't go away even in the bright light of day. Branson's was filled with support, with family ties that provided strength and continuity. With love. Now their two worlds had collided.

And once again Ashley's plea echoed through her mind. *Don't bring danger to the Randolphs.*

But she had done just that.

KELMAN, TEXAS. Kate had never expected to be back here so soon after her narrow escape the other night. She wouldn't be if she knew anywhere else to go. But Ricky was dead and she was not about to drag Lacy into this, not any more than she already had.

This was all a mistake, a really bad mistake. She'd known it the night she'd come home from work and found Ricky dead in their living room. It had something to do with that Randolph baby. Joshua Kincaid had always said the Randolphs of Kelman, Texas, were nothing but trouble. Now she knew exactly what he meant.

Still, her body ached and she was so very tired. She couldn't keep running without time to heal, without time to recover her strength.

So she was going to the only man who might be willing to help her. If not, he could make one phone call and it would all be over. It was a toss-up, but she had to trust someone.

THE SUN WAS LOW in the sky but a good hour from setting when Branson returned to the ranch. Fatigue rode his shoulders, and strain drew deep lines beneath his eyes. Lacy didn't have to ask if there had been any good news concerning the case. The answer was stamped across his face.

But she hadn't hesitated when he'd asked her if she'd like to go for a quick ride before dark. Only now that they were on their way to the corral, their shadows long and mingling in front of them, she wasn't certain this was a good idea.

"It's been years since I've ridden," he said. "I'm not sure I still know how."

"I have a horse you can handle, but we don't have to do this now, if you'd rather not. I just thought it might do you good. It's always therapy for me. Something to keep me from blowing my top completely."

"I can't imagine your ever needing therapy for that. You always seem so in control." Except for this afternoon when he'd talked of Betsy's parentage. She decided not to mention that just yet, though it had stayed on her mind.

Branson pushed open the gate to the corral and waited for her to walk through in front of him. "I usually am in control. Which is probably why I need therapy."

"You may have a point there." She looked around her. A brown beauty stood by the fence, his head high, his mane rippling in the breeze. Another walked toward them, stopping to neigh and tap his front foot when he was a few yards away.

Branson started a running monologue with the horse, talking in a smooth, reassuring tone all the while the animal approached them. "Silver's had a rough time of it lately," he said, addressing his words to Lacy, but still keeping the same tone that had assuaged the horse. "He was riding in a horse trailer that was involved in a collision. He's recuperating fine but doesn't always take well to strangers since the accident."

"So you have a way with animals as well as with frightened women."

"Much better. I've never been too good with the opposite sex. I don't do small talk. Don't pay enough compliments. Don't like to play games." He scratched Silver's nose. "Horses don't need all of that. We bond much faster. Now, let's find you a horse and get on our way. If we sit around jawing much longer, we won't have time to ride."

She studied Silver up close and personal and tried to imagine herself sitting that high off the ground.

"Do you have something in gentle, extra short? So I don't have far to fall if he decides he doesn't like carrying me."

Branson smiled and led the way to the stable. "I have something in gentle. No extra shorts. My suggestion is you stay in the saddle. South Texas ground is extremely hard."

She waited while he saddled his own horse, a big, sleek sorrel with a flaxen mane and tail. The horse stood still until Branson had finished cinching the saddle, then he pranced around as if he was eager to get started.

"I can put you on Surefire," Branson said, turning back to her. "He's Ashley's horse, but she doesn't get to ride him nearly enough now that she and Dillon are living in Austin so much of the year."

"If you don't think Ashley would mind."

"She'd be glad someone's taking him out."

A few minutes later Lacy was making Surefire's acquaintance. He was beautiful but definitely not an extra short.

"The first thing you want to do is let a horse smell you," Branson said as she stepped closer. "See. He's got his ears forward now. He's paying attention to you, wondering what you're up to." He took her hand and touched her fingers

to the horse's neck. "Talk to him while you rub his neck
and back. Don't move too quickly, and don't surprise him.
Horses like to know what's coming."

She followed Branson's instructions. By the time Surefire was saddled and ready for her to mount, she was a little
more at ease.

Branson made a step of his hands and she put one foot
in it, throwing the other over Surefire's back. She took the
reins, trying to remember what she knew about using them
to let the horse know what she wanted him to do.

"We'll take it slow," Branson said. "And remember,
you're in good hands. If you let him, Surefire will pamper
you the way you do Betsy. He's a pro."

They left the corral and, true to his word, Branson kept
the pace slow. The land was flat, dotted with clusters of
mesquite, patches of pear cacti and sagebrush almost as tall
as she was.

But the south Texas flora was not the only thing of interest. The horses stirred up traces of wildlife as well. A
jackrabbit hopped out of the brush in front of her and a
bevy of quail took to the air in a rush of feathers and wind.
She laughed out loud when a feisty roadrunner raced across
their path as if he were late for a very important appointment.

Therapy. It was that. The air seemed cleaner, the oranges
and golds of the sky brighter, the smells sharper and more
pungent than she'd remembered them being in a long time.
Out here, she could almost forget the horror that ruled her
life.

Almost.

After a half hour or so in the saddle, Branson slowed
and came back to ride alongside her. "There's a spring-fed
creek up ahead. We can dismount for a few minutes if you

like. I've seen deer there just before dark. If we're still and quiet, you might get a close-up look at some.''

"I'd like that, but shouldn't we get back to the house?''

"Why?''

"I don't know.'' She rode silently for a few minutes, her mind exploring the question she'd asked instinctively. "I guess it seems the world is too nice out here. That we shouldn't have this time with all that's going on.''

"We've done everything I know to do, Lacy. We're doing it even as we talk. Kate's in every cop's computer. We have her description out all over Texas. My friend on the San Antonio police force has officers on the streets, pulling favors from snitches to find out what they can about any guys Ricky might have crossed lately.''

"I know. It's just that I worry about my sister. I always have.''

"Has your worrying ever changed anything?''

"No, of course not.''

"Then maybe you should start looking out for yourself, Lacy. Unless Kate wants a different kind of life, she's going to keep finding trouble.''

Branson dismounted and then helped her to the ground. She walked away from him, swishing through the tall grass until she reached the muddy edge of the creek. A turtle ducked under the cover of water as she approached, and she jumped at the sound.

"Don't make judgments about Kate, Branson. You don't know her. You don't know what she's been through.''

Branson walked up behind her. "You're right. I don't know Kate. But someone tried to kill her, and she hasn't gone to the police with what she knows? That makes me think she's involved in this deeper than just by association.''

"She doesn't trust the police. She has no reason to.''

Lacy reached up and caught hold of a low-hanging branch above her head, one that jutted out over the water.

"No, she has you to run to. She was going to let you marry Charles, let you ruin your life to save her boyfriend from his own doings."

"I never told her that I was getting married because of her. I didn't want her to carry that kind of guilt around."

"Point made. You are a lot more worried about her than she is about you."

"That's not true. Kate's done more for me than I could ever do for her."

Branson touched his hands to Lacy's waist and turned her around to face him. "Tell me about Kate, Lacy. What makes you defend her so staunchly even when she's dragging you into danger."

"It's a long story."

"We have all night, and the more I know about her, the more likely I'll be able to figure out what's going on."

Lacy took a deep breath. There was no way to tell Branson about Kate without delving into the past, into the dark, secret places that she tried to avoid. But if talking about Kate and what she'd been through would help, then Lacy wouldn't back away from the truth.

"Okay, cowboy. You asked for it. Here's the story of my life."

Chapter Ten

Branson dropped to a spot where the grass grew in a thick carpet of green. Taking Lacy's hand, he tugged her down beside him. He leaned against the trunk of an oak tree, his long legs stretched in front of him. She sat close by, pulling up her knees and hunching over them while she decided where to begin.

"I told you that my mother died when I was ten."

"That would have made Kate sixteen?"

"Right. But my mother didn't die of natural causes. She took an overdose of tranquilizers. We never knew if it was intentional or if she'd just been trying to shut out the depression she lived with."

"That must have been a terrible shock for you and Kate."

"I still see her in my nightmares, lying there, her body stiff, her eyes vacant."

"It would be hard to forget an image like that."

"Impossible, though it's grown more manageable over the years." Lacy took a deep breath and forced herself to go on. "Mother had been diagnosed as having a personality disorder though I didn't know that at the time. All I knew was that one minute she would be laughing and happy, the next she'd be screaming at us for no reason. Then she'd go to her room and stay there for hours crying in the dark. I always thought it was my fault.''

''Were you close to your dad?''

''Apparently not. He walked out on my mom and Kate and me when I was eight. After that Mom's bad moments far outnumbered the good ones. I don't think she ever got over his leaving.''

Branson scooted closer. ''You don't have to tell me any more. I hate to see you upset like this.''

''No, I'd like to tell you. It's been bottled inside me too long. Besides, if it helps our search for Kate in any way, then it's worth it.''

''Whom did you live with after your mother died?''

''There was no family. The authorities came. I don't know who they were—men in suits, women in nice dresses. They said we had to move out of our little house and go live in foster homes, but no one was willing to take the both of us. I remember the day they separated me from Kate. I screamed and begged her not to let them take me. She just stood there with tears rolling down her cheeks.''

Branson muttered a string of mild curses. ''People in authority. No wonder you never trusted anyone after that.''

''Oh, it got worse. Finally after about six months, they took us to this foster picnic affair where all the families who kept children got together. It was the first time I'd seen Kate since the separation. We ran that day, started running and hiding out and Kate never really stopped. She did whatever she had to in order to buy food and let us be a family.''

''So that explains the bad checks.''

''Like I said, she did whatever she had to. She became my caretaker though she was little more than a child herself. We looked behind us constantly, waiting for some cop to tap us on the shoulder and take me back to foster care.

Now we realize they probably never even looked for us, but then we were just running scared.''

Branson reached over and took her hands in his. "I can see why you feel the way you do about Kate, but you can stop running, Lacy. I won't let you down."

She met his gaze and grew weak at the intensity of his stare. They had crossed a line somewhere. Maybe it had happened last night when he'd kissed her. Maybe it had happened the moment she'd felt his hands on her flesh as he'd unbuttoned her wedding gown. Whatever had passed between them, it was affecting their judgment.

"I know you want to help me, Branson, and I appreciate it more than you can possibly know. But I don't think my staying at the Burning Pear is a good idea."

"It's the only idea in all of this that *is* good. You're safe here. When I'm not around, Langley and Ryder will look out for you."

"I can't drag your family into danger. *You* can't do that to them."

"I didn't. I talked to both of my brothers this afternoon. They didn't hesitate for a second. They not only want you at the ranch, they relish the opportunity to protect you. You've won them over."

She swallowed hard and looked away. For years it had been just she and Kate against the world. Now a whole family of cowboys was willing to stand up for her, go up against a killer if they had to.

"I don't know what to say, Branson."

"Then don't say anything. Just stay with me. Stay with us. And somehow we'll find Kate. But if she's involved in kidnapping Betsy, she'll have to face charges. I can't keep that from happening."

"I understand." The colors of the sky were turning dark now, the horizon grabbing the sun and pulling it ever lower.

And the wind had gone from pleasant to chilling. "I'd like to go back now."

Branson helped her mount Surefire and then climbed into his own saddle. They left the creek and followed a fence line, moving south, close enough to talk, yet the silence grew heavy between them.

"How did your ranch come to be named the Burning Pear?" she asked, more to break the suffocating tension that surrounded them than anything else. "There must be a story behind that."

"We have frequent periods of drought in this part of Texas. Sometimes it's so bad, the creeks and rivers dry up and the grass stops growing or dies altogether. When that happens, we use a portable contraption that fits over the cactus and burns off the prickly spines. The cows follow us along as we work, chomping down as soon as the cactus is spine-free."

"And that's called burning pear?"

"That's what we say down here. And as you can tell, we have a lot of pear cacti to work with."

"Is all of this land part of your ranch?"

"It is on this side of the fence. The land on the other side is Maccabbe country. At least a small strip of it is."

"Milton Maccabbe?"

"You sound as if you know the man?"

"No, but I've heard Kate speak of him, or at least a man by that name. Does he work for Joshua Kincaid?"

"He used to. He was the foreman of Kincaid's ranch until a few months ago. Kincaid had bought out one of the small ranches that borders the Burning Pear a few years back when he was planning to expand his cattle business. He never did much with it, and he sold a strip of it to Maccabbe when the man decided to retire."

"So Milton Maccabbe's your next-door neighbor. It

would be a far piece to walk to borrow a cup of sugar though.''

''That's okay. I'll take wide-open spaces to neighbors any day. Especially when the neighbor's as strange as Maccabbe is. But, the man does know his cattle.''

She gave Surefire a little more rein, this time leaving Branson behind. But not for long. He caught up with her, riding beside her, the breeze in their faces. And together they rode back to the Burning Pear.

BETSY WAS BATHED and in her pajamas, so cute and cuddly, the honorary cowboy uncles were actually fighting over who should give her the bedtime bottle. Of course, they hadn't been fighting over who should bathe her. Lacy had had to enlist Branson's help for that and then convince him that Betsy wouldn't actually melt if he put warm water on her head to rinse away the baby shampoo.

The phone rang. She almost answered it, jerking her hand back just in time. No matter that the Randolph men made her feel as if this was her home, it wasn't.

Langley grabbed the kitchen extension. A minute later he stuck his head through the open door. ''It's for you, Lacy.''

''Who is it?''

''A man. The caller ID says out of area. Do you want me to ask his name?''

''No.'' Branson answered for her. ''You take the call in the kitchen, Lacy. I'll listen in on this extension.''

Anxiety stirred inside her like poison brewing in a witch's cauldron. She felt Langley and Ryder watching her as she walked determinedly to the kitchen. The only person who knew she was here was Charles, unless Adam Pascal and Joshua Kincaid had surmised it.

She picked up the phone, gearing up for the worst. "Hello."

"Hello, Lacy."

The voice was low, muffled. Sinister. Dread and fear converged inside her. "Who is this?"

"You'll find out soon enough."

"What do you want?"

"You. I want you, Lacy. I want you dead."

Her breath burned in her lungs. She wanted to sever the connection and stop the man's horrifying intrusion into her life. But even in this mind-numbing state of terror, she had to find out what she could. "Why are you doing this?" she asked, her voice a shaky cry. "Did you kill Ricky Carpenter?"

The man laughed, low, mocking. "I have to go now, Lacy. I just wanted you to know that I know where you are and I am coming to get you. Don't close your eyes. I am your nightmare."

The slam of the receiver did little to break the spell. She stumbled backward, leaning against the kitchen counter for support.

Branson was beside her in seconds. The cold fire of fury burned in his eyes, yet he appeared calm, solid, in control.

"Was that the same man who called you the day you were supposed to marry Charles?"

"I think so, but his voice is so strange, almost garbled. It was that day, too." She leaned into Branson, unable to resist his strength. He held her until she stopped shaking. Finally the questions that haunted her mind slipped from her tongue.

"What could I have done to that man, Branson? Why does he want to kill me?"

Branson released her from his arms but didn't move away. "Some people don't need a reason to hate. The madness is inside them. They just pick a target, a person they can direct their anger at.''

''But he knows me. He knows my name. He knows I'm here at the Burning Pear.''

''And that's what worries me most. He must have seen us together. It could be someone we know.''

''I didn't recognize the voice.''

''He didn't intend for you to, but that doesn't mean you don't know him. He was talking through some kind of filter. You can buy professional equipment to alter the voice or you can make your own device. It's no big deal if a man has reason to do it.''

''Which means it is someone I know, someone whose voice I would be able to identify.''

''You, or one of us.''

''No. This is my problem, mine and Kate's. There's no reason to think any of this is connected to you or your family. Except that I've brought these horrors into your home.''

''We were drawn in the night your sister delivered Betsy to our door. You didn't cause that to happen.''

Lacy clutched the edge of the counter, her backside pressed against the cold tile edge. ''When will it end? How will it end?''

''With this son of a—'' He threw up his hands. ''With the man or men responsible behind bars. Count on it.''

But all she could count on was fear so real she could taste it. Dread that iced her nerves and chilled her heart.

Branson stroked her cheek, his fingers brushing the bottom of her earlobe. She trembled. Not from fear this time, but desire so strong it jolted her senses.

A room away, two cowboys were rocking a baby to sleep and waiting to hear who the mystery caller had been. But in the kitchen, there were only Lacy and Branson and a need so palpable it took on an identity of its own.

Branson leaned closer, his lips inches from hers, his breath short, choppy, yet warm on her flesh. Her heart raced for a second and then seemed to stop altogether as Branson's mouth touched hers.

The kiss was intense, almost fierce, as if Branson hated himself for letting it happen. When he finally broke away, he lowered his gaze, their foreheads touching, their hands clasped, holding on for dear life.

"Damn." His voice was a rough whisper. "My job is to protect you, not seduce you."

"Does it matter that I wanted you to kiss me?"

"It matters. It just doesn't make it right."

"And do you always do what's right, Sheriff Branson Randolph?"

"I try."

"Because of the badge you wear?"

He let go of her hands and took a step backward, breaking the physical connection that had held them, but not the emotional one.

"The badge is important to me, Lacy, but this isn't about the badge or duty or honor. It's about you. And it's about a madman who obviously plans to be your assassin. If I get wrapped up in wanting you then I give the killer the edge. I don't plan to let that happen."

Ryder stepped into the room behind Branson. "I don't mean to interrupt, but was the phone call bad news?"

"You're not interrupting." Lacy managed a tentative smile and walked past the two of them. "Branson can fill you in on the phone call. I'm going to give Betsy a good-night hug. I need it."

"You'll have to hurry. She almost went to sleep before she finished her bottle. Langley is putting her to bed."

Lacy walked quickly through the house stopping at the open door of the nursery to peer inside. Langley was standing over Betsy, watching her sleep. She tiptoed in and stood beside him.

Langley reached down and eased the cotton blanket over Betsy's legs. "She's something, isn't she?" he whispered, letting his hand linger near the sleeping angel.

"She is. She fits into this family perfectly."

"I think so, too."

"The Randolphs are an unusual family," Lacy said. "Not everyone would take so quickly to a baby who'd been dropped off at their door."

Langley cracked a smile. "We're just plain folks doing what needs to be done."

"Old values on a modern ranch. It's a nice combination." She started back to the living room but stopped to study the framed photographs that dotted the corridor wall.

Most were of the Randolph boys as they were growing up. Branson on a tractor with his dad, a wide grin showing off his missing front teeth. Ryder on a horse, dressed up like a counterpart from the Wild, Wild West. All three boys in their Sunday best standing in front of a huge Christmas tree.

And an adorable picture of Betsy lying in the pine baby bed.

"Your mother must have really taken to Betsy fast. She's already given her a place of honor with the rest of the family. She had to have this picture taken, developed, framed and hung right after Kate dropped Betsy off."

Langley studied the picture over Lacy's shoulder. "My mom took to Betsy like a preacher to fried chicken, but that isn't Betsy in that picture. It's Branson."

Lacy stared at the photograph. Betsy and Branson. The same dark eyes, the same wispy curls… Disturbing thoughts pushed into her mind, but she refused to entertain them. Branson would never deny his own child.

But even if Betsy wasn't Branson's, she was almost surely a Randolph. The likeness was too close to suggest coincidence. Branson and his brothers might not realize that, but she was sure Mary Randolph had. No wonder she fought to keep Betsy, convinced Social Services to let her have temporary custody.

Lacy stood for a moment, trying to get a grip on all that was going on. A mystery baby. A murderer planning Lacy's death. Kate, lost and in danger. Charles Castile scheming to find a way to make her pay in blood for the fifty thousand dollars she had borrowed in vain.

And Lacy falling hard for a sheriff who was determined to keep his distance.

All of it boggled the mind and numbed the spirit. And the only thing Lacy could do about any of it tonight was go to sleep. And pray she had enough tomorrows to make a life.

LACY HAD BEEN SURPRISED to hear from him tonight. Imagine that. All settled in at the Randolph ranch. Cozying up to that sheriff. But the good sheriff couldn't save her.

No one could.

The wedding was off. The murders were on.

Ricky, Kate and Lacy. Ricky, Kate and Lacy. The names spun in his mind, faster and faster until he was dizzy. Drunk on the thought of what he was about to do. Three for the price of one.

He felt better and better with each passing day. Almost like his old self again. The way he'd felt the last time he'd had to do something like this.

Ricky, Kate and Lacy. But now only two were left. Kate and Lacy. Kate and Lacy. Kate and Lacy.

Lacy. Lacy. Lacy.

Chapter Eleven

Branson leaned against the wooden railing of the front porch, sipping from an icy glass of lemonade. There were a few late-afternoon clouds floating around in the sky, but it didn't look likely they'd produce rain or cooler temperatures.

"If today's any indication, I'd say summer will be a scorcher this year."

Lacy looked up from the magazine she'd been leafing through. "It is hot for May, but I like summer. I like wearing shorts and going barefoot." She put the porch swing back in motion, the chains producing a creaking that matched Branson's edgy mood.

It had been two days since she'd received the death threat at the Burning Pear, but he had little hope that the man had given up. That's why he had kept Lacy under his or one of his brother's watchful eyes every second.

That was proving to be one of the most difficult parts of this investigation. To eat at the same table with Lacy and not react to the sizzle that sparked between them. To live in the same house and not touch her when their paths crossed. To be with her and yet not be with her.

"I hate to even ask," she said, looking up to meet his gaze. "But how was your day?"

"I spent most of it in San Antonio. I finally got a chance to hit the streets with my detective buddy. We talked to snitches, dredging for information. And believe me, some of the spots we dug in shouldn't exist this side of hell. The story stayed the same. Ricky wasn't a gambling man. Never has been."

"And no one knew a thing about why he'd been murdered?"

"No. He had a string of past-due charge accounts, had his fancy car repossessed and was three months behind on mortgage payments. But no enemies. He was a good old boy. People liked him."

"I know Charles did. The few times Ricky came by the office with Kate, he and Charles got into long conversations about sports in general and football in particular. That was probably what made Ricky think of Charles when he needed money."

"So Charles liked Ricky, but you mentioned the other day that he hadn't liked Kate, though he'd gotten her a job with Kincaid."

"Ricky had played in the pros. That gave him status, and Charles was big on that."

Branson nudged his hat back on his head and then finished his lemonade. No matter how he ran the maze, he always came back to Charles Castile. And out on the fringes, he had Joshua Kincaid. The dead body in the center was Ricky Carpenter. So where did Kate and Lacy fit in? And Betsy?

Betsy *Randolph?*

Maybe. Maybe not. But in just a few short days, she had the whole family wrapped around her tiny fingers. She smiled, and they went gaga. She cried, and they jumped through hoops. Grown men making fools of themselves. Hell, he was one of them.

But could she be his child? Only Marilyn Cassaleta would have that answer. *If* she ever returned his call.

Marilyn Cassaleta. Not the woman he would have chosen to be the mother of his child, but had he come to that conclusion too late? Had the desires he'd known one night ten months ago bound him to a woman he hadn't really known at all and could never love?

Had the mystery surrounding Betsy's identity bound him to another? Bound him with emotions so unfamiliar he couldn't begin to understand them.

"I'd like to take a ride over to Milton Maccabbe's place, Lacy. Would you like to come along? We might pick up some scrap of info we could use."

"How could Milton possibly know anything that would help us?"

"I'm going for long shots now. Milton worked for Kincaid until a few months ago, so he's possibly met Ricky, and you said Kate had met him. Actually, Kate's car was found in the creek that borders his land. There's a chance he saw something, though he's already told Gordon he didn't."

"But a long shot is better than no shot. Count me in."

"Okay, but let me warn you. Milton Maccabbe marches to a different drummer than anyone else you will meet in Kelman."

"Is that good or bad?"

"Let's just say you will not be overwhelmed by his charm."

MILTON MACCABBE stood in the shade and watched the sheriff and Lacy Gilbraith get out of Branson's truck and walk up the back steps of his house. He knew they weren't making a social call. No one ever did. That was the way he liked it.

He'd been a loner all his life, and he wasn't interested in changing that now that he was old and sick. Now that his life was measured in days and months instead of years and decades.

No, he knew why the sheriff was knocking on his door. He was going to try to tie him to Ricky Carpenter's murder. He wasn't worried. The sheriff was bluffing. He didn't have Jack Squat on him.

He wiped his hands on the front of his jeans and stepped out into the open. It was time to greet his uninvited guests to the Running Deer. But he wasn't going to invite them in and serve tea and cookies. They could talk while he worked or find someone else to bother.

LACY STOOD in the shade of a pecan tree and watched Milton Maccabbe brandish the sharp filet knife as he expertly skinned the slippery fish. Branson had introduced her, but if Milton suspected she was Kate Gilbraith's sister, he didn't comment on it.

"Hope you and Miss Gilbraith don't mind talking out here, Sheriff. But I'm not much on sitting around inside when there's work to be done."

"This is fine, Milton. You catch a mess of fish, you have to clean them."

"Yep. They're not big, but they'll be perfect for frying whole." He dropped the cleaned fish into a pan of clear water that rested on the work table.

"You must have a lot more time for fishing now that you're no longer running Kincaid's ranch."

"Not enough. I'm still having to do some work for the boss. He sent one of his city boys down today to go over figures with the new foreman. Between the both of them, they couldn't figure out what they were doing. They had to bring their fancy charts over here for me to tell them how much feed to buy.''

"I guess you're a hard fellow to replace," Branson said.

"I wouldn't be if Kincaid had hired a foreman with the sense God gave a goose. As it is, I've got to go back over there and help with inoculating the new calves.''

Branson swatted at a mosquito that was courting his eyelashes and stepped a little closer to the fish-cleaning operation. "I was telling Miss Gilbraith before we came by that you know your cattle.''

"I always did my job. I guess you're doing yours, too, Sheriff. And you must think it involves me or you wouldn't be out here.''

"I was just wondering if you saw anything suspicious around here last Wednesday night.''

"I already told your deputy that I didn't.''

"I just thought you might have remembered something.''

Milton reached into the pail at his feet and pulled another bream from his stringer. The fish flopped from his hand and onto the worktable. He wiped his hands on the legs of his pants and stared at Branson.

"Say it plain, Sheriff. Kate Gilbraith was shot on her way to your house. Then Saturday night Ricky Carpenter's body showed up at your gate. Looks like you got yourself a regular crime wave here in Kelman, and you want to know what I know about it.''

"That's about as plain as it gets, all right. I didn't know the facts were common knowledge.''

"If one person in Kelman knows anything, we all do. It's that kind of town.''

"True, but I wouldn't have taken you for a gossiping man.''

"I keep my ears open. Not that I had to with the media picking up the story of an ex-pro player being murdered.

It was probably the first headline a backup player like Ricky ever made.'' He picked up the knife and pointed the tip of it toward Lacy. ''I am a little surprised to see you out here with the sheriff, though. More surprised that you're going by the name of Gilbraith. I don't imagine your new husband would be too happy if he knew that.''

His comment took Lacy by surprise. It shouldn't have. If he knew about Kate's being shot, he couldn't help but realize they had the same last name. But there was no way he should know about her so-called wedding to Charles Castile.

''If you listen to gossip, you should learn when to discount it,'' she said. ''I'm not married. Charles Castile and I had a change of plans.''

He smirked. ''Is that so? I guess I must have heard the story wrong then. I heard you had a private ceremony after all the guests went home.''

Lacy didn't bother to argue. She couldn't imagine why Charles was spreading these lies, but she knew he had his reasons. He never did anything without a reason.

''You sound as if you know a lot about the wedding,'' Branson observed. ''You and Charles must be close friends.''

''I worked for Joshua Kincaid in Austin for ten years before I took over his ranch. I met most of his business associates at one time or another. As for being friends, it didn't much matter. I didn't get paid for that.''

''What exactly did you do for Kincaid in Austin?''

Milton ran his finger along the edge of his knife. ''You're asking an awful lot of questions, Sheriff. You don't happen to have a warrant for my arrest, do you? 'Cause if you don't, I think I'm through talking.''

''No warrant, Milton. I just thought you might have seen something since we share a common border.''

"Didn't see a thing."

"Then I guess we might as well be going, Lacy. I don't want to waste any more of Milton's valuable time."

They started to walk away, but Milton's words stopped them.

"You need to take *real* good care of Lacy, Sheriff. I wouldn't let her out of my sight, if I were you."

Branson turned on a dime. "Is that a threat, Milton?"

He rubbed his chin with the back of his hand. "It's a suggestion, Sheriff. There's a killer stalking Kelman, Texas. You know it. I know it. Kate Gilbraith knows it."

Lacy trembled as the fear she'd lived with for days attacked with renewed force. "Do you know where Kate is? Have you seen her?"

"Your sister can take care of herself, Lacy. She knows the score and the players. It's you who needs to worry."

Branson thrust his body into Milton's space. "If you know something, Milton, you say so now."

"I've already told you what I know." Milton went back to cleaning his fish, dismissing them with his actions.

Branson led Lacy to the truck. She had the crazy feeling that someone was watching her. She looked back at Milton. It wasn't him.

But she didn't trust Milton. He was involved in this. She just wasn't sure how. She waited until they'd left Milton's land and started back down the highway before she put words to her suspicions. "Do you think Milton could have murdered Ricky?"

"He could have. He's killed before."

"I didn't know that. Why would Kincaid hire a murderer?"

"Kincaid's never been too particular about the kind of person he hires, but I didn't say Milton was a murderer. I said he'd killed before. He was a mercenary before he signed on with Kincaid. I guess he got too old for roaming the world and decided to settle down.''

"How did you find that out?''

"I talked to Joshua Kincaid last night. I asked him a few questions. He was cooperative for a change. He probably figures it pays to be, what with one of his employees shot and her boyfriend murdered.''

"So he knows now that Kate was shot?''

"I told him. There was no reason not to.''

Lacy felt her insides tightening again. She felt as if she were running an obstacle course that never ended, where the hurdles grew higher and thicker with each step.

Branson shot her a glance that had worry written all over it. He was probably afraid she was about to blow. He might just be right. She wasn't sure how much more she could take. She swallowed hard and forced her mind to focus on facts.

"So Milton worked as a mercenary before he went to work for Kincaid,'' she said. "Now he's retired and bought his own place.''

"He traveled all over the world and then settled on a ranch in south Texas. You have to like that about the man.''

"So, back to my original question,'' Lacy said. "Do you think he killed Ricky?''

"Not going on what we have right now.''

"Why not?''

"No motive,'' Branson said. "But after talking to him just now, I think he might know something more than he said. Which brings us right back to Charles Castile. Milton brought Charles's name into the conversation. Then he warned you and said he'd told us all he knew.''

"But even if Charles did kill Ricky or have him killed,'' Lacy observed, "if he tried to get his money back, why would he threaten me or Kate? At the time Kate was shot,

I was still planning to marry him. And my first threatening phone call came just before I was to say I do.''

Lacy closed her eyes. She was dizzy with frustration, sick with worry about Kate.

"Talk to me about something mundane, Branson. Remind me that there are still normal people out there doing everyday things. Convince me that this will be over one day, that the real killer will be behind bars and the rest of us will be walking in the sunshine.''

Branson didn't answer, but a few minutes later, he pulled off the highway onto a dirt road.

"Where are we going now?''

"This is one of the back gates to the Burning Pear. If it's an escape you're looking for, I know the perfect place. I'd almost forgotten about it until you started talking. I haven't been there in years.''

Branson took off across the hard, dry ground, not bothering with staying on a road. She couldn't imagine how he knew where he was going with acres of landmarks that all looked the same, but he drove as if on a mission. To find a perfect place.

A perfect place. Branson said he hadn't been there for years. He was way ahead of her. She'd never been there.

BRANSON STOPPED the truck and killed the engine. Lacy stared out the window. She wasn't sure what she'd been expecting, but definitely not this. "Is this your perfect spot?''

"Yeah. I guess it's really not that much. Maybe that's why I haven't been back here in so long.''

His haven was a hole of sorts that extended the creek bed into a pocket of deeper water. The pocket wasn't big enough to be called a pond, but it was larger than most backyard swimming pools.

A cluster of cows sat on the opposite bank, dining on grass in the shade of a Texas persimmon tree. Branson lowered his truck window and propped his elbow out. "It's not exactly like I remember it."

Lacy opened her door and jumped to the ground. The grass was high, almost to her knees in spots. She imagined rattlesnakes slithering through it or coiled and ready to spring. Her skin prickled.

A large oak guarded the end of the pond where Branson had parked his truck. The tree's gnarly roots had cracked through the earth to run their rugged tails toward the water. A squirrel stopped and looked at them before scurrying up the trunk and out on one of the lower branches.

Lacy followed its retreat. An old rope was still knotted around the branch, though the length of it was hairy and unraveled from sun, wind and rain. Her mind painted a picture to accompany it.

Branson and his brothers swinging from the rope, their long legs dangling from cutoffs as they swung over the water, laughing and kicking before letting go and landing with a loud splash.

Branson led the way, stamping through the grass in a direct path to the edge of the water. He picked up a rock and skipped it across the glassy surface.

"My grandpa had this swimming hole dug out when my dad was just a boy. Then when we came along, my dad renewed the tradition of coming out here every year on the first day of summer to swim and picnic. My mom came with us, too, so that she could yell at us to be careful and to cut down on the horseplay. That wasn't the only time we came, of course, but those were the times that stick in my mind."

"Family traditions." Branson's life was full of them. Her family had a few, too, but they were the ones she'd spent years trying to bury before they destroyed her. She had done a pretty good job of it until this week.

As fear and anxiety had reclaimed her heart, the memories had returned, as fresh as they had ever been. But even in the worst of times she'd always had Kate.

Don't worry about Kate. She can take care of herself. That's what Milton had said. There had been a time when Lacy had believed that. When she'd thought there was nothing in the world her big sister couldn't do.

The grass swished and crushed beneath Branson's feet as he stepped over to stand beside her. "A big tree, a little water, a few cows. I guess it's not so much to look at," he said.

He'd misread her silence. She hastened to assure him otherwise. "It's not that. I like it here. It's peaceful, exactly what I need."

"It wasn't peaceful back when I was a boy. Anything but. Four of us yelling and shoving and ducking each other. My dad right in there with us. Sometimes my mom even got into the fray. Said she had to help her baby. And when she and Ryder teamed up against you, you were going under."

"Nice memories."

"Ancient memories."

But they would be with him always. Until he died.

She chewed on her bottom lip as a ridiculous notion teased her brain. Childish, immature. But the longer it played midst the darkness and gloom she'd carried around for the past few days, the less ridiculous it seemed.

She grabbed a handful of hair and pulled it off her neck, holding it so that the warm breeze could tickle her flesh. "I'm going in, Branson." She said the words fast, without any fanfare, before she had time to back out. "I'm going for a swim."

"Now?"

"Now. I'm already years late in the memory-making department. Besides, if my would-be killer makes good on his threats, now may be all the time I have."

He caught her hand. "Don't talk like that. I won't let anything happen to you."

"Are you going to follow me around the rest of my life just so you can keep me from getting killed?"

"If it comes to that."

"Then you can protect me while I swim." She yanked off her boots. "Or you can come in and join the fun."

"We don't have bathing suits."

"The cows won't care and you've already seen me in my underwear, so we know you can handle me without my clothes on."

He shook his head. "You may know that. I definitely don't."

"I guess we'll find out." She stepped away from him, her fingers already flying at the buttons on her blouse. A quick swim in a pool of cool water wouldn't change anything, but now that the idea had sprung to life, she couldn't let go of it. For days, her life had been nothing but serial complications, compounded by the minute, like interest on a loan. One glimmer of hope countered by two heaps of gloom and a cup of fear.

When the last button fell loose, she turned her back to Branson and shrugged out of the blouse, dropping it to the ground. Now for the jeans. She tucked her fingers into the waistband and yanked on the snap. Branson could join her or not. His choice. But she was going for a swim. She would steal a few minutes of pleasure. It might be the only thing that would keep her sane until this was over.

Until Kate was found. Until the killer was stopped.

Shaking, she fit her fingers around the catch on the zipper and tugged.

BRANSON KNEW he should turn away, knew it the second Lacy started stripping away her blouse. He couldn't.

He would have never come here if he'd expected anything like this to happen. He was already haunted by the images of the white wedding dress sliding off Lacy's shoulders. Had grown rock-hard and harried more than once by the memory of her golden hips above the row of lace that banded her panties.

Now this. He swallowed hard. He was not the man he used to be. Not the man he'd been a few days ago when he'd met Lacy.

Her jeans slid to the ground, and his resolve plummeted with them. But it wasn't just the sight of Lacy's shapely body that was doing him in. If it had been, he might have been able to walk away. He might have been able to force himself to continue as the dispassionate lawman he'd always prided himself on being.

But the real draw was Lacy herself. Tough as a colt, brave as a mother wildcat. Soft as the flesh of a summer peach. She'd gone through hell and back the past few days, and she always came up fighting.

She eased one foot into the water, then stepped backward. Reaching behind her she loosened the clasp on her bra. It fell open and she let the straps slide down her arms. Without looking back, she tossed it to the ground behind her.

Branson watched, mesmerized, weak, his breath so tight he thought he might die of suffocation. But the sensual onslaught didn't let up. Lacy hooked her fingers into the waistband and tugged on her panties. The lacy scrap of material fell, sliding down her long bronzed legs. She bent and pulled them over her foot, once again tossing them behind her without turning around.

By the time she'd crossed the creek and stepped into the deeper water of the man-made pool, his own jeans were so tight against his aroused body that he could barely move.

She swam for a few minutes, her graceful body skimming the top of the water, her hair wet and shiny, floating like burnished gold on the surface of the pool. Then she swam back to a place where her feet would touch bottom. She slapped her hands against the water and sent a spray in his direction.

"Come on in. The water is cold at first, but once you get used to it, it's like floating in soft cream. I'll never want to go back to a chemical-laced concrete pool again."

"I'm glad you like it."

"Does that mean you're not coming in with me?"

"It wouldn't be a good idea."

"Chicken."

"More of a rooster right now."

Branson walked back to the truck and dug behind the seat for the Mexican blanket. He'd tossed it back there a couple weeks ago when he'd taken Petey with him to coach some of the neighbor boys with their barrel-racing skills. It was best to always be prepared with Petey. You never knew when he might tire out and need a place to nap. That day he hadn't even slowed down.

But the blanket would substitute as a towel for Lacy. He dropped it to the ground underneath the oak tree and sat down on it. Lacy was still at it, playing more than swimming. She reminded him of a kid, twirling in the water, ducking her head, floating on top.

And here he was sitting in the shade like an old man. An old lawman with rules and regulations. An old man of thirty-four who might never have this kind of opportunity again.

He'd said he had to stay away from Lacy, that to let her under his skin would hinder his ability to do his job. But she was already under his skin. Under his skin, playing with his mind, speeding up his heart. And tinkering with every other body part.

So why was he avoiding her now, refusing to play when she needed the break from reality so badly? Because he was a coward, that's why. He'd had his heart busted once. Busted and then run over with a John Deere tractor seven years later.

"I'm not going to beg you, Branson, but I wish you'd come in."

"You seem to be having a fine time by yourself."

"I'm making memories. Good ones for a change. Memories to take with me for the rest of my life. However long that might be." She put her hands out to him, a welcoming gesture, as warm as the beseeching smile on her wet lips. "The memories would be better if I shared them with you."

Branson gave up. He was fighting a battle to keep his heart under protective armor. But winning the battle would be losing.

"Okay, lady. You asked for it." He stood up and unbuttoned his shirt, ripping it open and slinging it to the ground. "I'm coming in."

LACY'S HEART RACED like a runaway colt. She'd lured the handsome sheriff in against his wishes. She should feel guilty. She didn't. He was an important part of her fantasy. The carefree memory she'd never had.

A man who was honest and good. Who made her feel as though she was somebody special when he looked at her. Who believed what she told him. Who had taken her in and made her feel like a part of his family.

A man like she had never met before and probably would never know again.

He stepped into the water, buck naked, his hard, bronzed body gleaming in the sun. He was magnificent, every inch of him. And every inch of her was responding in ways she'd never known they could.

Branson swam toward her. She ran her hand across the surface, sending a sheet of water into his face. He blinked and wiped the excess water from his eyes.

"So you want to play dirty, do you?" He dived and grabbed her by the waist, pulling her under.

She fought, wrapping her legs around him. They came up together in a crashing heap of tangled bodies.

But the fight had gone out of her. She found Branson's lips instead. Water dripped into her eyes, into their kiss, but all she felt was the heat inside her, hot liquid flames that licked their way up and down her body. Sensations more intense than she'd ever imagined.

Branson led her closer to the bank, not stopping until he could plant his feet on the muddy bottom. Then he found new places to fit his mouth. Her eyes, her nose, her neck, her breasts. She was dizzy with desire, so hungry for him that she ached. She thrust toward him, wrapping her legs around him.

"Oh, Lacy. I knew this would happen. But if it hadn't, I was going to go nuts with wanting you."

"Don't talk, Branson." She covered his mouth with her fingers. "Just let me have this moment. And I'll make it be enough." She put her mouth to his for one more earth-shattering kiss.

And then Branson lifted her body, his strong hands supporting her thighs, his fingers digging into her flesh with delicious force. He brought her down on the hard length of him, their bodies slick and hot against each other, the water trickling between them.

She cried out, the feeling of Branson inside her so powerful, so erotic, she thought her heart might explode inside her. He brought her down on him again and again, until he erupted in a spring of ecstasy, taking her with him all the way.

When the passion was spent, she fell against him, weak, but happy.

"You were right. This is the perfect place," she whispered as her legs slid down his and her feet found footing in the soft mud beneath them.

"Perfect," he agreed. "Perfect in every way."

RYDER MET Branson and Lacy at the back door. "About time you two got here," he announced as Lacy climbed out of the truck and slammed the door shut behind her.

She tucked her hair behind her ears and hoped Ryder and Langley didn't notice that it was still damp and a lot more tousled than usual. She'd dried it as much as she could with the blanket and then kept her window down all the way home.

"Don't tell me Betsy's not burping on demand again," she teased as she scurried by him.

"No. I was just starting to get worried."

"Since when did you start worrying about me?" Branson asked.

"It wasn't you I was worried about."

"Oh, so you were missing your baby-sitter," Lacy teased.

Branson took off his hat and slid it onto the pine shelf just left of the back door. Three men, three Stetsons, all side by side. It said a lot about their home, Lacy decided.

Langley walked into the kitchen to join the crew. He had Betsy in his arms. She was snuggled against his chest, her brown eyes open wide, looking as contented as a well-fed puppy.

"Hello, little Betsy, did you miss me?" Lacy cooed. "Let me wash my hands so I can hold you for a while."

"You might want to take a peak at those flowers on the table first," Langley said. "The deliveryman said they were for you."

Lacy turned and stared at the bouquet. Roses. At least a dozen. Blood red. The unopened card was still pinned to the white satin bow. Her legs went weak, and she leaned against the counter for support.

"Aren't you going to read the card?" Ryder asked.

Lacy looked to Branson. "Would you do it for me?" Her voice sounded strange, as if it had come from far away. No one had ever sent her flowers before. Now someone had.

But please don't let them be from a killer.

Chapter Twelve

Branson reached across the kitchen table and unpinned the envelope from the bouquet of roses. Holding it at the corner, he pulled out the acknowledgment card. "It's from Charles." He read it silently, and then handed the card to Lacy.

Her fingers shook as she read the typed message.

I miss you. I love you. Please forgive me and come home.

Your loving husband, Charles

She didn't need this. Not on top of everything she had to deal with. But it brought her back to reality with a vicious thud.

She threw the card to the table. There had never been a marriage. Charles knew she didn't love him, and she couldn't believe he really loved her. He'd just wanted her, another possession to add to his list.

But the mistake had been hers. She had made a bargain and broken it. Now the all-powerful attorney would make sure she paid for it.

She went to the sink and washed her hands, scrubbing them as if she could wash away all the evil that was crushing and grinding away at her will. It seemed as if she'd been running away from fear and heartbreak all her life, and no matter how capable a sheriff Branson might be, there was no end in sight.

Her thoughts were broken by the ringing of the phone. In her present state, she fully expected it to be for her, to be Charles wanting to talk to his *wife,* or her proclaimed assassin just calling to let her know he was still on the job.

But Ryder called Branson to the phone.

Branson glanced at the caller ID. "I'll take the call in the den," he said.

Langley handed Betsy to Lacy. She cradled her in her arms, and as if by magic, Lacy's heart lightened. Life. Precious. Unscarred. Trusting.

Betsy had no way of knowing she was the center of major controversy. Had no way of knowing that she was a mystery child without a mother or father. But Betsy could surely sense that she was surrounded by love.

In spite of everything, Betsy was one lucky baby.

BRANSON'S GRIP tightened on the phone as he heard the feminine greeting on the other end. He'd been waiting for this, and still it unnerved him. "I was hoping you'd return my call."

"Surely you knew that I would."

"I'm never sure of anything with you, Marilyn."

Branson debated with himself about how much he should say on the phone. He was a suspicious person by nature, but this time he had good reason not to trust the woman on the other end of the line. And finding out the full truth had never mattered more.

"Are you suggesting that I'm fickle, Branson?"

The teasing annoyed him, but he kept his voice calm. "I just didn't know if you'd call."

"Well, I must admit, I never expected to hear from you again."

"I never expected to call again."

"I hope this means you've forgiven me."

"There's nothing for me to forgive. I wasn't the one you betrayed, at least not lately."

Marilyn Cassaleta laughed, a soft, seductive tinkling that as recently as ten months ago would have had his heart racing. Tonight all he felt was dread and maybe a little sorrow for a woman who had given up her self-respect and gotten so little in return.

"I'd like to see you again, Branson. I have a surprise for you."

"When can I come by?"

"Not tonight. My husband and I are trying to make a go of it again. He's moved back home."

"I didn't know he'd ever moved out."

"He did, right after I saw you last. He's only been back about a month. But he hits the road again in the morning on a weeklong run. So how about tomorrow night? You say the word and I'll chill the wine. We'll make it a pleasant evening. A couple of old friends."

He held his tongue to keep from telling her it would take a lot more than wine to make their meeting pleasant. If he could have handled this his way, he would demand answers from her over the phone, come right out and ask if she'd had his baby.

But he needed to be with her when he pried for information, watch her eyes when she talked. Make it difficult for her to deceive him even though she was so good at it.

"Come to see me, Branson. We have things to talk about, you and I. Important matters."

"How about tomorrow morning, around ten?"

"No. I don't do mornings. You know that. I'm a night-time kind of gal."

She talked in that breathy way that used to drive him mad. She was flirting, trying to play with his mind. It didn't work anymore. Now it was hard to imagine that he had been so gullible in his youth. Harder still to believe he'd fallen back under her spell ten months ago for even a few hours.

"How about noon, Marilyn?"

She sighed as if she was making a great concession. "Four o'clock. That's as early as I can make it."

They said their goodbyes, and he hung up the phone. The question was, would he be ready for her. He wasn't so stupid that he'd just blurt out his fears. He wouldn't ask if she'd given birth to the baby girl who had been delivered to his doorstep.

Even if she wasn't already involved in this, Marilyn would smell the opportunity inherent in the situation. If she thought there was a way to milk money out of him or his family, she'd move on it faster than one of Ryder's broncos clearing the chute.

He sauntered back into the kitchen, angry for having put himself in this position. He stopped in the doorway. Lacy was in a straight-backed chair with Betsy lying in her lap. Betsy was waving her pudgy little arms, kicking her feet and cooing.

The sight tugged at Branson's wounded heart. It was the kind of picture a man could get used to. But it wasn't the time to think like that, the same way it hadn't been the time to make love to Lacy this afternoon. His body tightened as the memories awakened forbidden urges.

He struggled to keep them in check. He had no room in his life for feelings that addled his brain. He had to keep his mind clear.

Lacy looked up from playing with Betsy and smiled at him across the room. Her eyes held only a spark of the fire that had burned in them this afternoon, but a spark was enough to make him grow warm all over.

And he knew all his protestations were a bunch of bunk. As long as Lacy was in his house and in his life, his mind would never be clear of her.

The thought scared him to death.

Ryder propped his backside against the kitchen counter. "I have a little good news, Branson. It might make up for some of the bad you and Lacy have been getting."

"I need to get my hearing checked," Branson said. "I thought I heard you say *good* news."

"Your hearing's just fine."

"Do we need a drumroll?" Lacy asked.

"It wouldn't hurt. Mom's had a full battery of tests," Ryder said, "and the only thing they found wrong with her was—wait, I have to read this from my notes." He pulled a square of paper from his pocket. "Gastroesophageal reflux disease from a hiatal hernia."

"And that's good news?"

"A lot better than a heart attack," Langley exclaimed. "According to the doctors, Mom needs less stress, a better diet, and she needs to stop sneaking midnight snacks of salsa and chips. That's pretty much the treatment," Langley explained.

"Sounds like a fancy name for heartburn," Branson said, but he was as relieved as his brothers.

"The doctor did say it was fairly common and often confused with a heart attack," Ryder answered, raking his fingers through his hair and brushing it off his forehead.

"What about medicine?" Branson asked. "I'd think modern medical science had more to offer than good advice."

"The doc's prescribing something to aid digestion," Langley answered, "but he thinks she'll be just fine. He wants to keep her an extra day, to force her to rest, I expect. But she can come home day after tomorrow. We just have to decide who's going after her, and how to make her follow the doctor's orders."

"The second part of that is impossible, but I'll be glad to drive into San Antonio and pick her up," Ryder said.

"And leave me with Betsy all by myself. I don't think so, little brother." Langley leaned over and stroked Betsy under the chin. "Although she does like me. See. She's smiling. I think I'm her favorite Randolph."

"You'd have Mrs. Brown to help," Ryder said, still arguing his point. "That's not exactly by yourself."

"It's close."

"Why don't you both go?" Lacy said. "I'll stay here with Betsy."

Neither Ryder nor Langley jumped at her offer. They were both looking at Branson, waiting for his okay. He didn't give it.

"Why don't we decide this later?" he said. He walked over to the coffeepot and picked it up, shaking it so that the brew swirled in the glass pot. "This stuff looks like mud. How long ago did you make it?"

"Mrs. Brown made it before she left. It looked like mud then, too. Tastes worse."

Branson opened the cupboard above his head and grabbed a pottery mug, apparently willing to try the brew anyway. "Anyone care to join me?"

Lacy made a face. "I don't think so. You go ahead, and when you're finished you can have a turn holding Betsy while she's still awake."

"And dry," Ryder said. "I changed her. I'm getting pretty darn good at it if I do say so myself. And Betsy's only teasing Langley. I'm the one she's really crazy about.''

"Glad you finally found your niche, Ryder," Branson interjected. "Mom wants you to give up rodeoing. Maybe you could run a nursery."

"Very funny. Very, very funny."

Branson dropped into a chair, and Lacy slipped Betsy into his arms. He rearranged her, trying to find a position that felt natural. None did. It was taking him a while to get the hang of this baby holding.

"So, what do we want to do about supper?" Langley asked. "I'm getting a little tired of Ryder's cooking."

"We could eat the leftovers from that stew Mrs. Brown cooked at lunch," Ryder said. "Of course, it tasted like dishwater."

"You eat a lot of dishwater, do you, little brother?" Branson asked. "You rodeo champions have odd tastes in food."

"I can make a salad," Lacy offered.

"A salad *and*…?" Langley prompted.

"And steak, or a pork chop, or maybe a big hunk of roast beef with gravy," Branson offered. "I could go for that."

"A salad *is* a meal," Lacy said. "It's healthy."

"Darn right it is," Ryder said, limping a little more than usual as he walked over to link his elbow with Lacy's. "My brothers are seriously lacking in the art of healthy gourmet dining. You come into the kitchen with me and make a salad." Ryder shot his brothers a shaming look. "I'll make those barbarians a side dish to go with it."

"Try those porterhouses I took out of the freezer this afternoon," Langley shouted. "I wanted to be sure there wasn't a repeat of that stew."

"You guys don't worry about a thing. Lacy and I will

prepare a meal fit for kings, and, if you're nice, we may invite you."

Branson faked a cough, pretending to choke on the excess bull. "Would you listen to the man? He thinks the sun came up just to hear him crow."

The joviality was false, but Branson appreciated what his brothers were doing. Keeping the tone light, trying to take Lacy's mind off her missing sister. Make her forget that the beautiful red roses on the kitchen table were from a man who claimed to be her husband. Help her cope with the fact that some crazed killer had targeted her as his next victim.

When the going got tough, he could always count on his brothers.

He sniffed. The odor he picked up was neither fish nor fowl, but it was foul. Betsy grunted a little, her face turning red, and Branson felt the painful twinges of panic.

He could count on his brothers for some things. For others, he was strictly on his own. That's why he might as well accept the inevitable. Sheriff Branson Randolph was about to change his first dirty diaper.

LACY SAT in the porch swing beside Branson, the anxiety that had taken up residence inside her temporarily lulled by a full stomach and the healing effects of just being at the Burning Pear.

The day's work was done. Betsy was fed and tucked into bed for the night, and, in spite of Ryder's earlier proclamation, he and Langley had volunteered for kitchen duty.

Lacy slipped her feet out of her shoes and wiggled her toes. "It's a beautiful night," she said, "and this porch swing is fast becoming my favorite spot." She touched his hand. "Next to the swimming hole, of course."

He squeezed her hand in response. "It was a lot more exciting than I remembered it being."

She leaned back and closed her eyes.

"Are you tired?" he asked. He ran his hand along the back of the swing, touching her neck and massaging it gingerly.

"A little. Emotionally more than physically."

"You've handled everything amazingly well. In case I haven't told you, you are one hell of a woman."

She opened her eyes to find him staring at her. "I've had plenty of opportunity to deal with tough situations, but I still wasn't prepared for all of this. I don't know what I would have done if you hadn't happened into my life. I still can't imagine why you invited me into your home."

"Me neither, but I'm glad I did. In case you haven't noticed, I like having you here." He kept his left arm on the back of the swing, but he took her right hand in his. "I like it a lot."

"I like being here."

Branson rubbed his thumb along the back of her hand. "I need to explain something to you."

"If it's about this afternoon, you don't have to explain anything. I told you then, it was to make memories. And it did." She stared at his hand on hers. "I don't expect it to mean any more than that."

"Don't you?" He let go of her hand and tilted her chin so that she couldn't avoid meeting his gaze. His eyes were fathomless pools, dark and mysterious. "I don't know what kind of man you're used to, but when I make love with a woman, it means a lot. Which is why I need to say what's on my mind tonight."

Branson's intensity set off alarms in Lacy's mind. "You don't owe me any explanations, Branson."

"No, but I need to clear up a point of confusion. On the

day we met I told you that Betsy couldn't possibly be mine.''

''Vehemently, if I remember correctly.''

''Yeah, well, you know me. I'm good at vehement. It's finesse I'm short of. Anyway, when I made that claim, I thought Kate was Betsy's mother.''

''She definitely isn't.''

''I believe you. But that means that there is a chance that Betsy could be my daughter.''

Lacy shuddered, her stomach tying itself into tight knots. Branson and some other woman making love, making a baby together, making Betsy. The pictures moved through her mind in slow motion. But she was being ridiculous. She hadn't even known Branson then. And she had no claims on him now. She sucked in a shaky breath.

''Are you talking about the relationship you mentioned the other day, the love you declared you'd gotten over?''

''That's the one.'' Branson leaned forward, resting his elbows on his knees and running his fingers through his hair. ''Marilyn Cassaleta. Ten months ago I ran into her. Before that I hadn't seen her in seven years. We met one summer when I went back to the University of Texas to do some graduate work.''

''Had you been lovers then?''

''Lovers. Yeah, that pretty much sums it up, though at the time I thought we were a lot more. We split up the day before I left to come back to the Burning Pear. A very bitter parting.''

''That's too bad. Had she done something?''

''I thought so. I'd spent the morning shopping for an engagement ring. I was planing to ask her to marry me that night.''

''What changed your mind?''

"I went over to surprise her and found her in bed with a friend of mine—a married friend."

"That explains bitter. But that was years ago."

"Right. And you'd think I would have learned my lesson. But I was doing some legwork last year on a case up in Austin, checking out a man's alibi. I ran into Marilyn in a café. She invited me home with her for a drink. We talked. We kissed. And like a fool, I fell right back under her spell. The spell didn't last long, but long enough for me to make a big mistake."

"Have you seen her since then?"

"No, I left that night when she mentioned her husband, a truck driver who was out on the road. She said she wanted to see me again, but we'd have to keep it from him. It was a shock to realize her game was the same after all those years. I had just switched roles."

"I don't understand. Even if Marilyn had gotten pregnant with your child, how would she have kept it from her husband?"

"I wondered about that myself. She could have told him it was his, or maybe she thought it was and had just found out differently. Anyway, it turns out that they've been separated most of the ten months."

"But how would Kate have ended up with Marilyn's baby?"

"That's one of the questions I'll be asking Marilyn. Maybe she knows Ricky." Branson sat back in the swing and turned to face her. "I have no real reason to think Marilyn is Betsy's mother. I just want to rule out the possibility."

"Miss Cassaleta sounds like a real sweetheart. I can see how you fell for her."

"I never said I was smart where women are concerned.

That's why I go to so much effort to avoid them. That's also why I've stayed happily single for so long."

"Well, for Betsy's sake and yours, I hope this Marilyn creature is not Betsy's mother. But what will you do if she is?"

"I don't know. Whatever it takes to make Betsy's life as good as it can be. Right now I just want to know the truth. I could get DNA testing, of course, see if I'm the father scientifically, but I'd rather talk to Marilyn in person. I'm supposed to be at her house tomorrow afternoon at four."

"So you'll confront Marilyn face-to-face?"

"If it turns out that I am Betsy's father, I'd have to face Marilyn eventually. I'd just as soon do it now."

"Then you wouldn't deny Betsy your name?"

Branson stared straight ahead, his jaw clenched. "Give up my own flesh and blood? Not in this lifetime and ten more to come."

"You're a prince among men, Branson. A prince in denim and cowboy boots, but a prince all the same."

Branson stood and walked away, not turning to face her until he'd put a few feet's distance between them. "Not such a prince, Lacy. It was irresponsible sex, and I'm not blaming anyone but myself for buying into the fantasy that Marilyn had changed."

"You're being awful hard on yourself."

"Am I? If it turns out that Betsy is my daughter, who's going to tell her that her mom and dad were just fooling around one night and she was the accident that resulted?"

"I hope no one."

"So do I."

"Would you like for me to ride up to Austin with you? I don't think I should be there when you talk to Marilyn, but it's a long drive, and I could keep you company."

"I'd appreciate that. I thought about asking you, but I wasn't sure how you'd feel about it."

"Have you told your brothers any of this?"

"No, I haven't told anyone but you. I wanted to wait until I knew one way or the other."

Lacy swallowed hard, realizing once again how entangled her life had become with Branson's in just a few days. As close as Branson was to his brothers, he had kept this from them and yet he had told her.

Branson walked over and stood in front of the swing. "I shouldn't have piled my troubles on your shoulders. You already had more than enough of your own."

"That's what friends are for."

"Friends. Only I didn't feel like a friend this afternoon." He took her hands in his. "Let's get out of here, Lacy, before I start thinking about that and lose control again."

"Where do you want to go?"

"There's a bar on the edge of town—the Roadhouse. We'll get a cold beer and I'll try to cool off. Besides, there's always a few ranch hands hanging around in there, maybe some I've missed questioning. You just never know who might have seen a stranger hanging around Kelman during the past few days."

THE ROADHOUSE was pretty much as Lacy had pictured it from the description Branson had provided on the drive out. Cigarette smoke converged into a thick swirling cloud that danced just beneath the ceiling. A twangy country song about love gone bad blared from the jukebox. The lights were dim, the beer flowing.

"Here comes the law," someone boomed as soon as they'd cleared the door.

Branson made the rounds speaking to everyone. Claps on the back, joking, cattle talk. In here he was one of the guys, respected, but obviously liked. Yet another side of the multifaceted sheriff. Lacy didn't even attempt to remember the names of all the men and women she met.

The long, wooden bar was lined with wranglers in faded jeans and young women who laughed a lot and looked at the guys with adoring eyes. There were several couples and groups of men and women at the mismatched tables that clustered around the dance floor, drinking from bottles or from short, chubby glasses. A few couples were dancing.

Two guys moved over to make room for them at the bar, but Branson denied their invitation. He stayed long enough to snare a couple of beers and led her to a table at the back of the room where two men in their early twenties were sitting with their feet propped up on a chair.

"That looks like the sheriff," one of the men said as they walked up, "but you know it can't be. This man has a woman on his arm. A looker, I might add."

"Yeah," Branson agreed, "good-looking and all mine, so keep those nail-chewed, tobacco-stained hands to yourself." He hooked the toe of his boot around the rung of a chair and dragged it over. "Mind if we join you?"

"As long as you're not here to talk business," the man said. "I've been out in the sun all day putting in a new fence, and my mind is as parched as my throat."

"No business. I'm off duty. I just promised Lacy I'd introduce her to a few authentic cowboys. I thought the two of you could fool her."

"If we can't, nobody can. Hell, we got Joshua Kincaid fooled, and he pays our wages."

Branson introduced the two men as LeRoy Forte and Buster. She didn't catch Buster's last name what with the abundance of background noise, but she did learn that neither of them were from south Texas. Their drawl was distinctively different, though still southern.

LeRoy drank and talked with gusto. He explained how they had come over from Alabama to visit relatives and had fallen in love with the idea of being cowboys. Joshua Kincaid had met them in the Roadhouse one night and hired them on for the spring roundup and branding. That had been two years ago and they were still here and still working at the Kincaid ranch.

"So how's your new foreman doing these days?" Branson wrapped his fingers around the slender neck of his beer and took a long sip. "I haven't run into him in town lately."

"Guess not. Every other day or so Kincaid's been running down from San Antonio to make sure he knows what he's doing," LeRoy answered. "Kincaid or that fancy-dressing number cruncher who works for him."

"It sounds like everyone misses your former foreman."

Buster rubbed the first stubby harbingers of a red beard. "Yeah, Milton Maccabbe is a strange old buzzard, but he knew what he was doing. The new boss has got a lot of learning to do."

"Milton paid his dues. Even those who've been ranching for years have to keep learning. It's a tough business," Branson said.

"And speaking of business, you must be awful busy yourself these days, Sheriff, what with Kelman making the news in the crime department," Buster said. "A woman shot in the shoulder. A man murdered and dumped at the gate to the Burning Pear. Do you think it was the same shooter?"

"Could be."

"Have you got a suspect?"

"Not yet."

"Sounds like someone's got it in for you," Buster added, balancing on the back two legs of his chair and leaning against the wall. "Someone tired of living, I expect, or else he hasn't seen you handle that gun at your waist."

"And I'd rather not have to show him." Branson toyed with his beer bottle, rocking the bottom of it on the scarred wooden table. "Have either of you noticed any strangers hanging around Kelman of late?"

"Nope." Buster bounced his chair back to the floor. "Whoever this shooter is, he must be keeping a low profile or else he's long gone. This isn't a town you can just get lost in."

"Unless we're not talking about a stranger," LeRoy said. "It might be someone who lives around here."

"Good point," Branson said. "What about out at Kincaid's place? Do you have any guests staying out there?"

Buster shook his head. "We haven't had any guests staying at the ranch since Kincaid threw that big party back around Christmas. Now *there* were some fine women. I mean, we're talking *mucho fine*."

The talk moved from women to livestock, as it always did in cattle country. Lacy drifted back into her own dark thoughts as she scanned the bar and wondered if one of the cowboys sitting in this very room could be the man who wanted her dead.

Branson finished his one beer and they said their goodbyes. A gust of wind whipped her hair into her face as they walked across the dark parking lot in silence. Once again, she had the crazy sensation that she was being watched from the shadows.

She stopped and looked behind her. No one was around. But still the hair on her neck stood on end and she felt the prickly tingle of fear. And as always, she wondered where Kate was tonight and if she was safe.

THE MAN PARKED his truck in the brush at the side of the road and watched as the know-it-all sheriff and Lacy Gilbraith rode by. He could have killed her tonight. Could have put a bullet through her skull while she stood in the parking lot of the Roadhouse.

But he was glad he hadn't. Especially now that everything was working out the way he'd planned and schemed. He would kill the two sisters together, just as he'd always dreamed of doing. And he'd kill them real slow. He wanted them to suffer, to know that he was getting his revenge.

Time was running out for them. *Ticktock. Ticktock.*

Anticipation ravaged his brain. This was as good as it got. Lacy and Kate would die begging for mercy, and he'd walk away a free man.

He'd always known it could be done, and he would do it. Very soon now.

It wouldn't be the first time he'd killed and gotten away with it, but it would be the most satisfying.

Ticktock. Ticktock.

Chapter Thirteen

Lacy jerked upright, her mind still lost in that hazy world between sleep and wakefulness. Betsy let out a wail, and Lacy threw her legs over the side of the bed. Still groggy from the dregs of sleep, she stumbled the few feet to the crib and tried to focus.

Reaching into the crib, Lacy rescued the thrashing infant from her perceived injustices. Betsy continued to kick and to punch her tiny fists into the air like a boxer who couldn't find his opponent's nose.

Lacy held her close, rocking her in her arms. "What's the matter, precious? Did you think everybody had forgotten about you? Did you want some attention? Yes, you did."

Betsy stopped crying though her body still shook with erratic sobs and whimperings. Turning, Lacy located the luminous dial of the clock. It was half past four. Betsy had taken her last bottle at eleven last night. No wonder she'd decided to impersonate an alarm clock.

"Lacy."

She looked up. Branson filled the doorway. Bare-chested, hair rumpled, his gym shorts splitting the field of dark hairs that narrowed at his belly.

He filled the room with his presence. Powerful. All man.

Her body grew warm, and she felt the heat rise to her cheeks. No wonder. She should be blushing with what she was thinking. She struggled for a steadying breath and hoped her erotic yearnings were not transparent.

"You women are making a lot of racket in here."

"Only one of us." Lacy's voice was strained, still reeling from the unexpected effect of seeing Branson in his half-dressed state. She turned away from him, determined to regain control of her senses. "Betsy's hungry."

"From the volume of the wailing, my guess would be she's starving. I'll go get her a bottle. Can I get you anything while I'm at it?"

"A glass of water would be nice."

"Milk for the baby, water for the lady. Coming right up."

Branson disappeared through the door. Betsy started fussing again, and Lacy walked the room with her, patting her on the back, soothing her as best she could without nourishment to offer.

Milk for the baby. And then she'd be happy again. Full stomach, clean diaper, a little loving. Contentment came at such a reasonable price when you were an infant.

Perhaps it would stay that way for Betsy. She might truly be a Randolph. Born into a circle of love and support. Family ties so strong they'd be able to wrap around her and lift her over any obstacle life hurled in her path.

"Sweet Betsy, you might just be one of the lucky ones." She made the words into a lullaby and sang them softly as she dropped to the rocking chair to wait for Branson.

BRANSON HAD ALREADY been awake for over an hour when Betsy's cries had given him the opportunity for a little action. That's why he was more than happy to prepare Betsy's bottle. It was a welcome break from lying awake and trying to force mismatched puzzle pieces into place.

He padded back down the hall, bottle of lukewarm formula and glass of cold water in hand.

"Would you like to feed her?" Lacy asked when he reached the door to the nursery.

He hesitated. He'd managed to avoid the feeding experience so far. He felt as if he had ten thumbs when he was just holding her. Holding a nipple in her mouth had to be a lot more difficult.

"It's a good time to learn," Lacy coaxed.

"I can try," he said, wishing at the same time he hadn't.

"You take the rocker, and I'll hand her to you."

"I take it this requires a little more finesse than nipple-feeding a motherless calf," he said, settling in the chair.

"You'll get the hang of it soon enough. It just takes practice." She positioned Betsy in his arms. "You just hold the bottle so that the nipple always has milk in it. That keeps her from swallowing an excess of air."

He did as he was told and Betsy locked her lips onto the nipple. A second later she was sucking away, making soft mewing sounds that made her sound like a baby kitten.

A funny feeling settled inside him, kind of the way he felt when he helped bring a stubborn calf into the world. Lacy sat on the bed opposite him, smiling, her hair down and falling around her slender shoulders.

They could have passed for a married couple tending their first baby. The contrast between what it appeared to be and what the scene actually represented was so bizarre it boggled his mind. Betsy might be his daughter. He'd know soon enough. But Lacy was not his wife. And definitely not Betsy's mother.

How different it would be if she were. He and Lacy rocking their baby to sleep, reading her bedtime stories, dressing her in frilly dresses. And in the red cowboy boots he'd buy her.

And here he went again. Imagining a perfect life. Imagining himself happy and married all in the same thought. It wasn't like him at all.

He'd warned himself from the day he met Lacy not to get too close. Life-and-death situations were not the time to fall in love or even to dabble in lust. The adrenaline ran too hot, the danger level way too high to trust your emotions when you were chasing a killer.

So much for warnings.

He'd forgotten them all at the old swimming hole. The perfect spot. The perfect day. He wanted a lot more of them. And he wanted them with Lacy. That meant he had to stop a killer.

Clues. He needed clues. Opportunity, ability, and above all, motivation.

He finished feeding Betsy and lay her down in the crib, the same one he had slept in when he was a baby, the same one his brothers had slept in. The same one his and Lacy's children might sleep in one day.

There it was again.

He was already thinking like a man on the way to the altar. He'd definitely crossed the line between duty and desire, and now that he had, there was no going back.

Lacy stepped beside him. Their fingers touched as they both reached over to offer the comforting reassurance of a hand on Betsy's back as she adjusted to the move from Branson's arms to her bed. In seconds, she was fast asleep.

Branson, on the other hand, was wide awake. "I guess I should go and let you get a little more rest. We have a long day ahead of us."

"Okay," she said, mumbling through a wide yawn. "Though the sun is already coming up."

He lingered. "I doubt I'll go back to sleep. I have too much on my mind."

"Do you want to talk?"

He should say no. But they were both awake and... "Yeah, Lacy. If you're up to talking, I really do have some things I'd like to toss around with you."

"Then let's go to the kitchen or to your room. We don't want to wake Betsy again."

"My room is good." Branson led the way, walking as quietly as he could but still hearing the slapping of his own bare feet on the wooden planks of the hall floor. He didn't hear Lacy's, but he felt the nearness of her all the same.

In less than a week, he'd grown accustomed to having her around. He'd grown familiar with her fragrance, with the way she walked, the way she turned her head at a slight angle when she was angry or pursed her lips when she was unhappy. He'd grown accustomed and attached.

Lacy walked into his room a step behind him and sat in the chair by the window, pulling her legs under her. "So what is it you want to talk about at daybreak?"

"Charles Castile."

She pursed her lips and made a face. "That should be a real eye-opener."

"Did you know he was married before?"

"Yes, the divorce was final a few years before I met him. Charles complained regularly that his ex-wife had taken him to the cleaners. Didn't I mention that?"

"No, but I've been running a check on him. I still haven't gotten as much as I'd like, but what I have suggests he's not as wealthy as his life-style would indicate. Did you ever get any indication that he was having trouble with his finances?"

"No, he always seemed to have endless resources, but I

know he was upset recently when Joshua Kincaid started sending some of his business to another firm.''

Branson paced the room. He always thought better moving. ''But he was willing to buy a wife for fifty thousand dollars. Ricky must have been convinced Charles had big bucks if he thought he would lend that kind of money just because you asked him to.''

''Ricky had a lot more faith in that happening than I did. I expected Charles to laugh me out of his office.''

Branson stopped pacing and dropped to the edge of his bed. ''How long after you asked Charles for the money did he come up with the marriage offer?''

''Almost immediately. It was as if he was just waiting for the opportunity.'' Lacy put her hand over her mouth as if she'd just let a secret slip out. ''Now that I think about it, he could have had it planned. Within thirty minutes after I'd asked him, he was back in my office with the terms. But why? Could he have been that desperate for a wife?''

''He's desperate enough now that he's lying about it.''

''But if Ricky and Charles set me up, who beat the living daylights out of Ricky?''

''I don't know. Ricky needed money. Perhaps he asked for a loan and this was the deal Charles made with him. Maybe the bruises were painted on, and the gash could have been a mere skin cut with fake blood. Kind of like stage makeup.''

''It's possible, I guess. I know Charles lacks ethics.'' She rubbed the back of her neck and stared straight ahead as if lost in thought. ''But Charles is not a murderer.''

''No one is until they kill someone. People a lot less likely than Charles have crossed that line.''

''No. Not Charles. I don't believe it. That would mean that I almost married a madman. That a man who claims to be my husband wants me dead.''

"Most murders are committed by relatives or lovers."

"Now that's a comforting thought."

"Well, someone wants you dead, and it's likely the same person who's already shot Kate and killed Ricky. None of that is too comforting."

"I'll just be glad when this is over." She stood up and walked to the window, staring into the darkness. "I've been thinking, Branson. I don't think I should be here when your mother comes home from the hospital."

He stepped behind her. "Why not?"

"She's not supposed to have stress in her life. Having a woman in your house who's dodging a killer is stressful."

He circled her waist with his arms. "I've already thought this out. I don't plan to burden my mom with the details of this case, Lacy. There's no reason to."

"Then what will you tell her?"

"The truth. That you're the sister of the woman who was shot while delivering Betsy to us and that you're helping me find her."

Lacy continued to stare into the darkness. "Your mother will see through that. But even if she doesn't, she's not the only reason I think I should leave."

She hesitated and Branson dropped his hands from her waist, sensing he was not going to like what she had to say next.

"I think we're getting too close to each other," she said, her voice falling to a whispery low. "Our lives are becoming too entangled. As it is, it's going to be difficult for me to just walk away when this is over."

"Who says you have to?"

"What I am. What Kate is."

"You and Kate are not the same person."

"But she's my sister, and I'll always stand by her. Even if she's in trouble. Even if she breaks the law that you're sworn to uphold. I won't condone what she does, but I can't write her out of my life either."

"No one's asked you to." He turned her around to face him. The moonlight brushed her face with silver and shadows. He trailed his finger down her cheek, knowing he would always remember the way she looked right now, that in his mind he would always think of her draped in moonlight and wearing his pajama top. "I don't know what might happen between us, Lacy. Neither do you. But I've been slamming doors on relationships for years. I don't want to slam this door. Not unless I have to."

"You're infatuated with me now, Branson, but that will change over time. I won't fit into your life. I come with more baggage than a 747."

"I've got strong shoulders. I can handle it." Branson took her in his arms. He could feel the pounding of her heart against his bare chest. There was probably a lot more he should say, but he'd never been good with words.

He swept her up in his arms and carried her to his bed. Outside there was a world of danger and unanswered questions. But inside his room there were only him and Lacy. At least for as long as they could hold back the dawn.

HIS LEFT HAND on the steering wheel of his truck, Branson reached inside the briefcase that rested on the seat between him and Lacy. He pulled out a manila envelope and handed it to her. "This is everything I have on Charles including some faxes that came in this morning. Take a look at them and see what you think."

"What did today's faxes say?"

"One said that Charles hasn't cashed any big checks from Joshua Kincaid in the past six months. He has a half-dozen credit cards with mega credit limits—all maxed out."

"So why did he ever agree to pay fifty thousand dollars for a wife?"

"I don't know, considering he didn't have fifty thousand dollars in the bank when you wrote that check."

"What are you saying?"

"Just that the check you wrote for fifty thousand dollars never cleared the bank. It couldn't have because Charles's personal checking account has dwindled down to nearly nothing. The only check written to Ricky Carpenter that has cleared the bank as of yesterday was one for ten thousand dollars and that one was on the company account."

Lacy shook her head. "This is getting too bizarre. The check was for fifty thousand. I wrote it myself on Charles's personal checking account."

"Would you have married Charles for ten thousand dollars?"

"No, I could have come up with that myself. I'd have had to clean out all my bank accounts and sell my car, but I would have done that long before I would have agreed to marriage."

"And Charles probably knew that."

Lacy opened the file and started scanning the reports. She'd have plenty of time. They still had a five-hour drive in front of them. But unless they hit a major delay, they would easily make it to Austin and Marilyn Cassaleta's by four.

Branson tapped his hand on the steering wheel, working off the excess energy. In spite of the fact that he'd gotten up at four-thirty instead of six this morning, he hadn't needed much coffee. The adrenaline pumping though his veins was more than enough to keep him going at full speed.

Finally, a few things were starting to add up, although he wasn't sure if he was coming up with the right sum.

Motivation was still missing. Kate was on the run after having been shot through the back window of her car, her boyfriend Ricky had been murdered and Lacy was getting death threats. He was convinced that these events were all connected.

Branson felt certain that Charles Castile fit into this. So far he just wasn't sure how. He needed more to go on. And until he found it, a killer was on the loose. Desperate matters called for desperate measures.

"On the way back from Austin," he said, "I'd like to stop in at Charles's office."

"He won't be there that late."

"I'm counting on that. In fact I would like for us to go by so late that no one will be there except security and maybe the cleaning crew. We'll pay a surprise visit to your beloved husband."

"I was never beloved and I'm not Charles's wife."

"He says you are. He has a signed and witnessed marriage license."

"He has a *forged* marriage license. And I have no clue what that's about."

"If we're really lucky, we may find out on tonight's fact-finding mission."

"We can't just break into Charles's office and go through his records. Don't you have to have a search warrant for that? If you don't, the evidence is not admissible in court. I've watched enough TV police dramas to know that."

"*I* can't just go in. *You* can. You're his wife. There's a marriage license to prove it."

She perked up. "You're right. Charles wanted a wife. Now he has one. If he has anything to hide we'll find it."

"But you still have doubts that Charles could be our murderer, don't you?"

"About as many as I had buttons on that wedding dress the day you found me in Kate's apartment."

"Ah, yes, I remember that dress well. But do me a favor, will you?"

"I might." She rested her hand on his thigh. "Just what did you have in mind?"

"If you ever decide to wear a dress like that for me, could you use Velcro instead of buttons."

She made a fist and tapped him playfully on the arm. "No way, cowboy. Anticipation is half of the fun."

"Maybe for the woman. Definitely not for the man."

Lacy sat up straight in her seat and went back to examining the reports on her ex-boss. A few minutes later she shifted around so that she could face Branson. "You know, as much as I hate the thought of confronting Charles at home, I would like to pick up my car and some of my things while we're in San Antonio. If this little venture tonight doesn't go well and he finds out about it, he may toss all of my stuff into the trash."

"Then why don't we make a night of it? We'll visit Charles's office while he's at home, spend the rest of the night in a hotel and then go by Charles's house in the morning while he's at work."

"I do like the way your mind works."

"Me, too." He ran his hand along the back of the seat and caught his fingers in her hair. "Especially the hotel part."

In fact, he wished they were going there now. He wished they were going anywhere except where they were bound.

But Marilyn Cassaleta and a quest for truth was next on their agenda.

BRANSON TOOK the stairs up to the third floor. He could have hopped on the elevator, but it was still ten minutes before four, and he needed the exercise to unkink his back and legs after the drive and to gear up for the confrontation. He'd rehearsed in his mind what he should say, but he knew a lot would depend on Marilyn.

He rang the doorbell and waited. The hallway was quiet and empty. Most of the residents were probably working or running afternoon errands. He rang the bell again. Sweat formed on his forehead. He pulled a handkerchief from his back pocket and dabbed it away.

This time he knocked, banging his knuckles on the wood. Marilyn had said she would be here, but she was known to lie about far more important things than being home for an appointment.

Relief rushed through him as he finally heard the lock turn and watched the door creak open. Marilyn looked exactly as he remembered her—flawless skin, straight black hair falling around her shoulders.

"You're right on time, Branson. You haven't changed. You were always the most dependable guy I knew."

"I'm still dependable, but I *have* changed. I've gotten much wiser."

She swung the door open all the way and motioned him in. She was wearing a loose-fitting, flowing robe, with lots of layers of gauzy fabric. He was sure it was meant to be sexy, but the effect was lost on him.

She raised up on tiptoe to give him a welcoming kiss. He made sure it was no more than a casual peck.

"My, but you're in a lousy mood today," she pouted, "but I'm still glad you called and asked to come by. I have something to tell you."

"So you said, something about important matters we needed to discuss."

"Actually, it's more like a surprise. An exciting one. You'll think so, too."

Dread twisted inside Branson. It sounded as though his fears were about to be realized, but he was not going to give anything away. "What makes you think I'll be excited about your surprise."

"Because you're you. I know you say you've changed, but I'm sure you haven't. You're a Randolph, a family man through and through. But I'm being remiss in my hostess duties. Would you like a drink? I have the wine chilled, just like I promised."

He didn't *want* a drink. He *needed* one. But he could wait. Good or bad, he wanted this over with. The problem was that if she was about to tell him he was a father, he might never be through dealing with Marilyn. And that would be the worst irony of all.

"Nothing to drink for me, Marilyn."

"And nothing for me. Alcohol is off limits for me these days. It's part of my surprise." She twirled in front of him. "Okay, Branson, I can't wait." She cupped her hands beneath her stomach, balling up the gauzy material and pulling it tight. "So, what do you think?"

It took him a minute to catch on. When he did, relief flooded his senses, refreshing as a splash of ice water during branding time. Marilyn was pregnant. He didn't know much about these things, but from the size of her stomach, she had to be a few months along. Meaning she had not given birth to Betsy.

He grabbed her in a bear hug and kissed her on the cheek. "This is great news, Marilyn."

"See. I told you you'd be happy for me."

"And I am, happier than you could possibly imagine. But you could have told me your surprise over the phone."

"I didn't want to. I was afraid you wouldn't come to see me if I did. You know how lonesome I get when my hubby's on the road."

"Look, Marilyn, I know it's not my place to say any-thing, but you're going to be a mother now."

"No." She put her hand up to halt his lecture. "You don't have to say a word. I've already made up my mind. I'm going straight, Branson. I blew my relationship with you, and I was sorry for years. I'm not going to let that happen again. Especially not now." She patted her stom-ach. " The baby's my husband's. Even though we've been separated, we've spent time together. I'm going to be a mother, and I'm going to be a good one. A faithful wife, too. I am, if it kills me."

"It won't."

"So now, what was it you wanted to see me about."

"Nothing." He reached into his billfold and pulled out a hundred-dollar bill. "I just want to wish you a happy life. You and your husband and the baby." He dropped the bill on the table. "Buy the baby a present from me?"

"You don't have to do that."

"I know. I'd like to."

"What should I buy?"

"A pair of cowboy boots, when she, or he, is old enough to wear them."

Branson said his goodbyes and left. This time he took the stairs, running all the way. He felt years younger than he had going up them a few minutes ago. Not that he wouldn't be thrilled to have a baby like Betsy.

But he'd want to make babies with a woman he loved.

LACY SAT SIDEWAYS in the parked truck, watching Branson as he finished his account of his visit to Marilyn's apart-ment. "So the first girl who broke your heart is pregnant."

"Yes, with her husband's child, the way it should be."

"But if Betsy isn't your child, then one of your brothers must be her father."

"Not necessarily. Kate could have been mistaken."

Lacy nodded, but she was thinking that mistaken wouldn't explain why Betsy so closely resembled Branson when he was a baby. Or maybe it was just coincidence. She'd heard people say that all newborns looked alike, red and wrinkled. And, in Betsy's case, adorable.

Branson fit the key into the ignition. "One problem solved," he said, shoving his Stetson to the back of his head. "Next stop, the office of Charles Castile."

Lacy kicked off her shoes and pulled one foot under her knee. She'd never been comfortable riding like a lady. Lucky for her, Branson's truck was roomy enough that she could shift and squirm and ride with both feet tucked under her if she pleased.

That was another thing she'd miss like crazy when this was over. Just climbing into the truck beside Branson. Strange that in the midst of so much fear and dread, she'd found so many minutes of pleasure.

They rode in silence for a while and then Branson snaked his right arm along the back of the truck seat, grabbing her shoulder and giving it a robust squeeze. "So are you ready for this, Lacy? This will be your first taste of real police work."

Excitement buzzed in Branson's voice. She loved him this way. Loved the sound of him when confidence had him flying high. Loved the look of him, his eyes intense but flashing, his manner spirited. But then, when hadn't she been fully taken in by Sheriff Branson Randolph?

Still, the unsettling fingers of apprehension orchestrated her own reactions to all of this. Branson only needed a few more pieces and then he would be ready to sort them into neat little cubicles. Put the pieces away and then put Charles away.

But her life had never fit into neat little pieces, and she

couldn't imagine it would work that way this time either. Lacy and Kate Gilbraith waltzing away from trouble on the winning side. The rich and powerful Charles Castile being dragged away to jail. It was a great story, a movie of the week. Only where was the frightening twist at the end?

She trembled, suddenly overwhelmed with the feeling that she was about to discover the twist and that it would be uglier than either she or Branson could imagine.

Chapter Fourteen

"You're working mighty late tonight."

Lacy managed a nervous smile for the building's security guard. "I was working at home and realized I'd left some folders here that I needed. My friend offered to ride over with me to pick them up."

"That's probably a good idea. This city's no place for a woman alone at night. It's a shame what the world's coming to."

"It is that," Branson agreed.

The guard gave Branson a quick once-over while he talked. Fortunately Branson had exposed nothing that might identify him as a lawman and give them away. Just a worker and a friend coming into the office after hours. She'd done it often enough that the guard knew her on sight, as she had no identification on her.

"I'll be making the rounds of the building in a few minutes," the guard said, rattling the ring of keys that dangled from a loop at his waist. "So if I'm not down here when you're ready to leave, just ring the bell by the door. I'll come back downstairs and let you out."

"Thanks. We might be a while. I have to locate some files."

A few minutes later they stepped out of the elevator on

the fourteenth floor. The surroundings should have seemed as familiar to her as the coffee she'd drunk at breakfast. The same lingering odors of perfumes and aftershaves, the same sky-blue carpet and luxuriously appointed reception area. The same whir of the air conditioner.

But they didn't. *She* was different. Changed by a week of murder, explosions, threats. A missing sister. And changed by dread so strong it had altered her sense of reality.

And though she couldn't really deal with it now, couldn't spare the mental or emotional capacity it would take to comprehend the effects, she had been changed by her involvement with the sheriff at her side. Affected by Branson, Betsy and the whole Randolph clan.

A week ago, she had fit in here at Charles's firm, at least on the surface. Today she was an intruder, a spy. A police accomplice.

The offices were quiet, but the lights were still on, and the trash cans were full. Apparently the cleaning crew hadn't made it to the fourteenth floor yet. Lacy would have felt much more at ease if they'd come and gone.

She led the way to Charles's office, her heart beating a tattoo that could have served as backup for a frenzied hard-rock tune. Marriage license or not, under ordinary circumstances, she would have never considered prowling through Charles's private files. She wouldn't be doing it now if Branson were not at her side, armed and ready to protect.

But even if Charles was to walk in, a highly unlikely possibility, the worst he would do would be to erupt in cold fury. No matter what Branson thought about him, she was sure Charles was not a madman.

The office door was locked. That slowed Branson down for about sixty seconds. He picked the lock with the expertise of a cat burglar and then had her push the door open.

So technically he had not broken in. Lacy had just opened the door to her husband's office.

"You check the desk," Branson said. "I'll go through the file cabinet."

"What am I looking for?"

"Anything unusual. Anything that might explain why he was dealing with Ricky Carpenter, or why Ricky would go along with him in his forced-marriage scheme."

Lacy dropped into the leather swivel chair and started rummaging through the top middle drawer. She turned up the usual supply of pens, pencils, clips, staples and an official-looking envelope from the IRS. The envelope had been sliced neatly open. She reached inside, pulled out the typed letter and became riveted to the message.

Charles Castile was being investigated for possible fraud regarding monies he allegedly collected but did not report. The letter was dated a month ago, a few days before she and Charles made the wedding bargain. "You might want to read this, Branson. It looks like Charles was in deeper financial trouble than we suspected."

Branson took the letter and skimmed it. "Taking a little cream off the top. Not a smart move, especially if you get caught."

"If Charles was stealing money from the IRS, why was he broke."

"Maybe he wasn't stealing enough. Maybe he was the one with the gambling problem."

The next hour passed with a minimum of conversation and a maximum of frustration. Nothing else in the desk or the file cabinet indicated that Charles was anything except an honest, hardworking attorney with the best interests of his clients at heart. The only other evidence that he was in difficult financial straits was a letter from American Express saying his gold card had been canceled.

"I feel like a fox who just broke into a deserted hen-house," Lacy complained when she grew weary of reading boring files.

"You give up too easily." Branson trailed his fingers along the curve of her shoulders as he walked behind her. He stopped in front of a supersize glob of modern art in a chrome frame. Without a notice for the painting, he lifted the picture from the hook and propped the artwork against the wall by his feet.

"You've been watching too many James Bond movies, Branson. I worked here for almost two years. Charles isn't imaginative enough to have vaults hidden behind picture frames."

"Or maybe he's too imaginative." He removed one more picture and then walked over to stand in the middle of the room. He turned slowly. "The bookcases look a little unusual. Is there a matching set or maybe a closet on the other side of that wall?"

"No. They're just bookcases. I was here when Charles had them built. The workmen made such a mess that Charles closed this suite of offices altogether while they were under construction."

Branson walked over and stood in front of the bookcases for a few seconds before settling on his haunches to get a better look at the bottom edge of them. He tapped and knocked on the wood.

"Bingo!"

Lacy watched in amazement as Charles's leather-bound copies of antique law books slid to the left. And behind the bookcases stood a vault big enough to house the complete works of William Shakespeare in a print-size large enough to be read.

"I don't believe this," she said, moving in for a closer look. "I've walked by that bookcase a hundred times."

"I'm sure Charles planned it that way. Secret vaults are much more effective if they're secret."

"Do tell." She watched as Branson pulled a small leather case from his pocket and extricated a flat metal tool with a sharp, needlelike point, similar to the one he had used on the door, but more detailed.

"You do come prepared," she said. "A regular Boy Scout."

"Not me. I was 4-H, with a prizewinning bull to prove it."

A couple of stabs with the needle, a couple of jabs with the flat edge, a couple of clicks and the door eased open. Lacy stretched to get her first-ever peek of the insides of a secret vault. It was far different from what she'd expected. Basically it was a file cabinet, with drawers that slid out in the same manner as a traditional file cabinet.

Branson ran his finger along the upper edges, rippling the manila folders until he found one that appealed to him. He removed the folder and reached inside. The papers were legal-size, stapled in the left-hand corner.

"It's an insurance policy," Lacy said, looking over Branson's shoulders. "Surely Charles didn't build this elaborate device to house his insurance policies."

Branson tapped the first section of the form. "This policy is on Mrs. Charles Castile."

"Let me see that." She took it from him. The policy was on Charles's wife, one Lacy Castile. The effective date was the same as the date they had planned to be married. "He didn't waste any time insuring me, did he?" She scanned the small print for a dollar figure. Squinting, she counted the zeros. There were six of them.

"And now we know why he went to the trouble to have the marriage license forged. You're worth more to him as his wife."

"As his *dead* wife." The policy tumbled from her hands. "It was a setup, just like we said. Ricky had to have been in on this."

"It looks that way. Charles could insure his brand-new wife for a million dollars without arousing suspicion." Branson pulled out a second policy that had been in the same folder. "He increased the dollar value on his policy as well, which is probably why he told the insurance agent he was there in the first place. I'm sure the agent complimented him on his consideration for his new wife."

Lacy's mind struggled with the findings. "So why do you think he killed Ricky?"

"Maybe Ricky turned chicken and threatened to tell you. Or maybe Charles didn't want to take a chance on being blackmailed later. He probably had a variety of reasons."

"And Kate and I were next on the list. Me, for the money. And Kate for... Why Kate? Why was she shot? And how does Betsy fit into any of this?"

"Don't even think about it now, Lacy. The answers won't all come out until we have Charles in custody. And we may never know everything."

Lacy sat beside Branson as they pulled file after file. They uncovered plenty of reasons for the IRS to be after Charles. There was even a letter from Joshua Kincaid saying he was being questioned by the IRS regarding his return. Apparently that's when he'd decided to take his business elsewhere.

"Looks like your hubby was planning a trip," Branson said, pulling out a travel brochure on South America. "A honeymoon trip?"

"Only he was undoubtedly going alone."

"And probably on a one-way ticket."

Her stomach churned again. If Kate had shown up for

her wedding. If she hadn't run. If Branson hadn't popped into her life when he did.

She'd likely be dead by now or at least soon, and Charles would be waiting on his million so that he could leave the country and start a new life in style.

"We have enough, Branson. Can't we go now?"

But Branson just kept reading, making piles, making notes. The longer they stayed, the more nervous she became.

Lacy froze as a man's voice wafted beneath the office door. Charles. For some crazy reason he'd come down to the office this time of night. Maybe the guard had called him. Charles might have given him orders to call if she showed up. Footsteps approached the closed door.

"Sit tight, Lacy. Let me handle this."

"Be careful." The warning came out as a whisper, all but lost in the drumming of her heart as the doorknob turned and the door to Charles's office flew open.

But it was one of the janitorial team who poked his head inside. The man all but jumped out of his skin when he saw them.

"Just cleaning out a few files," Branson said. "Hope we didn't startle you."

"Yes, sir. I mean, no, sir. You just go right ahead. I didn't mean to bother you. I uh, uh, didn't know you were in here. Don't mind me."

"He's going for the guard," Lacy said, grabbing files and stuffing them back into the vault. "He didn't buy your explanation for a second. Not with the mess we have in here."

"From the look on his face, we scared the poor fellow so bad he may still be running."

She looked around her. Charles's usually spotless office

was a mess. Papers spilled out on the carpet. Pictures on the floor. File-cabinet doors ajar.

And a stain spreading under the door from the adjoining conference room. She walked over to check. Stepping over the stain, she turned the knob and opened the door. She opened her mouth. The scream never came out.

Charles Castile had been here all the time.

Chapter Fifteen

Lacy was still in shock when the local police arrived on the scene to investigate the suicide of attorney Charles Castile. She did more listening than talking when Branson shared the evidence they'd found with the investigating crime detail. But even when she heard Branson's very lucid explanation that Charles had planned to kill her for a cool million dollars, she still had trouble believing the facts.

Under the circumstances, the cops weren't at all surprised that Charles had chosen to take his own life, especially coupled with his problems with the IRS and his burgeoning debt. Neither was Branson. Lacy was no longer sure what she believed. She certainly couldn't trust her own instincts.

She had worked for Charles for almost two years, dated him, even been infatuated with him for a while. She'd eventually grown to distrust his business ethics, but she had never imagined him capable of murder or even suspected he was in such serious financial trouble.

She propped one elbow on the arm of the waiting-room chair and rested her head in her hand. Two men walked by her, wheeling out the body. Her stomach turned a new series of flip-flops.

"Are you all right?"

She looked up at the sound of Branson's voice.

"No."

"You will be. The worst is over." He stepped in front of her. "I know we'd planned to spend the night in town, but I'm so wide awake now, I'd never fall asleep anyway. Would you mind if we just drove on home tonight?"

Home. The word sounded warm, inviting. The only problem was, she didn't have one. And now that Charles was dead, she wouldn't need to remain in protective custody.

She stood and started toward the elevator. "I don't mind if you drive back to the Burning Pear tonight, but I'd still like to go by Charles's house and pick up my own car and some of my things."

"It's past midnight."

"We won't bother Charles."

"True, but I don't think your driving back to the Burning Pear alone tonight is a good idea."

"Neither do I. I'll get a room in town."

He took her arm and pulled her to a stop. "What's this about?"

"It's over, Branson. Charles was behind the threats. He's dead. Case closed. You don't have to protect me any longer."

He stared at her hard, the look on his face as pained as if she'd slapped him. "Is that what you want, Lacy, to get away from me and the Burning Pear as fast as you can?"

"I told you this morning. I can't stay there forever."

"But you can stay tonight. Langley and Ryder will have a million questions to ask you. And Betsy would miss you." He trailed his finger up her arm. "Besides, we still have to find Kate," he said, catching her hand with his. "That's why we teamed up originally, remember?"

"How could I forget?" She took a deep breath and resigned herself to what had to be done. Branson wouldn't understand, but she had to find her own life, move on before she started believing that a lasting relationship between them was actually possible.

"I'll stay at the Burning Pear tonight, Branson, if that's what you want, but I'd like to go to Charles's house and pick up my things and my car."

"Okay. I'll follow you back to Kelman."

Walking at Branson's side, Lacy left the office where she'd spent the biggest part of the past two years of her life. She wouldn't be returning. One more part of her life that had come to an end.

She stepped onto the elevator, relieved that the mystery had been solved, that the killing had been stopped. But the worry was not over for her. She wouldn't be able to breathe easy until she could see for herself that Kate was alive and well.

"If you had actually gone through with your wedding to Charles, you'd be a widow tonight."

"More likely I'd be dead and Charles would be a million dollars richer and living on some exotic island. I still find it hard to accept that Charles actually killed Ricky and then dumped his body at the Burning Pear," Lacy said as the elevator started its drop. "It just doesn't fit with his meticulous nature. He's not a do-it-yourself kind of guy when it comes to dirty work."

"He probably thought he'd run out of alternatives."

"Do you think Ricky would have actually gone to the police? He was in this pretty deep himself."

"It doesn't matter what I think. It's what Charles thought that counted. Besides, he didn't need Ricky anymore and he might have been afraid he would eventually spill his guts to the wrong person, like Kate. If Charles killed him, he wouldn't ever have to worry. Dead people never squeal."

"But in the end, none of that would have mattered. He killed himself." The elevator bumped to a stop and the doors opened into the first-floor hallway. They wouldn't have to ring for the guard. He was standing by the door and chatting on a cell phone, no doubt telling a wife or friend all about his exciting night.

He stopped his phone conversation long enough to let them out and to remark on how upsetting it must have been to find the body. Lacy assured him that it was. As soon as they were out the door, she sucked in a lungful of fresh air.

"What about Betsy, Branson? Can Charles possibly have had something to do with Kate bringing her to the Burning Pear?"

"I guess we won't know that until we find Kate."

And Kate could be anywhere. She'd run before and disappeared completely, dodging cops every step of the way. She was a pro, one of the best at what she did. It was only that what she did was not the best. Now Lacy only prayed that wherever her sister had run, she hadn't ended up the way Charles and Ricky had.

"It's nice to have this case pretty much settled," Branson said as they climbed into his truck. "I'm sure there will be a celebration at the Burning Pear tomorrow for Mom's homecoming. This will make it a lot more special."

"Is your mother up to a celebration?"

"It will just be family, and we'll have to keep it low-key. But everyone will want to be there to welcome her home."

The *family* would all be there. And Lacy wasn't part of it. She'd make sure she was gone before the celebrating started.

"OH, PALEEEZE, Uncle Ryder. Take me out to ride the horses. I want to practice for the rodeo."

"All right, but don't let your grandma hear you say that, Petey. She'll have my hide if she thinks I'm making a rodeo junkie of her favorite grandson."

"Let's hurry before my mom makes me take a nap."

"I heard that," Ashley called from the kitchen.

Lacy sat in the den rocker, feeding Betsy and listening to the chatter. The house was bustling with activity, getting ready for the celebration Branson had predicted. A family dinner in honor of Mary Randolph's return from the hospital.

Ashley had come down for the day to help with the cooking. She was preparing all of Mary's favorites except for salsa, and Ashley had vowed she was cutting back on the spices. Fried chicken, creamed potatoes with gravy, butter beans, corn on the cob, homemade biscuits and blackberry cobbler.

The vegetables were from Mary's garden via the freezer. The fryers had been raised on a neighbor's farm. The odors had to be straight from heaven, Lacy decided as she lifted Betsy to her shoulder for burping.

Lacy had spent the morning with Branson, sitting in his small office in Kelman, going over every detail. Branson was convinced Charles was the man behind everything.

She still had doubts. She could buy that he'd done the scheming, but she still couldn't picture him doing the dirty work of killing Ricky, storing the bloody body somewhere and then carrying it in his fancy car all the way to Kelman.

And the best theory, the only theory, Branson had come up with about Betsy was that either Charles or Ricky had gotten her from somewhere, maybe a new mother who had thought she was giving the baby up for adoption. They had decided to use the baby to try to get money from the Randolphs. Perhaps it was their last-ditch effort to get money without resorting to murder.

If that was the case, Kate had spoiled that for them when she'd brought the baby to the Randolphs. That action might have actually sealed Ricky's fate and ultimately Charles's.

Lacy stared at the baby in her arms. Baby Betsy. If Branson's theory was correct, she wasn't a Randolph at all. But to Lacy's way of thinking, the baby pictures in the hall suggested otherwise.

Ryder hoisted Petey onto his shoulders, his limp more noticeable now that he was bearing extra weight. "We men are going out on the range," Ryder teased, "while you women take care of the kitchen and baby-tending work."

"Yeah, Mom, we men have to go do ranch stuff. We're cowboys, aren't we, Uncle Ryder?"

"You betcha." Ryder stuck his Stetson on his head and ducked as he went out the door so that Petey's head didn't collide with the transom.

Lacy finished feeding Betsy and then took her back to the nursery for her afternoon nap. "I'll miss you, sweetheart," she crooned to the sleepy infant. The words twisted at her heart. She would miss Betsy and everything about the Burning Pear.

Most of all, she would miss Branson. But this was his life. Basically trouble free until she'd stepped into it. Reason enough that he didn't need her on a permanent basis. It would be far better to leave on her own before he pushed her out.

She heard footsteps behind her and looked up to find Ashley standing in the doorway. "Is Betsy sleeping?"

"Just about. She's fighting to keep her eyes open, but she's losing the battle."

Ashley walked over to stand beside Lacy. "She's such a darling. It's too bad she's not really a Randolph. These guys need a girl around here, someone who could soften their rough edges and wrap their big cowboy egos around her pudgy little fingers.''

''They're all crazy about her.''

''They're crazy about you, too, Lacy. Especially Branson.''

Lacy tried to answer, but the protest stuck in the lump that had formed in her throat.

''I know I was a little harsh that first day we met. I was out of place. I may be out of place again, but there's something I feel I have to say.''

''You don't have to worry, Ashley. I'm not out to trap Branson. I know I'm not the woman for him. The truth is, I plan to be gone when he gets home tonight.''

''You mean you'd just leave without saying goodbye to him?''

''I'll call him from town. It will be easier that way.''

''No.'' Ashley's dark eyes were flashing. ''You can't do this to Branson, Lacy. He doesn't deserve it. You can't just walk out of his life.''

''Branson likes his life the way it is.''

''Did he tell you that?''

''Yes, when we first met.''

Ashley shook her head. ''That's his protective shield. He doesn't mean it. He's always been bitter and suspicious where women were concerned. Dillon says he has his reasons. I don't know about that, but I do know Branson's different with you. He's let down his guard in a way he's never done with any other woman in all the time I've known him.''

''I can't stay, Ashley. I'm not the woman you think I am. I carry trouble with me the way some women carry an umbrella.''

''Do you care for him?''

Lacy gave Betsy a parting touch and then turned to face Ashley. She could say no and walk away, but they would both know she was lying. "I love him. That's not the issue."

"If you love him, you won't walk away. You won't throw away your chance at happiness, yours and Branson's."

"And what will happen when trouble follows me right into his life, when my family heritage taints all of the Randolphs?"

"Branson wouldn't be marrying your family. He'd be marrying you."

"It doesn't work that way and you know it. If my sister runs crosswise of the law, it wouldn't be tucked away on the back pages of the paper the way it used to be. She'd make bold, black headlines. Sister-in-law of Sheriff Branson Randolph arrested. Senator Dillon Randolph refused to comment on charges."

"The Randolphs would handle it," Ashley insisted. "Believe me, if anyone could put them to the test, I did. Our lives are not so different, Lacy. My mom didn't die like yours did, but she deserted me shortly after my birth. I was raised in foster homes. My brother was killed while being apprehended for robbing a bank. A lot of people, including my brother's accomplice, were convinced that I had possession of the stolen money. He followed me right here to the Burning Pear."

"I didn't know. The Randolphs are all so crazy about you."

"And I'm crazy about them. But even if we weren't so compatible, they would accept me because Dillon loves me and because I love him. And they will love you the same way if you give them half a chance. They are a remarkable family."

Ashley stepped backward, moving toward the door. "Give Branson a chance, Lacy. Give love a chance."

Lacy turned back to the crib as Ashley walked away. Her throat burned and a stinging tear pushed its way from her eyes. *Give love a chance.* It seemed so right when Ashley said it. But could she bear to give it a chance and lose?

LACY PULLED the warm clothes from the dryer. The shirts she'd borrowed from Ashley. The jeans. And Branson's pajama top. She held it to her cheek, absorbing the feel of it to tuck away with her memories. Leaving the Burning Pear and Branson might well be the hardest thing she'd ever have to do.

"Lacy, the phone's for you."

Startled, Lacy let the pajama top slip from her hands. "Is it Branson?"

"No," Ashley called. "It's a man who says he has news about your sister."

"About Kate!" Lacy hurried past Ashley, not stopping until she reached the extension in the den. "Who is this?"

"Surely you recognize my voice."

"Adam! Have you heard from Kate?" she gasped, her heart racing so that the words seemed to fly out of her mouth. "Do you know where she is? Have you seen her?"

"What happened to hello, Adam? It's nice of you to call."

"Don't play games, Adam. If you know anything about Kate, just tell me. You must know how worried I am about her."

"You always worry about her. A lot more than you ever worried about me. More than you ever worried about Charles either, I'll bet. What about the sheriff, Lacy? Where does he rate on your list of priorities?"

"Did you call just to hurl accusations, Adam?" She

came close to slamming down the receiver. She didn't. You could never be sure with Adam. He might just know something, but he'd take his own sweet time about getting it out.

"I called to tell you where your sister is, but if you're not interested in talking to me...."

"I'm sorry. I am interested. Please tell me about Kate." Adam wanted pleading. She'd give him pleading.

"She's staying with a friend of hers, a neighbor of the Randolphs'. You might want to call and tell her that it's safe to come out of hiding now."

"Where is she?"

"Milton Maccabbe's place."

Lacy's hope plunged. Adam was lying. She'd almost bet on it. "Why would she have gone to Milton's? She hardly knows him."

"She knows him better than you think. She went out to the ranch a few times after she started dating Ricky. Joshua likes hanging out with pro football players, even has-beens. And Milton likes his women a little on the trashy side. He and Kate were a good match."

Lacy bit back her anger. "How did you find out Kate was at Milton Maccabbe's?"

"It doesn't matter. If you think I'm lying, pick up the phone and call. See for yourself."

"I'll do that." She would, right away, but she had little faith that she'd find Kate there.

"We have a bad connection, Lacy. I didn't hear you say thank you."

"Thank you, Adam. If I find Kate at Milton's, I'll thank you forever."

She hung up the phone and rang information for Milton's number. It was unlisted. Just her luck. She could call Adam back, but it was only a twenty-minute drive to Milton's place, and most of that was on the road leading from the Randolphs' house to the highway.

"I'm going out for a while, Ashley."

Ashley joined her in the den. "Don't you think you should call and tell Branson?"

"No, he said he was way behind on paperwork. I'll catch him later."

Lacy rushed out the door, the keys to her car in hand. She shouldn't get her hopes up. But then Kate had to be somewhere. Maybe she'd misjudged Adam. Perhaps he wasn't as bad as he seemed.

KATE GAVE UP her attempts to spit the horrible choking rag from her mouth as Adam hung up his cell phone. Then she watched in horror as he took a knife from the table and sliced Milton's phone line as easily as if it were thread.

Her hands burned from the ragged ropes that held them, and her ankles were chafed and starting to bleed. She managed to rock her chair back and forth on the wooden floor. It was the only movement she could control at all.

Adam strode across the floor and yanked the rag from her mouth. "Don't be so impatient. I'm sure your sister is on her way."

"You low-down, filthy, son of a—"

"You have such a nasty mouth, Kate. Didn't anyone ever tell you it's not ladylike to talk like that?"

"No one ever taught me anything. But I still had better sense than to date a piece of garbage like you."

"Now, now. Flattery will get you nowhere. The only reason you didn't date me was because you didn't want your sister's leftovers. But the biggest mistake *she* ever made was to leave me for Charles Castile."

"She didn't leave you for Charles. She left you because you're nuts. And it was the *smartest* thing she ever did."

"We'll see how smart she is. She should be here any minute."

"She won't come out here. You told her to call. I heard you."

"And when she can't call, she'll come running."

"No, it's Milton who'll be back any minute, and when he is, he'll string you up like those fish he catches."

Adam laughed, a harsh, ridiculing sound, the kind a madman might make. Fear rolled inside Kate, a sickening, violent motion that turned her stomach inside out.

"Milton won't be back until tonight. He's working at Kincaid's ranch today."

"So that's why you came over here the other day, to ask Milton for his help."

"Not for me. The help is for Kincaid's green foreman. I was just taking care of business and happened to hit the jackpot. I'd been searching for you everywhere, and you were practically under my nose. Under Sheriff Branson Randolph's nose as well."

"Milton should have shot you that day and left you for the buzzards."

"He might have if he'd known I'd caught a glimpse of you."

"I didn't even know you'd seen me. If I had, I would have been gone from here by now."

"I know. I saw how quickly you turned the horse around and galloped off in the opposite direction. You were like a vision with that long blond hair flowing behind you. Stunning, like your sister."

He crossed the room and grabbed a handful of her hair, pulling it until tears squeezed from her eyes. "The beautiful Gilbraith sisters. You both thought you were too good for the likes of Alan Potter. But you weren't good enough."

"Alan Potter? I never met the man."

"You're talking to him right now. Adam Pascal was only an alias, but I don't need to use an alias with you. You'll never live to give my secrets away."

"I won't have to. You called Lacy. Everyone will know you led her into a trap."

"Wrong. I called Lacy from my cell phone. Milton will get the blame for your murders. Poor, weird Milton. Most people think he's crazy anyway. They won't be shocked at all that he has such a violent nature."

"Buy why—"

He let go of her hair and dangled the red work rag in front of her face. "No more talking or I'll have to stuff this back in your mouth. We're just going to wait together. We're going to wait on Lacy. She'll be here soon. Time is flying by now." He cupped a hand to his ear. "Listen, you can hear it. *Ticktock. Ticktock.*"

BRANSON SCOOTED a stack of papers across his desk and uttered a low string of curses. His neat little package had fallen apart. Charles Castile had not dumped Ricky Carpenter's body at the Burning Pear. He had been out of town that night, in New Orleans on business. Several people had verified that.

Which meant there was another person involved in this.

A hit man? Probably. But surely now that Charles had killed himself, the hit man would back off. He'd know there was no money coming his way, so why risk getting arrested for murder? Lacy should be safe enough. Kate, too.

So why did he suddenly feel a hell of a lot more apprehensive than he had a few minutes ago? He shuffled through his notes and stopped on the name of Adam Pascal.

Opportunity? He was definitely physically capable. He'd probably been to Kelman before with Joshua Kincaid, though Branson had never run into him.

Motive? Money, of course. A hit man could make a nice little bonus.

And there was jealousy. Lacy had dumped him and then started going out with Charles Castile. He thought of Adam's parting words to Lacy the other night.

You look like a million dollars. Charles knows how to play his cards.

That might not have been his exact words, but that was the gist of them. A million dollars. The value of the insurance policy Charles had held on Lacy's life. And now that Branson thought more about it, Adam hadn't registered surprise when Lacy told him the wedding hadn't taken place.

Adam had known the truth even though Charles was making a point of telling everyone that Lacy was his wife.

Branson sifted through the police data he'd requested on every possible suspect, adrenaline pumping like crazy as he checked Adam's profile. Clean. No past record of any kind, and honest businessmen didn't often make murder their first crime.

But maybe Adam's file was too clean. He picked up the phone and punched in a number that could get him an instant credit report.

It was spotless. In fact, it didn't exist.

Branson had a sudden, overpowering urge to hear Lacy's voice. He grabbed his phone again, this time punching in the number for the Burning Pear.

LACY DROVE UP to Milton's house and parked near the back door of the small cottage. The other day Milton had met them outside. Today he was nowhere in sight.

"Please, Kate, be here," she whispered as she left the truck. "Don't let this be one of Adam's sick tricks."

She knocked, but no one answered. A shadow moved behind her. She spun around just in time to see Adam. Just in time to see the gun in his hand as it came down and slammed against her skull.

Chapter Sixteen

Lacy groaned and opened her eyes. For a minute she saw double. Two blinding ceiling lights, two scarred Formica tables, two sharp-edged knives.

Two Adam Pascals.

She tried to get out of the chair she was sitting in, but her feet were tied at the ankles and her hands were bound behind her back. Slowly her brain creaked into gear and she blinked until her surroundings slid back into focus.

Kate was a few feet away, bound to her chair in the same fashion. Lacy could hear her labored breathing, but her eyes were closed and her head was slumping over. Her right eye was swollen, the tissue around it an ugly shade of purple.

Adam crossed the room, not stopping until he was so close the toes of his shoes touched Lacy's. She stretched her neck back to look up at him, and crashing waves of pain shot through her.

"What's going on?" she demanded, her words echoing in her throbbing head.

"So you finally came to," he said. His voice was calm and steady, frighteningly cold. "Kate and I have been waiting on you to join us. Haven't we, Kate?"

Kate had opened her eyes, alert as soon as the first words had come out of Lacy's mouth. Now she stared at Lacy, her eyes dark mirrors of the same dread that was clawing away at Lacy's control. But they locked gazes, and as always, they drew on each other's strength. No terror was ever quite as harrowing as long as they had each other.

"I'm sorry, Lacy. Someone tried to kill me. I came here to hide. I didn't want to drag you into the danger. It looks as if I did anyway." Her voice was hoarse and scratchy, and Lacy ached to put her arms around her sister.

"It's not your fault," Lacy assured her. "This is all Charles's doing. You were right to get upset that I was marrying him. It was all a dirty trick."

A dirty trick that Kate's boyfriend had been in on, but Lacy let that slide for now. She'd worry about telling her the truth about Ricky later, if there was a later.

Lacy turned to Adam, some of her fear swallowed up in the anger that roared through her senses. "If you're killing me as a favor to Charles, you're wasting your time, Adam. He's dead. He committed suicide last night in his office."

Adam laughed, and the hysterical sound of it sent new shudders rocking through her.

"So the police did buy into that. Just like I knew they would. And I bet your cowboy sheriff was the first in line."

"Charles killed himself, Adam. I saw the body. I saw the gun in his hand."

"Yeah. And I put it there. I killed that whimpering excuse of a man the same way I killed Ricky."

"It was you who killed him?" Kate cried. "And you claimed to be his friend."

"So what do you know—looks like I'm a liar, too."

Lacy tried to understand, but nothing made sense. Maybe it was the roaring in her ears and the brain-splitting pain in the back of her head. But she forced her lips to form the question that rolled in her mind. "Why did you kill Charles?"

"Why did I kill Charles? Because he chickened out on me. He was afraid of Branson Randolph. Afraid the pretty-boy sheriff would pin your murder on him even though I was going to make it look like an accident."

"An accident. Then it was you who bombed Ricky's town house?"

"As a matter of fact it was. But that wasn't to kill you. You were supposed to be getting married then. That was to cover my tracks. And it worked. No one will pin Ricky's murder on me. And they won't get me for these two, either."

"Ricky didn't do anything to you, Adam. He didn't," Kate insisted. "Why did you have to kill him?"

Adam paced the kitchen, his eyes darting from one of them to the other. Lacy had never seen him like this.

"Ricky's the real Judas," he stammered. "He delivered Lacy into Charles's hands for money to get his house out of hock. Only he thought Charles was just looking for a hot young wife. He didn't know that Charles was going to have Lacy killed so that he could collect the insurance money."

"I still don't see why you had to kill him," Lacy argued. She didn't care so much about the deadly facts now. She just wanted to keep Adam talking.

Adam went to the faucet and filled a tall glass with water. He fished a couple of pills from his shirt pocket and swallowed them before downing the water in huge, dripping gulps. When he finished, he pulled out a chair and sat in front of Lacy.

"You didn't answer me, Adam. Why did you kill Ricky?"

"I don't have to answer you." He raised his hand as if he was going to slap her, but stopped before he did. "Ricky tried to stop Charles from killing you. He threatened to turn

Charles in to the police, and you know the good attorney couldn't let that happen. So he called on me. Adam to the rescue. He paid me to kill Ricky and Kate to keep them quiet, just in case Ricky had told Kate anything.''

"And then you were supposed to kill me so that Charles could collect the insurance money?"

"Insurance on his wife. But you blew that when you walked out on him at the altar, and you had the man running scared. I told him not to panic, assured him that we could still pull this off. But then you hooked up with that cowboy with a badge, and Charles fell apart.''

"But it's over now, Adam. Charles is dead. You don't have to kill me anymore. You don't have to kill Kate. Charles can't pay you."

"I never cared about the money. It was Ricky and Charles who loved money. I wanted you, Lacy. I loved you, but you left me for Charles and his big bucks. Now the joke's on you. There is no Charles Castile. And there is no money. He gambled it all away." He reached over and stroked her face. "Now there will be no you."

"Don't do this, Adam. Please don't do this," she begged. "You'll be sorry if you kill us."

"Why? They'll never catch me. They'll blame this on Milton Maccabbe. Everyone knows he's strange. And even if they do catch me, they'd hang me as quick for one murder as they would for three or four. So, you see, I have no reason *not* to kill you. Besides, I've waited a long time to get my revenge."

He reached behind him and took a knife from the table, the same sharp knife Milton had used to clean his fish. "I want this to be slow and painful, Lacy. I want you to feel every cut, every gush of blood. And I'll kill Kate first, so you can watch."

Lacy felt the blood drain from her head in an onslaught

of panic. "No, don't. Please don't, Adam. I'll do whatever you want me to do."

"It's too late. You made a bad choice, Lacy. Now you'll have to pay the price. You and Kate."

Adam took the point of the knife and poked it into the flesh at the base of Lacy's neck. "But tell her, Kate. My name is not Adam Pascal. It's Alan Potter. And you won't be the first women I've killed. I will *not* be brushed off by a bitch."

"You won't get away with this, Adam, or Alan, whoever you are. You won't."

"But I will. I'll do the deed and then just leave town and disappear into someone else's identity. It's so easy. It happens all the time. Ask any cop, even Branson. Only, you'll never get the chance. And you won't be around to flirt with some other guy and crush his spirit the way you did mine. Actually, I'm probably doing Branson a favor."

"No, Adam, no. I care for you. I do. I always have, right from the first." She was lying, buying time. She couldn't reason with Adam, so she'd have to find a way out of this. And she had to find it quick.

"Sure you do. That's why you refused to go out with me once that prissy attorney started buying you all those expensive things. Do you think I don't know that about you? That you can be bought? Does Branson know that? Did you tell him?"

"Branson doesn't mean anything to me."

"You lie. I saw you dance with him the other afternoon. You were all over him." He pushed the tip of the knife against her flesh.

Lacy shuddered as the first hot drops of blood rolled down her chest.

"You're the one who lies," Kate cried. "You said you were going to kill me first, and now you're about to cut

Lacy's throat. Come on over here, or are you afraid of me?''

"Yeah, right, you piece of trash. Like I'm *real* afraid of you.''

But Lacy knew that Kate was only drawing his attention away from her. It worked. Adam stepped to Kate's chair. His movements were jerky now, and sweat had started to bead on his forehead. He had lost the little bit of control he'd had a few minutes earlier.

Adam was sliding over the edge into total madness. A place he'd evidently visited before.

"One, two, three, you'll never catch me. Four, five, six, I'm up to your tricks.''

Lacy turned in horror. Kate was taunting Adam, singing a song they'd made when they were frightened little girls. But then they'd been afraid of the nonexistent bogeyman.

"Stop that! Stop that *now!*'' Adam threw back his arm, holding the knife high over his head. Lacy started a scream that died in her throat. Someone was coming. She could see the dust flying in the driveway.

Without hesitating, she bounced her chair up and down, knocking into Kate's chair just as the knife came crashing down. The blade buried itself deep in the wooden arm. But Adam had crossed the line completely now. His eyes were glowing, the muscles in his arms taut, his mouth twisted into an ugly snarl.

She bounced once more, this time pushing into him just as he retrieved the knife from its grave of wood. He yelled a bloodcurdling scream that reverberated off the walls and ceiling.

She threw herself, chair and all in front of Kate. Her ears rang from the terror. Pain hit then, a jabbing blow to her chest. She looked down, but all she could see was blood, a thick crimson syrup that covered her shirt and was dripping onto her thighs.

And all she could hear was Kate crying her name.

Adam was holding the knife over Kate's head now, dementia haunting his eyes.

"Don't cry, Kate. Don't cry. I love you. Please don't cry," Lacy pleaded.

The knife was coming down. It was too late to cry. But at least the Gilbraith sisters would die together.

Lacy only wished she'd talked to Branson first. She wished she had told him that she loved him.

Chapter Seventeen

Lacy screamed one last time as the sound of fear cracked through the room. Only this time it was Adam who was falling. It was Adam whose face was distorted from pain.

"Oh, no." A string of curses followed, low, almost a cry themselves.

Lacy looked up. Branson was standing in the door, his pistol drawn, his face ghostly white. Ryder was there, too, but he was already moving toward Adam's fallen body.

Branson crossed the room in a heartbeat and fell to his knees in front of her. "Are you all right?"

She shook her head. "Probably not. But I'm alive."

She was falling herself, back into time. She'd said those same words before, the day Branson had saved her from the bomb. "You must be getting a little tired of riding to my rescue, cowboy."

"Never." His voice broke, but his hands were strong and sure as he checked Lacy's wound. "How about you, Kate? Are you all right?"

"The knife missed me altogether, thanks to Lacy."

"And thank God, Lacy's wound is not as deep as it looked at first."

"It stings like crazy," she said, holding her stomach and sucking up the pain.

"I know, but just hold on. I'll get you to the hospital, but first I need to slow the bleeding." Hands flying, Branson stripped off his shirt and made a bandage of it. "You must have swerved and knocked Adam off balance. It's more a ragged gash than a stab."

Lacy leaned her head against his shoulder. "Kate, I want you to meet Sheriff Branson Randolph."

"We've met," she said. "I wasn't too crazy about him then, but he sure looks good tonight."

"I wish I could say the same for you two ladies."

"How's Adam?" Branson asked without taking his eyes off Lacy.

"He's not dead," Ryder announced, kneeling over Adam's prostrate body. "He's only going to wish he were."

Adam's only response was a whispered curse as the handcuffs clanged shut around his wrists. He'd been the one to take a bullet, and it had ripped the fight right out of him.

Branson reached behind Lacy and sliced the rope that bound her hands. He did the same at her ankles while Ryder left his prisoner long enough to do the same for Kate.

As soon as Kate was free, she fell to her knees and wrapped her arms around Lacy. "If I ever even think about flirting with trouble again, remind me of this, Lacy. Just say the words *Adam Pascal,* and I swear I'll go so straight they'll be asking me to preach on Sunday morning."

"Deal," Lacy said. "But this wasn't your fault."

"All I have is my truck," Branson announced, all business again. "But it will still be quicker than waiting on the ambulance. I'll call it for Adam, though, and I'll call my deputy to come over and ride along with him. Ryder can wait with Adam until Gordon relieves him. Is that okay with you, Ryder?"

"Oh, yeah. This is the most excitement I've had since I got kicked by that angry bronc up in Fort Worth. Of course, it would've been a lot more exciting if I'd been the one to pull the trigger on this scumbag here."

"I'll keep that in mind. I could always use a good deputy. Right now, how about helping Kate to the truck? I don't think your prisoner's going anywhere. I'll carry Lacy."

Branson lifted Lacy in his arms. "Keep your arms up. It looks like the bleeding has about stopped and we don't want it to start again."

She buried her head against his chest. "How did you know where to find me?"

"Ryder saw you heading this way when he and Petey were out on the horses."

"How did you know I was in trouble?"

"I'll tell you all about it later. When we're home."

Home. The Burning Pear. Where people laughed, and loved and trusted. She wanted to tell Branson that she loved him. She wanted to tell Ashley that she was ready to take that chance they'd talked about. But her mouth was dry, and her head was spinning. She'd just have to tell them later.

At home.

LACY SAT between Kate and Branson on the couch. The Randolphs, all except Petey and Betsy who were already in bed, sat nearby, sipping their after-dinner coffee. Ryder was accompanying his with his third helping of blackberry cobbler.

Lacy tried to follow the conversation, a continuous series of questions about the afternoon's narrow escape, but she kept losing her train of thought.

The doctor had stitched her wound, bandaged it and

given Branson orders that he was not to let her do anything but eat, drink plenty of liquids and rest. He'd also given her a shot of something that had killed the pain and dulled the senses so that she seemed to be floating a little outside the realm of reality. Under the circumstances, it wasn't an altogether bad place to be.

"Well, I'm just glad Branson and Ryder made it there in time," Mary Randolph said, not for the first time. "But, Branson, I'm still not clear about what made you rush off looking for Lacy. Ashley said the last she'd heard, the man who'd threatened to kill Lacy was dead."

"New evidence made it clear that even though Charles had tricked Lacy into agreeing to marry him so that he could kill her and collect the insurance money, he hadn't dumped Ricky's body at our gate. That meant someone else had to be in on this." Branson leaned back and crossed a foot over his knee. "I started trying to come up with possibilities."

"And you came up with Adam Pascal?"

"Actually, it was something he said as we were leaving Kincaid's the other night. He said that Lacy looked like a million dollars. And then he made some remark about Charles playing his cards right."

"And you realized his words had a double meaning, that he was talking about the million-dollar insurance policy?" Langley leaned forward, propping his elbows on his knees. "That still wasn't much to go on."

"No, but it also hit me that Adam had been the only one who wasn't surprised to hear that Lacy and Charles weren't really married."

"Meaning, Charles had to have told him the truth even though he'd forged a license and lied to everyone else."

"Right. And then when I ran a quick credit check on Adam this morning, I realized he had none. Absolutely nothing. No car note, no credit cards, no mortgage. The same blank sheets had shown up in the state computer system when we had run his original background check.''

"A clean record. I don't get it," Kate said. "Why would that make you think something was wrong?''

"Too clean. That's a frequent profile when someone has either assumed someone else's identity or created a fake identity from scratch. Apparently Adam did the latter.''

"That's right. I'd almost forgotten,'' Langley said. "Kate said he confessed his real name to her when he was about to kill her.''

"So did Alan Potter have a record?'' Ashley asked, rocking forward and stretching her legs toward the hearth. "He sounds as if his heart must be totally black.''

Branson set his empty mug on the end table at his elbow. "He'd been convicted for killing a girlfriend in Louisiana. He served a few years and then got off on a technicality. The prison psychologist recommended treatment, said that Adam should be hospitalized. He was for about six weeks. Then another psychologist released him. It was all a matter of public record once we had his real name.''

"I'm just glad we have caller ID on the phone at the ranch,'' Ashley said. "I knew the second I gave Adam's number to Branson that something was dreadfully wrong.''

"Same here,'' Ryder said. "When I saw Lacy driving toward Milton Maccabbe's house, something told me I needed to alert Branson.''

"I owe all of you a lot,'' Lacy said.

Kate reached over and squeezed her hand. "We both do.''

"And Milton Maccabbe truly had nothing to do with this,'' Langley remarked. "He's such a strange bird, I figured he was involved somehow.''

"Just the opposite,'' Kate said. "He was the only person

I thought I could count on. And I knew he lived alone. It seemed the perfect place to hide. And it was safe until Adam showed up."

"I just wish you'd called Lacy," Branson told Kate. "Then today would never have had to happen. You could have both been put in protective custody."

"Hindsight," Kate said. "It's a wonderful thing. But all I knew was that I didn't want to drag Lacy into any more trouble. I'd already done that way too many times."

"Well, I say let's put the whole thing behind us," Mary Randolph said. "Except for what Kate has to tell us about Betsy."

Kate exhaled, her mouth twisting into a frown. "And I don't know what to tell you. All I know is that Ricky called me at work and said I should hurry home. He said some woman had come to the house looking for me. She said she had a baby whose father was one of the Randolphs of Kelman, Texas. He was going to call you and demand a ransom, but I begged him not to do anything until I got home. I thought I could stop him."

Kate's voice grew low and labored. "But when I got home, Ricky was dead. I grabbed the baby and ran from the house. I wasn't going to demand a ransom. I just wanted the baby to be safe."

"Only Adam waited until dark to come back for the body," Branson explained. "He admitted tonight that he saw Kate leaving in the car and followed her with the intention of killing her. He had no idea who the baby was or that Kate was bringing her here."

"I thought once that someone was following me," Kate said, "but then there was a string of cars on the highway and I forgot about it until I turned off on the road to your ranch. That's when Adam fired on my car."

"Then you really don't know who Betsy's parents are?"

Sadness crept into Mary Randolph's face and cracked her voice.

"No. I'm sorry I dragged all of you into this. I really am. I don't know where Ricky got the baby, but there's no reason to think she's really a Randolph. I think he'd just heard Kincaid talk about the Randolphs and thought you were rich enough to pay a large ransom for a baby if he could convince you she was your own flesh and blood."

"There's no record of a missing baby anywhere around here," Branson said. "Not one."

"But someone had to give birth to that precious baby," Mary said. "And I tell you, no one's taking her away from the Burning Pear unless I know they're the real parents. If the mother said to get the baby to us, that's good enough for me."

"Now, Mother."

"Don't now, Mother, me in that tone, Dillon Randolph. That baby needs love. And I'm perfectly capable of giving it to her. Where better could she be than here at the Burning Pear if she's not with her real family?"

Where better indeed? Lacy thought. Where better could anyone be? She leaned her head back and closed her eyes.

"Ashley, why don't you go with Lacy and see that she gets to bed? She's looks as if she's about to pass out on us."

"And you are going right behind her," Dillon said. He walked over and took his mother's arm. "And no complaining. Doctor's orders."

"I'll tell you what," Ashley said. "Why don't you see that Mother Randolph gets to bed, Dillon. I'll escort Kate to the upstairs guest room and point out where she can find towels and any toiletries she might need. And Branson can make sure Lacy gets to bed all right." She gave Branson a conspiratorial wink. "Can you handle that, brother-in-law?"

"I believe I can."

LACY'S EYES were already closed. They had been since two seconds after she'd lain her head on the pillow. He should clear out and let her rest, but he couldn't bear to walk away.

He'd gone through hell and back today when he'd stepped inside Milton Maccabbe's kitchen and seen her tied to the chair and covered in blood. If he'd been too late, if he'd lost her to a madman—no, he couldn't even bear to think what life would be like without her.

"I love you, Lacy." He eased down to the side of the bed and took her hand in his. She was asleep. It didn't matter. He was saying the words for himself. He'd say them to her again later, when the day's trauma was over.

"I know I said once that I wasn't the marrying kind, and maybe I'm not. But I love you, Lacy, and want to share my life with you. I've never been more sure of anything in my life."

Her lashes fluttered, and she half opened her eyes. She reached up with her left arm and pulled him closer. "I heard that, cowboy."

"And I guess you plan to hold me to it."

"Only for forever."

Epilogue

Five months later

Branson hurried Lacy down the hallway and into his bedroom. The reception that should have been over an hour ago was still going strong. Their guests spilled out of the house and onto the grounds of the Burning Pear, still eating, drinking, laughing and dancing. He'd tried to coax Lacy away earlier, but everyone had wanted to gush over how beautiful she looked and wish them well.

Worse, Lacy had insisted on having their picture taken with everyone in the family at least once and with Betsy a half-dozen times. Now they had exactly half an hour before they had to leave to catch a plane bound for Hawaii.

Lacy swirled her full skirts and turned her back to him. "I'll need help getting out of this dress."

Branson took one look at the row of tiny pearl buttons and groaned. A half hour. It would take him that long just to work his way though the buttons.

"I think this is where I came in," he moaned.

"But this time the end result will be a little different."

"Only if I get the dress off before we have to leave for the airport."

"But undressing is half the fun."

"I've had that half before."

"You've had the other half, too," Lacy teased.

"Not with my wife." He nibbled her earlobe and then trailed kisses down the back of her neck. Pulling her closer, he circled her tiny waist, clasping his hands just under her breasts. "You should have gotten the Velcro I suggested before. You knew I'd be in no condition to manipulate buttons."

"Velcro on a wedding dress?"

"Especially on a wedding dress."

He fumbled with the first button. Nothing happened. "This isn't going to work. What do you say we just rip it off?"

"Absolutely not. One of our daughters may get married in this dress one day."

"We don't have a daughter."

"Not yet. But I hope we have a houseful. Sons, too." She reached behind her neck and under the first button.

Branson watched as the dress opened at her touch. That's when he saw the silvery teeth of the hidden zipper.

"You sneaky devil," he whispered. He took the zipper and pulled. The white satin and lace parted, revealing soft bronzed flesh that narrowed at the waist and then swelled into beautiful hips. His heart raced. His mouth grew dry. The rest of him grew hard.

He pushed the fabric from her shoulders and the yards of white fell in a snowy heap at her feet. Lacy stripped away her underwear as he watched in exquisite agony. He was breathing hard when she turned and faced him. All but gasping by the time she swayed against him, his body so hot he thought he might explode.

"Something tells me we may not make it to Hawaii, Mrs. Randolph."

"Sure we will, cowboy. One day. After all, we have the rest of our lives."

And then her lips touched his and he was lost in the thrill of it. He'd never expected to find a woman like Lacy, and now that he had, he was certain that one lifetime of loving her would never be enough.

"I love you, Lacy," he whispered when they surfaced for air. "I love you more than I ever dreamed possible."

"And I love you, Branson Randolph. All my life, I thought I was destined for loneliness and heartache," she whispered. "Now it turns out I'm the luckiest woman in the world. I found you. I found a place where I belong."

"And always will. Welcome home, Mrs. Randolph. Welcome home."

* * * * *

So who is the mystery father of baby Betsy?
Find out as Joanna Wayne continues her

RANDOLPH FAMILY TIES

miniseries with

THE STRANGER NEXT DOOR

available wherever
Harlequin Intrigue books are sold!

Chapter One

Langley Randolph ducked out of the rain and into the front door of Gus's Corner Café. He shook the moisture from his Stetson hat and stamped the mud from his boots.

"Not a fit night out for man nor beast," Gus called from behind the counter. He wiped his hands on the white work apron that stretched over his ample paunch. "What brings you into town?"

"Work. The storm triggered the alarm at Higgins's Supermarket. I expected as much, but I had to eyeball the place and make certain it was nothing else."

"Higgins needs to shell out a little cash and update that system. His alarm goes off if the wind blows crooked. Still, I'm glad for your company. Can I get you a cup of coffee?"

"You can." Langley shed his jacket and tossed it over one of the spare hooks supplied for the purpose. "I can use the caffeine. I've got a little more work to do before I can call it a night."

"Looks like you're serious about your temporary stint as sheriff."

"Not by choice. I'll take my cud-chewing critters t trouble-causing humans any day."

"Well, you can't blame your brother for wanting a h

eymoon. If I had a wife half as pretty as Lacy, I might even chuck my boots under the bed and pull on one of them flowered Hi-waiin shirts.''

''Yeah, well, it would take more than a woman for me to wear that getup.''

''You just haven't met the right woman yet. Everyone said Branson would never take the plunge and he was grinnin' like a mule eatin' thistles when the preacher tightened that marriage knot around his neck.''

''That was Branson. This is me.'' Langley settled onto a bar stool at the counter.

''This is a new brand of coffee,'' Gus said, setting a mug of steaming brew in front of Langley. ''All the big restaurants in San Antonio have switched to it. At least that's what my supplier said.''

Langley tried it while Gus watched.

''How's it taste?'' he asked before Langley placed the cup back on the counter.

''Like a new brand.''

''I mean, do you like it?''

''It's coffee. I liked the old brand just fine.''

''You're stuck in your ways, Langley Randolph. Do you know that?'' Gus leaned over the table and wiped at a stain that didn't want to give up. ''Just plain stuck in your ways about everything except your cows. You got to have all the latest breeding methods on your ranch, but you want everything else about your life to stay the same. That's why you don't have a wife.''

''Right, so how about one of those same-old cheeseburgers you make? And a side of those same-old onion rings?''

Gus grinned. ''Well, at least you've got good taste. I'll fix me one and join you. I doubt I'll get any more paying customers tonight in this downpour. Everybody's home propping their feet under their own table."

"Yeah. Too bad we didn't get this rain about August when my grass was dying from the drought."

"Well, then we wouldn't be living in south Texas, would we?"

Gus grabbed a couple of beef patties from the cooler and plopped them onto the hot grill. They spit and sputtered, and Langley's stomach reacted appropriately. He'd have preferred to be one of the folks with their feet stretched under their own table tonight, but if he had to be out, Gus was as good company as any. Actually better than most he'd talked to today. At least Gus didn't have any complaints he wanted to report to the acting sheriff.

Three days into his new role, and Langley was eager to give the lawman job back to Branson. He liked running the ranch, tending his cattle, researching the latest methods for producing the best beef in the most economical fashion.

But the Randolphs always stuck together, so he couldn't very well turn down his brother's request to fill in for him for two weeks while he honeymooned. Branson had his young deputy Gordon on the payroll, but he didn't trust Gordon with too much authority just yet. He said he didn't want to come home and find half the population in jail from some minor infractions that Gordon had blown out of proportion.

The bell over the door tinkled, and Langley stretched his neck and looked around. Gus had been wrong when he'd said no one would be out in the storm. One more person had ventured out. A stranger. Drenched, but still attractive enough to make any red-blooded male take notice. He was no exception.

She raked a handful of wet hair from her face, tucking it behind her right ear before crossing her arms over her chest. The pose successfully hid the soft mounds of breast that the wet T-shirt had revealed. What she couldn't hide were the tinges of purple and dark blue, remnants of bruises that covered her face and arms. Instinctively, Langley's guard went up.

The woman stepped toward the counter. "Can I help you?" Gus said. "You surely didn't come out in this thunderstorm for a burger and fries."

"No, I'm looking for the sheriff. I was told he might be able to help me. Do you know where I could find him?"

Trouble. Langley knew it, the way a man knows his horse is about to buck or that the branding iron's not quite hot enough to do the job. He didn't know how he knew it. He just did.

He slid from his stool. "I'm Langley Randolph," he said, "the county sheriff—at least I am this week. What can I do for you?"

"I hate to ask on a night like this, but I'd appreciate a lift to the Running Deer Ranch."

He studied the woman. Even soaked through to the skin, she had a sophistication about her. And an accent he didn't recognize. "Do you have business at the Running Deer?"

She nodded. "I'm Danielle, Milton Maccabbe's niece. I'm here to see him."

Langley ran his hands deep into his front pockets, debating with himself on how he should tell the dripping stranger with a strange accent that the man she was planning to visit had died two weeks ago. "I'd be happy to give you a ride, but—"

"Good," she broke in. "I'm anxious to get out there, and I'm without transportation."

"Then how did you get to Kelman? We're a long walk from nowhere."

"I came by bus."

So that explained why she was soaking wet. Kelman didn't have a regular bus station, but if there was someone to pick up or let off, the bus stopped at Phil Klinger's feed store. But it was half past seven. The place would be locked up tight this time of night.

"The driver suggested I call the sheriff from the pay phone where he dropped me off, but it wasn't working. I guess the storm had knocked it out. I saw the sign for the café and took a chance it would be open." She hugged her arms more tightly around her chest. "I didn't expect to be lucky enough to walk right into the sheriff."

"If Langley hadn't been here, I'd have given you a ride," Gus hastened to assure her. "We Texans don't leave a woman on her own if we can help it."

"I'll drive you wherever you'd like to go," Langley said. "But I'd like to eat that burger Gus is cooking before I take off in the storm again. You might like to do the same. Gus makes the best burger in south Texas."

"The best burger in *all* of Texas," Gus corrected.

The woman turned toward the sound of the sputtering meat, her eyes wide. But she shook her head and directed her gaze back toward him. "I'm not hungry, but you go ahead. I'll wait and eat something at the ranch."

Of course, she expected to have dinner with her uncle. Which meant he couldn't put off the inevitable. "I hate to be the bearer of bad news," Langley said, deciding the straight approach was the best.

"What kind of bad news?"

Langley swallowed hard and wished there was a way

around what he had to say. But there wasn't. "Milton Maccabbe died a couple of weeks ago."

She lowered her head and directed her gaze to the toes of her muddy tennis shoes. "I knew he was sick," she said. "I just hadn't heard that he'd died."

"In his sleep. The doctor said it was a peaceful way to go."

"I'm glad. I just wish I'd been here."

Her voice cracked on the words, but she didn't cry. For the first time in a long time, Langley wished he was more like his brothers, wished that talking to strange women came easier for him. Instead, he was standing around like an awkward schoolboy, wondering if he should say something more or offer a shoulder to cry on.

Finally, she broke the silence. "Who's staying at the ranch now to look after the cattle?"

"Joshua Kincaid's hands are taking care of the place. Milton was foreman at Kincaid's ranch before he retired and bought the Running Deer. But no one lives there. The place is deserted once the sun goes down."

"Then I'd still appreciate a ride to the ranch, if you don't mind."

"It's not the sort of place to visit at night," Langley advised.

"I won't be visiting. I'll be moving in."

Langley rocked back on his heels. His gaze lowered from her dripping hair to the wet clothes that clung to her body like a second skin and then back to her bruised face. "I'm not sure I heard you right," he said, knowing that he had but hoping he was wrong.

"If Uncle Milton is dead, then the ranch is mine. He left it to me. I have it in writing."

"Are you a rancher?"

"No, but I can learn."

"Yep," Gus interrupted, "and if you have any trouble, you can call on Langley. He lives practically in hollering range. If there's anything about cows he don't know, it hasn't been discovered yet."

She propped a foot on the boot rail of one of the stools and leaned against the counter. "It's nice to know that expert advice will be so readily available."

"I'll be glad to help out if you have questions," Langley said. "Any of the Randolphs will, but don't put any stock in Gus's claims. Every rancher around these parts has his own way of doing things, and we all think our way's best."

"Nonetheless, I appreciate the offer." Danielle looked up at Langley, her dark eyes shadowed and mysterious, her lips parted, the flesh beneath the bruises raw. "But I'm sure I'll be selling the place as soon as I can."

Something in the way she spoke and moved reminded Langley of a frightened calf. It might just be the news of her uncle's death, but he had the strange suspicion that it was something more than grief that strained her voice and haunted her ebony eyes. More like fear. After all, Someone had recently branded her with the telltale signs of violence.

"You can call on me as a rancher or as a *sheriff*," he said. "We don't cater to abuse or abusers in Kelman."

"I don't know what you're talking about, Sheriff."

He stepped closer and trailed a finger along the purple marks that ran the length of her arm. She trembled at his touch and then backed away. An unfamiliar sensation swept through Langley, an awareness that set his nerves on edge.

A beautiful woman with dangerous secrets—one who was about to become his neighbor.

And suddenly Langley knew exactly how it must feel to be caught standing in the middle of a stampede with no way of escape.

Shh!

HARLEQUIN®

I N T R I G U E®

has a secret...

September 2000

Back by popular demand are

DEBBIE MACOMBER's
MIDNIGHT SONS

Hard Luck, Alaska, is a town that needs women!
And the O'Halloran brothers are just
the fellows to fly them in.

Starting in March 2000 this beloved series returns
in special 2-in-1 collector's editions:

MAIL-ORDER MARRIAGES, featuring
Brides for Brothers and *The Marriage Risk*
On sale March 2000

FAMILY MEN, featuring
Daddy's Little Helper and *Because of the Baby*
On sale May 2000

THE LAST TWO BACHELORS, featuring
Falling for Him and *Ending in Marriage*
On sale July 2000

Collect and enjoy each MIDNIGHT SONS story!

Available at your favorite retail outlet.

HARLEQUIN®
Makes any time special ™

COMING NEXT MONTH

#573 THE STRANGER NEXT DOOR by Joanna Wayne
Randolph Family Ties

First a baby was left on the family's doorstep, then a beautiful woman with no memory inherited the ranch next door. Langley Randolph wasn't sure what was going on, but he intended to find out. Danger lurked, but the passion aroused by his mysterious new neighbor, Danielle, made protecting her his duty—and having her his heart's desire.

#574 INNOCENT WITNESS by Leona Karr

After witnessing a murder, Deanna Drake's four-year-old daughter was traumatized into silence. With the help of Dr. Steve Sherman and his young son, her daughter found her voice—and incited the killer to attack again. But to get to Deanna and her daughter, the madman would have to go through Steve first....

#575 BLACKMAILED BRIDE by Sylvie Kurtz

For two weeks, Cathlynn O'Connell agreed to play the role of wife to the enigmatic researcher Jonas Shades. But alone in his secluded mansion, what began as a temporary arrangement soon spiraled into an intricate web of deceit, danger and disguised passions. Someone knew Cathlynn was an impostor. What they didn't know was that Jonas intended to make a proper bride of Cathlynn—if he could keep her alive.

#576 A MAN OF HONOR by Tina Leonard

Intuition told Cord Greer that things were not what they seemed. When two men came in search of Tessa Draper, Cord's first instinct was to protect. But now that the pregnant Tessa shared the intimacy of Cord's solitary ranch, he had to rethink his actions. Someone was out there watching, waiting to take away the only woman he'd ever loved and the child he considered his own.

Visit us at www.eHarlequin.com